...ANDS

Playing the Game

PAN BOOKS

First published 2003 by

This edition published 2003 by Pan Books
an imprint of Pan Macmillan Ltd
Pan Macmillan, 20 New Wharf Road
Basingstoke and Oxford
Associated companies throughout the world
www.panmacmillan.com

ISBN 0 330 49369 8

A CIP catalogue record for this book is available from
the British Library.

Typeset by SetSystems Ltd, Saffron Walden, Essex
Printed and bound in Great Britain by
Mackays of Chatham plc, Chatham, Kent

To my parents

With thanks to Peter Straus and Imogen Taylor

Chapter 1

Patti Ward sat in front of the long, fluorescent-lit mirror. Laid out before her was a comprehensive set of sable make-up brushes, from the narrow, moistened eyeliner applicator to the soft, chunky brush that she swept across her cheeks. She preferred to do this pre-camera ritual herself. The make-up girls, or, as they were now called in the latest round of title inflation, facial practitioners, were too attentive and indiscreet to be allowed uncontrolled access to Patti's face.

One girl, sponging foundation onto Patti's tense forehead, had marvelled at her lack of frown lines. Another had jabbed nosily at her eyelids. A week later, a newspaper diarist had asked, through the press office, whether television's most famous newsreader had been missing from the screen for over three weeks because she had had an 'eye job'. Some coincidence. Patti laughed off the suggestion, then privately phoned the diarist to tell her that the hospital visit to which she referred was to tackle the early stages of skin cancer. She had not told her infirm parents, who would be heartbroken by the news. The diarist stammered her sympathies and was indeed so mortified that she soon gave up her newspaper shifts in order to work for the Green

Party, announcing piously that she wished to save lives rather than destroy them.

Patti had survived twenty years at the top of her profession by maintaining a subtle balance in her public appeal. She sought admiration, shot through with pity. If she were simply beautiful, clever and successful, she would irritate and bore people. So she also cultivated a tragic strain which stopped others, mainly women, from disliking her. It was a persona which had served her well in the press, on whom she lavished attention and occasionally employed a stun gun. Who's afraid? Jenny, the facial practitioner supervisor, popped her head round the door.

'Hi, Patti, need any extra blusher?' Despite Jenny's seniority in her field, she had very little feel for her work. Presenters in her care looked boiled in front of a camera, as if they were suffering from dangerously high blood pressure. Still, she was thought to have a good personality, which meant chatty sympathy and occasional blubbing in the ladies lavatory. On location the description had the added conotation of being sexually companionable.

'Sure, sweetie, come in. How are you?' said Patti. Jenny hoped she would ask.

'Oh, I am fine. Great actually. Tim is taking me out to dinner for a kind of late birthday present – so amazing he remembered.'

Patti's expression was that of unconditional happiness. 'That's fantastic, Jenny. Is this a proposal?'

Jenny replied, flustered, 'No, he warned me in advance that it didn't mean anything but, you know, it might mean something. Men don't always realize what they mean, do they?'

Patti sighed. 'Be careful, sweetie. You have your own

job, your own flat, and, I imagine, your own cats. Don't let him humiliate you. Want my advice? Indifference is the only secure basis for a relationship. It is a much underestimated non-emotion.'

Jenny gave a brave, hurt smile. 'Any news on the programme? I heard that you had done a pilot?'

Patti shrugged, smoothing her beechwood-coloured hair, stroking the considerable length of her flesh-coloured stockings. 'Yes, but nothing is signed yet. Maybe they can't decide whether they really want an old bag like me presenting their flagship news show.' Modestly dismissing Jenny's protest she finished lightly, 'It is a drag actually, because the other side are nagging at me to join them for a truly obscene sum I can't tell you. You would think it'd be great to be pursued so hard, but it is surprisingly stressful. Like having someone going on and on at you about settling down. You know, we have all been there.'

Jenny breathed out and asked: 'Has Mark been assigned to the programme yet?'

'He wants to do it,' smiled Patti. 'Depends whether he has a good election. He mustn't keep banging on about the poor because it looks like bias. And he must stop flirting with me on camera. He called me darling when we were discussing the budget surplus. Can you believe it?'

Jenny giggled and went to fetch her coat. Patti crept out after her, filched a bottle of champagne from the VIP fridge and put it in Jenny's bag, with a note from her saying happy birthday and big hugs. It was important that Jenny should leak the story about the audacious attempts to poach Patti with the maximum conviction.

*

Patti had been calculating her effect on other people for so long that she could hardly remember her unstudied behaviour. Fame only exacerbated her self-consciousness. As well as over-generous tips, she forced herself to take a scrupulous interest in everyone she encountered. She assumed a heightened goodwill that would be unnatural in any unknown person.

Grumpiness was magnified into bad temper. Sadness into failure and tiredness, old age. Patti was forty-nine when she last checked with *Who's Who*, and she was disinclined to get any older.

Then again she had the temperament for fame. It was not just that she was vain or insecure. She did not need to be loved. It was just that love was a stepping stone to power if you had to begin your journey from first base.

Even before she became a journalist, she learned to ask questions. The more men answered questions about themselves, the more they liked Patti. They praised her wit and insight, which amounted to a critical appreciation of their own dazzling verbal displays. Meanwhile she was building up a vast human database to which she constantly cross-referred. She was never as crude as politicians with their simple briefing notes. She avoided showy exhibitions of memorizing the names and ages of other people's children. She concentrated on their unrecognized achievements. Something very clever that they had said or done, ideally something for which someone else had taken credit. She knew that grievance was as strong a motivating force as vanity. The only time that she stopped directing those around her was when she was in front of the camera. This was her true self, her own out of body experience, seen by millions, beyond the reach of anyone. As the studio staff receded into shadows, Patti yielded to the camera's energy and light and delivered her opening line, 'Good evening.'

Patti's pristine white Holland Park house shone in the darkness. The trees in the wide street were sprouting their baby-doll blossom, despite the nip in the air. She pushed open the wrought-iron gate and skipped up the steps to the door. She imagined Jenny descending the steps to her red-brick flat, ten minutes away but tragically in an 0208 area.

If Patti had taken a tumble, no one was to blame; it was the glorious indifference of the market. Patti had done pretty well out of feminism but only while her ideological commitment was accompanied by the radiance of youth. Once she reached middle age she was no longer described as a feminist but as a career woman, which is of course a euphemism for unloved. Bad things happened to career women. They were perceived as ridiculous, selfish and barren. Only the love of a rich man could save them.

Patti caught sight of herself in her hall mirror as she mused on this. The heavy tan of television make-up rendered her handsome but hard. Patti knew the art of beauty lay, over the passage of time, in the lighting. She required more candles here.

The house was spare and fragrant. There were framed photographs across the hall of Patti with heads of states, and various New Labour donors. It was a purely public endorsement. There were no photographs of her young self nor her family, not in the bedroom, nor the bathroom nor in any of her drawers. She was a fastidious editor of her life.

She opened the post: gym membership newsletter, charity appeals (Why the presumption of compassion? She paid

40 per cent tax, used no public services apart from roads which, incidentally, she paid for through speeding fines. It was not unreasonable to ask whether she was the only one prepared to take responsibility for herself. What about a no-benefits-claims bonus?) and another scratchy-ink letter.

Dear Patty, You have not replied to my previous correspondence. This delay is vexatious to me. I must have an answer re whether you will have intercourse with me. Not for the first time you winked at me during your broadcast on the subject of asylum seekers. I am sure you are at one with my views that these so called 'victims' are gippos and maggots on the face of the earth. Did you know that 2001 is the real date of the millennium? This is a fact missed by politicians and the homosexuals who built the Dome. And you know what the millennium means? As Marx said, the scum of the earth will rise up. I flatter myself that I can save you from war and catastrophe which is coming even though you media are suppressing the information. No doubt your bosses are in the pay of the darkies and have generously availed themselves of supplies of oil. But I have conducted my own investigations. Oh yes, terror, terror will be unleashed on us all but I have found out and have written to Her Majesty. On a different note, you look like a lady so why did you have nothing on under the suit you wore on television last night? You dirty slut. Yours faithfully, Arthur

Patti pursed her lips. Why couldn't he spell her name right? She knew perfectly well who he was. He had written similar letters to most of the presenters and television actresses of her generation. An earnest researcher from the crime programme had contacted her yesterday to ask if she had received any 'unpleasant' letters and if she had, would she appear on the programme. As the researcher read out the creakingly period piece names of fellow victims, Patti grimaced. Angela, Susan, Carol, Margaret, Joan. Didn't they all scream 'over fifty'? This was becoming a sociological study of two channel, black and white television.

'No, sorry,' Patti said cutting the girl short. Her only letters were from well-adjusted people, who were all, curiously, leaders in their field. 'Fortunately, I am not a magnet for perverts,' she said, reeling off a list of more probable victims. The researcher thanked her profusely.

'Patti is so nice, she always makes time for other people,' she reported back to her producer, who squinted at her knowingly.

Patti climbed the stairs to her bedroom. The house hummed with the silence. She liked it that way. Some people reached for the CD player or the television to lessen the sense of being alone. She simply commanded the space. What would it be like to share this space with Mark? To have his crumpled suits thrown down on the bedroom floor, his shaving kit on the basin. To cook and care for him. To be confident enough of his love that she could afford to be poor – or ill or unhappy. Wasn't that the point of marriage? That it was an investment in one's own decline. The dividends were all in the worse rather than the better. What could Mark possibly add to her position? No money to speak of, no status. Less than the sum of her parts. What was the value of companionship? She honestly did not know. It was a foreign currency.

Patti sank onto her bed. She had spent a fortune on the mattress but still she seemed to keep breast-feeding hours. At 3 a.m. she always awoke. This was when she heard a cry from the baby in the house next door. She took a pill and fell back into sleep, or rather to the same dream sequence. She was being wheeled back into a ward full of young women. There were spots of blood on her white smock. An Irish nurse stroked her cheek. 'Everything went fine. It is just the anaesthetic that is making you cry.'

Chapter 2

Leaving her Sloane Street shopping bags in the boot of her car, and pulling out her call sheet, Patti hurried through the lobby of the National Television Corporation, stopping only to share a joke with the security guards, the receptionist and the colleagues whom she greeted warmly but did not recognize. Underneath the easy exchanges she brimmed with impatience. She could not stand it when someone pushed a different lift button to her own. On the seventh floor a group of young temps piled in, filling the confined space with their perfume and breath and laughter.

'It was when he said, "Where have you been all my life", it cracked me up. I could see you making faces at me, it cracked me up.' The group sighed, wiping mock tears from their eyes.

'Don't start, you give me a stomach ache.' There was a pause as they directed their fading smiles at Patti. She smiled back, encouragingly and moved backwards behind an invisible cordon.

'Morning, Patti, we were talking about our girls' night out. We had such a laugh, didn't we?' Patti took her mobile phone out of her bag and fiddled with it until the group pushed out onto the eighth. She relaxed again.

The midday news conference was underway. Sally Fletcher, the programme editor in charge of making news coverage relevant to the lives of viewers who were uninterested in news, handed out lists as if she were organizing cricket teas.

'There we are, something to work from, have you already got one?'

'Sal, hi, am I late?' asked Patti rhetorically. 'I stopped to give blood. The biscuits have improved in case that is putting anybody off.' Sally glanced at her mildly.

'Well, good for you. Maybe we should be doing a piece about blood donation. I think there is still a shortage, you get adverts on radio. And there are some quirky angles. British blood is a no-no abroad because they think we all have foot-and-mouth.' There was a rustle of laughter round the room, which cheered Sally. Her role, according to the memos, was strategic enabler, but in real life this translated as organizer, conciliator and guardian of the holiday rota. This made her one of the most senior women executives.

'Patti, have you met our new health correspondent? Alexandra Khan meet Patti Ward, Patti meet Alexandra.'

A pretty, athletic-looking woman in her late twenties with thick, cropped hair and caramel skin stood up. 'Gosh, hi, wow. My father won't believe it when I tell him that I am breathing the same air. My family are all big fans of yours.'

Irony or self-confidence from this child of television? Patti was always surprised by the directness of young women journalists. Personal exchanges, particularly of a flattering kind, should be handled more delicately. She did not like to be bombarded with flattery. This kind of open eagerness was the most blatant form of ambition.

'Oh yes, most of my fans these days are people's dads,' said Patti, her voice low and stagy. 'Over on Channel Three people ask presenters for autographs for their children. Here we provide signatures for the elderly. It's only a matter of time before some focus group declares us irrelevant and we lose our franchise, but there we are, we battle on, don't we, Sally?' Alex laughed hesitantly. Patti was practised in audience reaction and knew how to toy with it. She shook the younger woman's hand enthusiastically.

'My what a pretty top. We so rarely get to see belly buttons in conferences these days. Mark, there you are. Steve, hi, I saw the big game when I was in Washington. Quite something.'

'Watched it in Washington. As you do,' rocked Steve Green, mirthfully. Patti turned her back on him. 'Shall we get on?'

'Get it on, get it on, get it on,' sang Steve. Patti winced and closed her eyes. She opened them bright and blue as a doll's, drawing Mark into her heartless gaze.

The group rattled through the news events of the day. Alexandra slipped on a denim jacket. Patti was discomforting, both sexy and austere, part Cannes Film Festival, part headmistress.

She was beautiful, with exaggerated features which looked best on screen. When Alex was later asked by her girlfriends for a more precise description of Patti's appearance she screwed up her nose, rolled a cigarette and said: 'She is expensive.'

It was the fabric of her clothes and her skin. She slid out of a jacket so fine that it took on the contours of the back of her chair. A soft white T-shirt beneath emphasized the artful gleam of her flesh. The palest beige of her arms blended with the softness of watercolour into the ivory of her long hands and shining pale fingernails. A thin platinum and diamond bracelet hung loosely on her little wrist, from which rose layers of aromatic scent. Alex frowned at her own boyish hands and chewed nails. A gulf of grooming lay between the two women. Alex felt a wave of insecurity. Her thrift shop chic seemed suddenly defenceless rather than bohemian. This was a suit moment: the big swivel chairs, the amazing view over the Thames and Patti Ward staring at her.

'What do you think, Alexandra?'

'Oh shit, what? What?'

Sally Fletcher intervened. 'We are just kicking round ideas at this stage. We really need some original angles. What do you think the health issues might be in the election campaign?'

'Well, there is a feeling of betrayal, I think, among GPs and, um, health workers. Blair hasn't delivered, he seems to be looking for scapegoats. He got some doctors to speak at the Labour conference and I think, I guess, I could find them and see what they say now?'

'Yes, *The Times* did that,' said Patti thoughtfully. 'But we could follow it, could we, Sally?'

Alexandra felt the blush spread to her shoulders. 'I have one other idea. It is a bit vague but my friends and I were saying in the bar last night that health has really taken the place of religion now. There were some figures I can dig out that say we are an almost totally secular society now. There is all this material wealth but no beliefs. So something has to fill the vacuum. Maybe there will be a backlash among the young, I don't know. There are some Muslim crazies who are desperate for a kind of religious ruck, a jihad. But I doubt that will amount to anything.'

Steve rubbed his hands together. 'What's that, a kind of lap dancing? I'm up for a bit of a jihad anytime.' Alexandra blinked at him. Patti sighed.

'Sorry, Alison, Steve is here on a subsidized Government scheme to find work for the unemployable. Do carry on.' Steve gave a yelp, happy to be the centre of attention but at a momentary loss for a knockout bantering response. Alexandra wondered whether it would be rude to correct Patti about her name. She was surprised that Patti had got it wrong because she was a famous stickler for accuracy. She remembered an essay Patti had written for her well-thumbed journalists' handbook in which she had defended the derided local reporter whose first question to a bomb victim was: 'And could you spell your second name for me?'

'I am Alex,' she said, uncomfortably aware of the inherent aggression of the rebuke.

'Yes, *Alex*,' said Patti ironically. 'Do carry on.' Alex had lost her train of thought. She started to tear at a nitch in her fingernail. There was an atmosphere of quiet impatience in the room.

'Because of course Patti is here as part of the Government's grey army,' shouted Steve, his toothy grin immediately frozen in remorse. There was further silence but for the usual unnoticed office noises of shoes scuffing the carpet, and the soft, sealed, aeroplane drone of computers.

Alex struggled on, 'Uh, uh, I think health seems to be filling this spiritual vacuum at the moment. It is our secular religion, so to speak. Uh, um, because like the Princess of Wales had a feel for all this, and in a way I think Cherie

Blair sort of reflects what a lot of women think. Everyone is obsessed with health, nutrition, all that stuff. Like, everyone believes in it, everyone worships it. No one expects to get ill. People have their different sects, homeopathic, high-tech. And Tony Blair is promising to lead everyone to the Promised Land of infinite health resources for everyone. Maybe now that social and economic differences are less apparent, I mean everyone has access to TV and mobile phones and travel, the real divide, the final injustice is health. But you see expectations are so high and people are getting angrier that he can't deliver this thing, this perfect health. Blair is the body politic, in a way. I mean you could compare church attendance with gym membership. Does this make any sense?'

The sports editor started to whistle a Spice Girls medley. Sally nodded encouragingly. 'I know what you mean. It is bold thinking, and that is what we need right now. But I think we have to try to get all these thoughts into a more newsy format,' she said.

Patti gently lifted Mark's baggy trouser leg with the tip of her sculpted shoe under the table and beamed at Alexandra. Sally noticed Patti's change of posture and the fact that she had no plaster on her left arm. Of course she had not given blood.

Flirtation was often Patti's way of thinking. She had to decide what course of action was needed to deal with the new recruit, about whom, by the way, she had not been consulted. Patti, for all her playfulness, had two bottom line responses to the people she met. One, were they useful to her? Two, were they a threat to her? Everyone else could be treated with benign indifference.

It was not outrageous that younger, talented women

should be joining the organization. But Patti was of a generation of women who had charted their way in a male landscape. This made her a feminist in theory and a minx in practice. Her femaleness was her weapon. Should she now lie down and make way for other women? She had been in the field of battle too long for that.

She was fully aware of the channel's youth drive, and of the cruel inequality of it. Patti was a woman, a positive. But she was an older woman, a negative. She knew that fresh thinking equalled young women. Her fight against ageing was harder, more humiliating, than her fight against men. But she was experienced and cool headed. Younger women were dormant until proved guilty. It was a matter of risk assessment.

Patti caught up with Alexandra in the corridor and fell into step with her. 'Alex, I just wanted to say that you were really impressive. It is an ordeal. And I thought your ideas could be good with a little more – focus. Health is the issue of our times. Especially with our ageing population. Not that you have to worry about it just yet.'

Alexandra looked awkward. She sensed that she had made a fool of herself. She was a bright child from a large family and had always been encouraged to speak up. She was head of the school debating society. At Oxford her views had been treated with grave consideration. Now, for the first time, she did not feel confident and articulate. She knew that she should shut up.

Patti did not look her up and down. Rather, she surveyed her in parts. A glance at Alex's hair, her waist, her habitual, soft leather ankle boots. She smiled at her all the while, a glossy ripple which never went as far as a grin. 'Do you want a coffee?' she asked finally.

Alex had arranged to meet her flatmates, Emily and Lisa. She had been looking forward to regaling them with tales from the adult world of work, especially Emily who got the point of things and was a great mimic. They would reassure her that she had not sounded totally stupid. They would examine their newly acquired diaries to agree on their next lunch date. Three was not a symmetrical number and sometimes two of them would break ranks and see a movie, for which they would be guiltily apologetic. Simple choreography became increasingly difficult as they became absorbed in their adult lives. But Alex thought she should accept Patti's offer and so they wandered across to Starbucks, Patti graciously introducing Alex to colleagues, while failing to pass on their names. Patti was both proud and subversive about the television company. Naturally, such reckless confidence had to be earned.

After Patti questioned Alex casually and exhaustively over coffee and sandwiches, while offering only a mysterious and sorrowful shrug about her own past, a spontaneous thought seemed to occur to her.

'What are you up to this afternoon, Alex?' Alex replied with untrained honesty that she intended to read the newspapers more thoroughly and come up with some better ideas for the following day's conference.

'Oh, there is no point in planning anything,' said Patti airily. 'News just happens. The controller of Channel One is giving a talk about women and diversity in studio three. It is for my little group, Women in Broadcasting, there'll be sandwiches and disgusting wine. Why don't you come?'

Alexandra dutifully followed Patti through countless sets of fire doors. She was proud to be seen with her and desperate to be free of her.

Janice Gordon, the Channel One controller, was just starting her speech when Patti slipped into the back row of chairs with Alexandra, causing just enough disruption to be noticed.

'Why is it, I ask myself, that women represent half of the population but only a fifth of this corporation?' asked Janice, peering over her winged blue spectacles.

'This is why I call this the National Toss-Off Corporation. Do we want real programme makers, or just more public school boys?' Patti caught the eye of Sir David Leach, CEO of the National Television Corporation, standing in the doorway. She raised an eyebrow.

'Tell me, Alex,' she whispered after politely applauding the speech, 'do you feel held back by being a woman? Do you?'

Alexandra looked anxious, tucking her short, copper-lit hair behind her ears, rubbing at her thick, dark eyebrow.

'I, I just can't agree with that. I mean my girlfriends and I really feel that we are competing equally with men. You know, I don't think there is a difference. It just doesn't feel complicated. We want jobs as much as men, just as they want children as much as we do. It is all totally shared.'

Patti shrugged. 'Well there we are, the complacency of a new generation. We just have to see if you can all last the course. Come and meet Sir David. I take a very foot-and-mouth approach to employment. If they know your name it is much harder for them to cull you. Male or female.'

'David, hi, how are you? Great quotes from you in *American Broadcast* magazine. Very inspiring. And I had no idea that you were interested in tropical fish! Amazing what you find out about people.'

Sir David Leach, a portly figure who had recently given

up wearing a tie with his suit and looked uncomfortable as a result, nodded excitedly.

'Christ, I didn't know that anyone read that magazine. But it is true, I do think that we are moving forward into some very interesting growth areas.'

'Meet our new star,' smiled Patti. 'This is Alexandra Khan. She is going to make you very proud.'

Alexandra blushed and shook the CEO's hand. Then she left the two to chat. Once out of sight, she skipped down the corridor. This was her first day at work and she had already been singled out as a high flyer. Patti may be overwhelming, but she had obviously taken a shine to her. Alex was prepared to worship Patti for this act alone. Patti would be her guiding star.

Despite Patti's allusions to an unspecified misery, there was nothing extraordinary about her past.

The curious feature of Patti's childhood was how little she could remember of it. Her first, or was it her second, husband had accused her of being in denial about her pre-school years. She replied, sincerely, that there was nothing worth remembering about this placid passage. Discontentment was the human spur. Her first clear recollection was of aggressively hurling her school satchel against the thin wall of a suburban hallway. She was not angry, merely bored – by her mother's unexceptional domestic order, by the smell of slow unimaginative cooking, by the smothering sameness of her existence. She must have been about nine years old. Her mother's tired face was lit by a table lamp as she sat marking school papers. The only sudden movement came from the ginger cat, which leaped from the chair next to her and darted off into the kitchen as Patti approached.

'Did you have a good day, dear?' asked her mother vaguely, her spectacles sliding down her nose. Patti shuddered and went to look for biscuits in the kitchen cupboards, scraping her ugly lace-up shoes on the floor.

'Mind the carpet, dear,' her mother said, correcting the word 'surprising' in the defaced exercise book in front of her. 'And leave some room for supper.'

Patti's father, a civil servant, kept predictable hours. He did not work late nor did he ever once phone from a pub. The headlights, from the car he drove from the train station, flashed through the net curtains minutes before the garage door slammed shut and his measured footsteps crunched down the drive. 'Is that your father?' Patti's mother would ask, gathering up her books, as if it could possibly be anyone else. It was at meal-times, when the conversation was on autopilot and even the cutlery grated to the same tune, that Patti first practised the art of psychological warfare. She punctuated the silences with sniffs, each intake jangling her mother's nerves. When the impact diminished she developed a form of asthma, medically undetectable but socially menacing. Once, when Patti was older, she supposed about eleven, her heart began thumping in the middle of a maths class and she asked to be excused. Willing a breathlessness, she sought out the headmistress' study. She sobbingly confessed to the shadowy, grey-haired woman that her parents were planning to divorce and she could no longer bear the atmosphere of violent conflict. After a phone call to her mother, Patti was allowed home early.

Despite dealing with children all day, her mother was nonplussed by her daughter and Patti remained sullenly silent. She listened from the stairs to her parents' hushed, worried voices that night and ran back to her bedroom when she heard the worn-out tread of her father's shoes approaching. He sat on the edge of her bed and looked at her in honest bewilderment.

'Your mother and I wonder what you have been watching on television,' he said.

Patti wriggled down into her blankets, wound her finger into her hair and burst into loud, dry sobs. 'I don't feel very wwwwwell,' she wailed.

'What a funny little thing you are,' said her father, patting the top of her head. The episode was never mentioned, although her mother sent back the innocuous television and would not have Lord Reith's name mentioned in the house. Patti could only remember one significant exchange since. She had been looking at herself in her bedroom mirror, trying to arrange her face into a more regular composition – she had an angular bone structure that became logical in adulthood and took on a poetry through a camera lens but as a child was thought harsh – when Patti had caught sight of her mother in the mirror's reflection.

'You are vain,' said her mother angrily.

Patti cried, 'No, I am not.'

'Yes you are,' her mother cried.

Patti spent her teenage years round at friends' houses, attributing her voluntary exile to her parents' impending divorce. Her friends tended to be gentler, weaker than she. They adopted her mannerisms and Patti in turn adopted their parents.

When boys swarmed round her with their soft facial hair and their first cars, Patti asked them to drop her off some distance from grand houses that she implied were her own. She did not wish them to witness the gothic scenes of home life. They were full of admiration and pity for her life as an abused heiress. 'Why don't you run away with me?' her suitors asked in turn. Once they had uttered the correct line in her curious psycho-drama she ditched them. 'I can't,' she would sigh, walking head down towards the long driveways until the headlights turned and she took a rapid turn towards her ordinary suburban street.

One day, a friend grew jealous of the classroom gang who gathered around Patti in the morning, trembling with sympathy for her plight. 'Patti is a terrible actress,' said Susan Parks crossly. 'She is always making things up. My parents know hers and they say they are not getting divorced and that it is nonsense about her being beaten. You are such a liar, Patti.'

Patti's followers refuted the claims angrily but they were troubled. They individually counted up their personal sacrifices, of money, boyfriends and revision notes and Patti, seeing them take stock, realized the moment had come for her to make a substantial gesture. Sure enough, by noon, an ambulance arrived at the school and the girls gathered wide-eyed to watch at the classroom window. Half the staff crowded round a stretcher; the girls could only glimpse a maroon blanket out of which poked a young mousy head. The victim, or rather heroine, was not identified until the next day, which added to the general sense of hysteria. Pupils sobbed and held hands as they listened to the short announcement in morning assembly. Patti had given school life a mysterious, important new dimension and she was duly rewarded by her peers. When Patti returned, a week later, no one was allowed to mention her wrists, although she skilfully displayed them by putting up her hand in class or stretching out her arms behind her head for the benefit of the four back rows. It was agreed among the class that Susan must be sent to Coventry until the end of the summer term, after which she was transferred to a school in Basingstoke.

Patti's parents never divorced so far as she knew although she experimented with the notion that they had died. She could not check, on account of losing their new address. After several of their letters were returned unopened, they concluded that Patti had discarded the chapter of her childhood.

When she left school, she threw her English prize, an inscribed novel, from the car window. Her headmistress noted that it was a typically dramatic gesture. Patti always wanted to be a heroine from a novel rather than a run-of-the-mill Home Counties girl.

Chapter 3

After telephoning her parents with a full account of her first day at the television corporation, Alexandra text messaged her boyfriend to meet her at Pizza Express. It was past ten but she was youthfully overexcited. She wanted to replay the day in a way that made clear her prodigy status. Alex was no vainer than her contemporaries, and as easily deflated, but it was a special day. Great job, new flat. She had a glorious sense of life unfolding.

Adam Berluscoli was loyally waiting with two vodkas when she arrived. He was easy to spot, with his Mediterranean good looks and familiar grunge city overcoat. Adam still had the air of an undergraduate, as yet undefined by career or financial status. His concerns were boyish: sport, sex and the funding of public services. When he drank, sex assumed a towering priority.

It was Alex who had a new professional sheen as she waved at him and walked over to his table with a confident deportment.

'Hi, darling, God I need that drink, how was your day?'

Adam was a junior doctor. His day was a blurred crowd scene of the aggrieved and the profane. For every patient he tended to, another made a more forceful claim. A frightened, dizzy pensioner was abandoned for a sweating, vomiting heroin addict. The addict had to wait for a tax-paying businessman with suspected angina. The business-man was put on hold for the sake of a feverish child. However unique the suffering, however virtuous the patient, a rigorous, split-second selection process had to be applied. The histrionic were not necessarily the most deserv-ing. Fortunately, Adam did not have time to question his judgements. But his head ached with the fear of litigation, or worse, ghostly reproach from those he had failed. Every time he said: 'Now, what can I do for you?' he felt dishonest. This was not, after all his vocation. But he could not let his mother down. Some roles in life were thrust upon you. He did not discuss his worries. Adam had been the man of the house since he was a small boy. He was acutely aware of the fragility of others and repressive of his own. There was only so much sensitivity to go round.

Alex had been together with Adam for five years now. She enjoyed counting the time, surprised by any relation-ship that exceeded the six month cut off. It was her first statistical measure of the past. She now added to it the years since she had left home, the time she had held down a job, and her cumulative National Insurance payments.

Adam had been on the fringes of her group, the boy-friend of a friend's friend. She savoured her first sighting of him, a diffident figure with childish black curls and wide adult shoulders stretching an old v-necked jersey. He had not approached her, just smiled and nodded and watched. It was Alexandra who had introduced herself. It was she who had steered the conversation to films, and one in particular that neither had seen. Alex was good looking and self-confident enough to lead from the front, so far as boys were concerned. As her school reports had said: 'Alexandra does not need to be told what to do all the time.' The film about which Alex and Adam violently disagreed, forcing them to continue their discussion at a bar over the road, was followed by weekly, then daily, dates to theatres and concerts during which his thigh would touch hers as they buried themselves in the programme. After a fortnight they had seen every cultural event in London and were completely broke. This seemed the right moment to begin sleeping with each other.

Some men were natural boyfriends. You would always pick Adam in a romantic identity parade. He was made to be a photograph in your purse. But the particular thrill of him lay in two features. There was his named Adam's apple. And there was his smell, which meant that you would choose him in an identity parade even if you were blind-folded. Alex had known better-looking men whose musty sourness made them unaccountably less attractive. Adam's smell was a chemical imperative.

This evening Adam was dog tired and his eyelids drooped as Alex recounted every detail of her day. 'So, I couldn't believe it when Patti said: "This is Alexandra Khan, she is our new star." Well, of course, she didn't mean it, but it was nice of her to say it, don't you think? I couldn't believe it.'

She pushed away her plate and lit a cigarette. 'God, what do I sound like. Me, me, me. But it was still nice of her. Do you think she meant it?'

Adam's eyelashes trailed onto the shadows beneath. He had an expressive actorly face, beloved of casting directors. He had toyed with the idea of auditioning for RADA but he had too much to live up to. His mother had never asked him to go into medicine, but his duty had always been clear. His father should have been in the House of Lords by now, in recognition of his pioneering work as a fertility doctor. At least so his mother said every time she scanned a new honours list. Instead, he was remembered for putting his head in an oven.

Alexandra was playing with his hand, coaxing away the fist. 'Oh, darling, you look whacked,' she said. 'What is it?'

'I am fine,' Adam said, brightly, as he always did. 'Let's have another drink.' He tried to attract the waiter who refused to catch his eye. Alex raised her head in an indefinably more commanding manner and ordered two more vodkas. Then she turned to Adam, beaming.

'And did you speak to the solicitor?'

He pushed his hand through his hair, his peculiar signal of defeat. 'I couldn't get hold of him.'

Alex tried not to look irritated. 'We have to pin him down,' she said. 'I mean we really need to exchange by the end of the week if we are going to complete on time. Shall I try tomorrow?'

'No,' said Adam, with pained dignity. 'I'll do it. He should have phoned me back today.'

'You just have to keep trying,' said Alex. 'You can't just phone once. You have to make a real nuisance of yourself.'

'I know that, Alex,' said Adam, feeling for his credit card in his coat pocket. But Alex had already paid the bill.

Alex had not quite understood the etiquette of the ideas conference. When Sally had told her that an investigation into the relationship between health and religion was interesting, she had meant it as a kindly dismissal. Otherwise she would have said go ahead. But Alex was now determined to make it work. She trawled the Internet for source material and badgered Adam for names of doctors who were philosophically inclined, or rather media savvy.

She visited a cross-section of gyms, although to save time, they all happened to be in west London. She practised her interview techniques as prescribed by her post-graduate journalism degree. What, where, how, did not easily translate into spiritual matters, but she persevered. Some of her subject matter was best covered by suggestive camera angles. The spire of a church, a shot of a pair of trainers.

When Adam turned up to see her after a night shift at the hospital and a morning spent conquering the administration of solicitors, local authority planning officers and mortgage advisors, she greeted him eagerly with new tangents on her thesis. He was wan, but always patient.

The project took longer than Alex had anticipated and was constantly interrupted by stories of the day, a seemingly endless publication of quasi-medical studies commissioned by social think tanks, drug companies or women's magazines. As the general election approached, the Government also became hyperactive in its proposed initiatives, all of which had to be reported with a balancing response from the Opposition.

Finally, during an end-of-the-week lull, Alex made her pitch at morning conference.

'I'd like to go to first principles on these health issues,' she said. 'If you can all spare me ten minutes.' There was an immediate round of fidgeting. Ten minutes is an interminable time in a news room. But Sally gave a judge's nod for her to continue. Alex felt both intensely nervous and deeply calm. This was, she supposed, a definition of professional adrenalin.

'Well, I have been doing some work on my idea I mentioned before about health becoming a religion in this country. I think this has vital implications for this election,' she had improvised this line over dinner with Adam the night before and was rather pleased with it.

'It seems to me to work in news terms. I've got the health secretary to agree that health is a kind of religion, which gives me the news peg.'

Patti looked up from her doodling on a piece of paper – she was playing noughts and crosses with herself.

'Did you say the health secretary agreed this or independently believed it? In my experience, politicians will say almost anything to be polite.'

Alex was thrown. 'But that doesn't matter if they say it, does it?'

Patti shrugged. 'I'm just pointing out that there is a difference between them forming this notion independently and simply nodding in agreement when you prompt them.'

'Let Alex finish,' said Sally sharply. 'Carry on, Alex.'

Alex cleared her throat, her voice a shade more uncertain. 'Well, after the health secretary talks about this new religion, I also talk to doctors who say, without any prompting from me, that they have to fill the role of priests.'

Patti leaned back in her chair. 'Sorry, just to be clear, you have a doctor who genuinely believes that?'

'Yes,' said Alex hotly.

'Can I ask his name, out of interest?'

'Well there are a few, as I said,' replied Alex. 'One is called Adam Berluscoli, he is a junior doctor. But there are others as well.'

Patti straightened and looked thoughtful. Then she lowered her eyes and gestured with her hand for Alex to go on. Sally looked crossly at her.

Alex was also annoyed at Patti's obstructiveness. Why was she trying to undermine her? Was she jealous of her idea? Alex liked to think so, although her thesis suddenly felt as unwieldy and woolly as the last time she had raised it. 'You can't save a bad recipe with icing sugar,' her mother used to say.

Still, she ploughed on. 'My point is, that the churches are empty but the hospitals are overflowing.'

'What does that say? That hymns can't cure a broken leg?' murmured Patti under her breath. Her gladiatorial enjoyment of the event was slipping.

'It says, to me, that health is seen as a fundamental human right and as the answer to life's problems,' said Alex. 'No one cares about the spirit any more. Or rather, people don't make the distinction. I thought that I would film this GP who says that his most prescribed drug is Prozac. One in five people are suffering from depression, like there seems to be some kind of national breakdown. But no one will look into the causes. We talk about stress, but what does that mean? Could it be that we are missing some kind of spiritual dimension? And will there be a religious backlash? They say that we have all the conditions for an explosive religious resurgence, they just don't know where it will come from.'

'They say,' interrupted Patti with savage pleasure. 'Don't you love that "they say".'

The sports editor gave an apologetic cough. 'Sorry, Alex, I have to go and see the England manager. Would you excuse me? Love the talk.' He tiptoed from the room, on his comically small and beefy frame. Then, confused and remorseful, he stopped and returned to his chair, whispering that he had a few minutes in hand.

Alex looked flustered. 'Am I running over time?' she asked Sally. Sally looked slightly worried.

'No, Alex, do go on, but if you could start to wrap it up now.'

'Yes, of course. I think the next scene could work well, visually. We cut to this little country church that I went to visit last Sunday. There are only three pews full and it's mostly old women. But there is one father with a disabled child, the child is big and a little too strong. He starts to get very anxious when it gets to Communion. You think there is going to be the kind of scene you get in casualty departments every day, when patients need to be physically restrained. But his limbs suddenly drop and he looks peaceful.

'And the vicar, who is a woman, blesses everyone and the camera goes along these three occupied pews and you see these people standing shoulder to shoulder, because of the angle of the lens. So that is a way of portraying England's residual faith. Then finally you cut to a London gym at 10 a.m. on Sunday which is heaving with people. It is a different kind of worship. And, of course, the message is that there is no room for the weak who are, generally, clogging up our society. Suffering inspires a religious sense and we don't have enough suffering, or at least we don't want to know about the suffering that exists. Certainly we don't care about suffering in the rest of the world. We are so damned insular. We would prefer to go on a diet instead.'

Sally waited a second to establish that Alex had finished

and then gave a cheerful nod. 'Well, this isn't orthodox news, and it is a very ambitious point that you are trying to make. But why not break out of our conventions? I think that it could be a real water-cooler moment. We need to have the courage of our convictions in presenting it. It needs a bit more clarity, a few bulletin points, but we are almost there. Am I looking at putting this first in the running order? Let's be bold about it.'

Patti was smiling warmly. 'It sounds really interesting. It is sort of *Songs of Praise* with attitude, isn't it? It is a great feature. But too soft to lead the news, surely? I mean what happens, Bong! Health is a bit like religion "they say". Bong! What is the meaning of life? Bong! Is this chair real?'

Alexandra attempted a chuckle but it caught in her windpipe. Stray tears wobbled on her eyelashes. She looked down, gaining self-control through short, shallow breaths.

Sally came to her defence, through maternal sympathy as much as professional judgement. 'I think that you are being deliberately flippant, Patti. This is a lot better than announcing some new Government initiative that we know will never happen.'

'Also,' said Patti, in her low, modulated voice, 'what are you trying to say? Religion is better, kinder, gentler? It sounds a bit patronizing to me. What is so bad about people wanting to pursue good health? Physical or mental. Note, I say mental rather than spiritual. Let's not bring God into this. We can get on fine without him. Health is the first principle of self-reliance. We all know that life is third rate if you feel lousy. It is lousy for you and worse for everyone who has to look after you. If a pill can make you happy and stop you from spreading misery all around you, then hallelujah.

'If you want to examine religion seriously, then you had better take in the world's most vicious, stupid and expensive conflicts that religion starts but the infinitely superior secular world has to sort out.

'What is the comparative harm of Westerners paying their gym subscriptions and getting some rare tax rebate from their GPs. Let's speak up for the individual sometimes, shall we? I don't want to share some bloody pew. I don't believe in society, let alone the tyranny of faith. I want to opt out.'

Alexandra fired back: 'OK, everyone for themselves. But who is going to look after you when you are older, I mean old, Patti? The health budget can't cope with that, only people who do believe in a moral society.'

The sports editor scraped back his chair, and broke into song. 'When I get older, losing my hair, many years from now . . .' He cleared his throat. 'This is getting a bit heavy for me.'

Patti's eyes were as narrow as a cat's. But her lips were arranged into a smile. 'Just testing you, Alex. We've left our university seminars behind now. I think what you have is the beginnings of a book. It has nothing to do with news, which is merely facts.'

'Right,' said Alex, 'well, thanks for your opinion.' She picked up her bag, the one Patti called her school satchel, and left the room. There was a few moments of silence as Steve looked to Sally for guidance and Mark stretched out his legs, carefully examining a point on the ceiling. Despite his enthusiasm for world conflict he avoided personal confrontation.

'That wasn't helpful, Patti,' said Sally severely. 'We should be encouraging passion in this place. I thought that was what you and I stood for when we were setting out all those years ago. When did you become the voice of the news establishment?'

'I think you misunderstood me,' said Patti coldly. 'I wanted to report news not to subvert the genre. Also, I wanted to be treated as an equal, which used to mean getting the shit kicked out of you. Now nobody is allowed to have hurt feelings. So we have to praise the young, however shoddy their work might actually be. Well done, you have drawn a star. I wanted to be a journalist, not a nursery school teacher.'

'Girls, girls,' said Steve.

'Fuck off,' said Patti and Sally simultaneously.

Mark laughed. 'Here endeth the lesson, can we go and have a drink?'

Sally Fletcher decided to walk to Kensington High Street tube station, stopping off at Safeway. It was the first properly warm day of the year. Not the usual flirtatious spring temperatures but a steady massaging heat. Women were pulling off jerseys and carrying coats. Cleavages were suddenly magically on display. The kind of men who carried their passports in their wallets now produced unseasonal sunglasses. Aluminium chairs were confidently pushed onto pavements outside cafes. The urban community was coming to life after the months of hibernation.

Sally slowed down to look in the shop windows, where fashion competed with nature in jaunty spring colours. Reflected in the windows was a stout woman in a belted raincoat whom Sally was reluctant to acknowledge. She knew from Patti's amused appraisals that she thought Sally insufficiently disciplined about her appearance. Her hair was inconsistently done, depending on when she could fit in an appointment, and her clothes were worn according to what came back from the dry cleaners, which was usually closed. Sally had always kept faith with 'separates' which were recommended by women's magazines as an interesting economical way of 'mix and matching'. But they would not mix and did not match. She felt short and dowdy, not least because she had recently renounced the expense of fine, ladder-prone tights in favour of lasting coarse brown ones. She juggled her food shopping from one hand to another to prevent deepening weals, sighing at the flaking dryness and the multiple burns evident on her bare arms, acquired through years of ironing and ovens. Celebrities in magazines spoke radiantly of their self-imposed flaws, such as post-pregnancy stomachs, but never displayed the smaller wear and tear of maternal sacrifice. Sometimes Sally paid attention to her appearance, ripping out bikini diets from the women-friendly pages of newspapers and putting them by the hob next to her recipes. Her bursts of determination tended to follow Patti's off-hand insults. Patti's criticisms were always vicarious; she would observe that a female politician could not get her shoes right, or a charity worker looked dowdy. Sally would bristle defensively, replying in a similarly veiled manner that the person might have more important things on her mind. If she felt particularly offended she would state that dress sense was the prerogative of the childless.

Of course, Sally liked buying clothes for a special occasion or in the sales, but she got far greater pleasure from shopping for her children, especially her twelve-year-old daughter. Even GAP had got a bit tarty nowadays, but she liked choosing the ensembles and she was pleased when Sophie expressed enthusiasm for her taste.

She popped into Urban Outfitters to find something to cheer Sophie up. She picked up a shrunken white T-shirt that said 'Hi!', a parent-proof version of the T-shirt next to it, which said 'Dirty'. A young woman asked, with insolent sympathy, whether Sally would like to leave her bags of food by the door 'so you are not tempted'. Sally's professional authority deserted her as she perceived herself through the eyes of the shop assistant. She muttered dissent but meekly put down her bags nevertheless. All her enjoyment of the shopping expedition left her and she hurried to the Underground where she squeezed onto a waiting train, apologizing for the sharp, bulky, breaking carrier bags which dug into the knees of the other passengers.

Eight stops, a short bus ride and she reached the row of shops which she grandiosely described as a high street. This comprised an Indian restaurant, a unisex hairdresser and a doomed gift shop. Local estate agents had been promising the arrival of an aspirational coffee shop chain but it had been put on hold because of a planning dispute or, more likely, fears of a recession. Residents felt socially excluded and undeserving. The journey time was disproportionately long in relation to the distance, a fact of life within the M25. Sally was struck daily by the distortions of her time. When she was not working she found extra hours added to her day. No lunches, no commuting. On the other hand she liked the mathematical apportioning of time that went with office life. A slice of the circle to commuting, a segment for lunch, programmes divided precisely into minutes and seconds. Accountability of time is a kind of madness. Sally liked to entertain at home but sometimes felt panicked by its open-ended nature. Guests were invited to arrive at eight but there was no stated time for departure. There was no controlling the slice. Gordon, her husband, was altogether better at ignoring the clock as he slumped in his favourite armchair. He did not feel compelled to leap up and cook or clean or make phone calls. Sally was training herself to sit quietly beside him and waste away the evenings. But for now she was preoccupied by immediate tasks. Sophie had sent an oblique text message. **Still hurts, have put skirt etc in wash. Can you come home?** And when Sally arrived home, Sophie was curled up with her duvet on the sofa, watching *The Simpsons.*

'Hi, Mum,' she said, lifting her tousled head and hot cheeks. The room was untidy and airless and Sally immediately opened the window, always her first gesture when she got home. It was a side effect of being a working mother that the windows had to be closed during the day.

Sally found the gear shifts between work and home troublesome. Her mind was too often at the other place. She worried when her home number came up on her mobile in the office and she felt awkward taking work calls in between wiping the kitchen surface. You could either make harassed-sounding jokes about noisy children and saucepans boiling over, or pretend that you were running a multinational company from the sink and that the roar of the kettle is only the fax machine. Both were role play.

Being organized by nature, Sally fretted about not seeing her work through. On Wednesday evening, she handed her week's schedule over to another editor, but work and life did not split so neatly, and she jealously guarded both.

Still, these were small frustrations. She did not want

family life in the abstract. She loved the messy, demanding reality of her husband and two children. All her emotional life was here and it had given her a compass through life's unfamiliar territory.

She had recently been feeling mildly out of sorts, with her intermittent heavy periods and strange swings of body temperature. Odd that she felt so physically sluggish when she was almost invisible at work. Sometimes she could walk the whole length of the building without being noticed. Just another middle-aged woman trying to hold herself together.

Sally did not feel invisible at home. She may have passed her unremarkable prettinesss on to her daughter, but this gift of love infused her with radiance.

'I'll make you a hot water bottle,' she said, pushing her daughter's silken brown hair behind her ears. 'Don't worry, darling, everything's fine.'

Patti, meanwhile, was being driven to Downing Street. She wound down the windows, breathing in the warm wafts of carbon dioxide so that she could upset the driver's precious air conditioning and agreeably contemplate office workers searching for a patch of grass to put down their coats and eat their sandwiches. Like other members of the ruling class she avoided public spaces and had forgotten how to use public transport. There had been an uncomfortable moment a couple of years ago when a television boss had suggested taking the Underground and they had both searched in vain for the right place to insert their tickets, to the amusement of a group of students. She had not repeated the pointless affectation. The route down Whitehall was part of her personal *A to Z*. The policeman at Downing Street waved her through without checking and she exchanged friendly nods with the small groups of political staff who wandered up and down the empty street as if it were a university cloister. It was her kind of neighbourhood. Outside the gate, a small crowd craned their necks, excited at last to see someone whom they recognized. Patti assumed a serious but humble expression. She was the people's broadcaster.

Patti had known the previous three Prime Ministers quite well, particularly Mrs Thatcher. Mrs Thatcher had greeted her approvingly, telling her that she was so glad to find 'one of us' at the National-socialist Television Corporation. Patti was not sure if this was a reference to her sex or her presumed politics. Since Mrs Thatcher had from then on spoken only to the male guests, she admiringly concluded that sisterhood was not uppermost in the Prime Minister's mind.

Tony Blair was always solicitous to her, remembering her birthday while being vague about her age. If asked about her relationship with the Prime Minister, she expressed a preference for the lonely eccentricity of the Chancellor, which suggested authenticity. The person she really liked, however, was Alastair Campbell. They clasped hands bruisingly, like the couple of street fighters that they were.

Tony Blair was full of public school charm, profoundly self-confident for all his studied diffidence. He murmured to her about mutual friends and shared holiday destinations as he led the way past the pram in the hallway, which Patti glanced at meltingly. 'Not the enemy of promise, after all,' she murmured.

He offered to show her the Cabinet room, but she demurred. They ascended the grand staircase together into a sunlit first-floor dining room. He implied flatteringly that she would not be impressed by properties this size in central London and probably owned one. They could have been a couple of investment bankers in the middle of a property boom.

Like Prince Charles, whom Patti also knew well, Tony Blair was fussy about his food which had to be fresh and exquisite. While he picked at his chicken he engaged Patti in the Big Ideas of the election, asking her with his steady, sapphire gaze, 'But what do YOU think, Patti?'

In turn, she held him with her own bright gaze. The sun bathed the room and, more importantly, her hair in light as she dabbed her mouth with a white linen napkin. It was a perfect environment for discussing Socialism. Resting her fork in her hand she told him, 'I think that you can afford to be radical, Prime Minister.'

He nodded vigorously. Campbell asked Patti what she meant exactly.

'I mean that you are capable of greatness. Your Government, your Chancellor, understand good administration and we need that.' She hesitated as if she could hardly contain her passionate conviction. 'But you, Prime Minister, are a visionary. You could take on the problems of the world. I think that you are a man of destiny, a man for the new millennium.'

Campbell cleared his throat gruffly. 'I don't think we want to remind people of the Dome in this election.'

Tony Blair broke off a crust of bread and stared at Patti with Disney ardour. 'Do you really think so, Patti?'

'Yes, sir, I do. Forget Middle England. Forget the voters, you can afford to. Think of the disenfranchised. Here, but also in the rest of the world. We have to think globally now. You can change this country, Prime Minister, you can change people's lives. But, my God, we also need a world statesman, a new Churchill. That is an awesome responsibility.'

Alastair Campbell winced sardonically. 'I'd never thought of you as a bleeding heart, Patti.'

Patti pursed her soft, slender lips. 'Alastair, I come from a poor background, but I have fought my way up. I think others should have the opportunity to do the same. Don't you think that is right, Prime Minister?'

The blue sea washed up against the rocks. 'Yes, of course,' said Blair. 'Opportunity for all. That is what this election is all about.'

'What about taxes,' said Campbell. 'Are you happy to pay for it, Patti, or is it just rhetoric?' Patti was shameless at the best of times but even she had her limits. She gave a little yelp and concentrated hard on her quivering fruit pudding.

At a quarter to three, the Prime Minister reluctantly folded his napkin and pulled back his chair. They all followed his example, standing ready to leave. 'Thank you so much for coming, Patti, I do value your opinion.' Patti glanced sideways at Alastair who made a small parodic bow. She mimicked a curtsey back. It was a bore that he no longer drank and was so uxorious.

The Prime Minister took his benign leave, promising vaguely that 'we must do something for Patti'.

Patti did not want to be in the House of Lords. It was not an adequate power base. As Campbell led her to the car, tantalizingly close to her, she said: 'Alastair, I need something, now.' He nodded warily.

'The reshuffle is good,' he said. 'Tony is showing just how tough he can be.'

Patti passed Alexandra's desk on her way to the make-up room. A simple bunch of flowers was half unwrapped after an obvious tussle with the tighter cellophane bands round the stalks. A card was propped up by Alexandra's computer.

Go for it, Alex. All my love, Adam.

'That's so sweet,' murmured Patti to Mark, who was perched on a stool, his lips moving as his eyes scanned the bundle of notes. 'I'll just put these in water for her, I hate to see flowers die under the studio lights.' Patti's nurturing side was more public than private. She held the bouquet, bridelike, until she reached the green room and thrust it at Jenny. 'Could you do something with this, sweetie?' Patti then sat before her little altar and gazed at her reflection. The geometric contours of her face formed a resolute composition. It was a beautiful face but it was not kind. She artfully created a softness by tilting her head to one side and smiling as if at a nativity scene. Patti's buffed and massaged skin absorbed her foundation rapidly, and the blusher followed on the natural sculpture of her face, despite Jenny's shaking hand.

Patti made a note to show concern for Jenny's obvious emotional turmoil, but not immediately. The problems of others had to be convenient. Half an hour later, gleaming and scented, Patti inclined her face lovingly towards the camera, and put down her pen.

'Good evening, tonight the National Television Corporation has an exclusive report about the imminent Cabinet reshuffle. A source close to the Prime Minster told us that Tony Blair is showing just how tough he can be.

'Fighting continues in the divided territories of Sri Lanka. And in the second half of the programme Alexandra Khan has been comparing gyms with churches.' She smiled pertly. 'That certainly demands some mental gymnastics. Now, over to Mark in our Westminster studio.'

As Patti left the news room, a phone was ringing insistently. She did not answer it. If Sally chose to be at home, she could not expect to control events at the office. If you want to succeed, you had to make choices.

Patti was not sociable in a journalistic sense. She did not go out for drinks with her colleagues, she certainly did not volunteer for late night curries. Patti felt there was nothing to gain from friendship and its raft of petty obligations. Sometimes she shone her blinding beam on a colleague who was of use to her and it was switched off as abruptly once she had achieved her aim. The rest of the time she regarded people she knew as extras rather than protagonists. Only the powerful had distinctive presences and Patti tripped across their magnetic fields. What she really loved was the fusion of power. She always read the City pages first in newspapers in case there were reports of business mergers. The more hyphens the better. The kind of parties Patti liked were grand and corporate where names and titles counted for more than conversation. This was so relaxing.

She particularly wanted to unwind after her effortful day and fortuitously a large American bank was sponsoring a party called Meet the Movers and Shakers at Tate Modern.

She liked the escape routes from the gallery's vast lobby and the light was flattering. A couple of bores and nobodies waved at her and she looked in the other direction, a pleasant, distracted smile bobbing on her delicate lips.

She caught sight of Sir David Leach. 'David, good to see you. Did you manage to catch tonight's programme? We think we'll get a good follow from the papers.'

Sir David looked like an overweight school boy caught out missing rugby practice. 'Oh, Patti, do you know I didn't, damn, I had to drive the boys back to boarding school and then I had early drinks with the PM. He spoke very well of you; of course, everybody does.'

'Thank you,' said Patti modestly looking down at her champagne glass. 'Oh look, there is your wife, she seems to have some trouble getting in. Shall I give her a hand and show her where the cloakrooms are?'

Sir David shook his head. 'No, I had better go. I am afraid my wife just doesn't have your sense of style, Patti, though she is of course indispensable in many ways.'

Patti nodded in enthusiastic agreement and wandered off. She was taller than many of the guests and had a clear view over their heads. As she was scanning the gallery for Mark she felt a finger run down her spine. She spun round, wrapping herself into Mark's embrace like an ice skater.

'Is this Britain's most gorgeous newscaster?' whispered Mark, moving his lips across her forehead.

'Is this Britain's most brilliant political reporter?' she murmured. She pressed herself against Mark's thin chest, warm beneath his crumpled linen suit. Patti nestled her lips into his floppy, light brown hair which smelled of booze, sweat and cigarettes.

As she inclined her head towards him in order to hear him above the noise of the party he grunted and lunged at her mouth. Patti was tipsy and exhilarated.

She heard a woman's voice piping up across the crowd. 'Patti, Patti. I'm Judith Walker. Do you remember me? Patti Borkowski, eh? Do you remember? I was Simon's friend. I came to your wedding. Ring any bells, if you'll excuse the pun, ha, ha. Patti, oh, oh, she didn't hear me.'

Patti took Mark's hand steering him rapidly across the room and down the stairs. 'Who was that woman?' asked Mark, his hand moving in the darkness down the back of Patti's skirt and fingering her suspender belt.

'Oh, don't know, no one, some journalist. Coming home with me?'

'Try and stop me,' he whispered. 'Actually, do we have to wait that long?'

The funny thing about the press, thought Patti afterwards, is how little they find out. It is astonishing what does not get into the papers. Mark had pulled over on the Embankment and they had staggered out, dragging at each other's clothing until they found a shadowy stretch under the bridge.

Minutes later, they tucked themselves in, and returned to the car. Mark drove her home in his Golf, one hand resting gratefully in her lap. He pulled up outside Patti's house and switched off the ignition. He leaned over to kiss her again, the beginning, he hoped, of a trail of lovemaking leading to the bedroom.

Patti moved her face away. 'Mark, I am so tired. Champagne always knocks me out, I should stick to whisky. Forgive me, darling?'

Curious really, thought Patti later, that she was prepared to have rough sex beneath a bridge but not let her boyfriend sleep with her. She would have liked the comfort of his sinewy arm across her. But the morning light was so hostile nowadays. At night she and Mark were comrades. In the morning, devoid of make-up and television lighting, she felt the twelve-year chasm between them. He became a bloody spy.

At 3 a.m. the baby next door cried and Patti woke. She sipped the water on her bedside table, pushing aside a historical biography, and banged her head determinedly onto the pillow. Her mind was too brightly lit for sleep. There in front of her was the undistinguished suburban house with its stained glass door.

There was Simon to meet her as she hobbled weakly down the front steps. Both were as pale as paper, bad diet, bad drugs plus the unacknowledged enormity of their loss. With awful clarity, she saw the red bus pull up and felt Simon's grip as he helped her up the stairs and onto the first seat, for the disabled and young mothers. She did not look at Simon's handsome, Slavic profile, nor touch his broad shoulders. Their decision, casually made, had severed their easy intimacy.

Nonetheless, as is statistically common in these circumstances, Patti immediately resolved to get pregnant. Simon stopped going to tutorials and Patti feigned illness to get her out of doing hospital radio. Instead, they retreated to Simon's bedsit, where they rarely moved from their unwashed sheets and ignored the increasing pile of dirty crockery in the sink. They listened to the Kinks and to Bob Dylan, they had sex and they smoked pot with tears flowing down their cheeks. Being young, their determined self-destruction made no mark at all on their lovely faces. Lovemaking covered the cracks in their relationship. They were physically suited to one another, his arm encircling her at the right height, his strong build emphasizing her slenderness. They had enough common references, music, youth, pleasure, to sustain a bond, although beneath all this they were hopelessly different. Simon had a Polish father and an English mother. He was culturally displaced, whereas Patti, for all her imagined orphan status, had roots. She hated his silly, guttural, foreign conversations with his father and the oily, prosaic recipes his mother cooked for them. She hated his crying and his rages. Her anger was of a deadly, sarcastic kind. Patti teased and impersonated and humiliated him. She became a passionate Communist, enrolling in the North London branch in order to spite him. Her abortion, was, as much as anything, a slight to his manly Catholicism. It was also a crude, clinical rebuke to his poetry, which was florid and humourless. She had been afraid of the fierce, demanding changes to her body and was obsessed with expelling the growing thing. Only after it had been ripped from her, leaving her punctured and bruised did she feel the first flickering of love and a profound longing. She had been punished for her deed and she wanted to punish Simon for being a horrified accomplice. It was his fault for believing in her. But she also desired him. She liked to rest her head on his tapered hips, stretching out her arm against his rising and falling chest. Patti narrowed her eyes to avoid seeing the red and gold book of poetry he held aloft. She loathed poetry, with its infuriating superiority of feeling. She blocked her ears to Simon's solemn, war-heavy, Polish utterances of love. It was not a relationship founded on empathy.

One afternoon, when Simon was serenely stoned, he told Patti that he had booked the registry office. They knocked on the door of a university friend of his, Judith Walker, and asked her to be witness. Judith, who was writing her thesis on the romantic poets, was taken aback by her friend's impulsiveness and tugged at the sleeve of her droopy smock while she considered.

'Why me?' she asked blinking through her spectacles at the large-framed Polish boy with whom she had hoped to share some of life's adventures.

'Because we love and trust you,' said Simon reaching out a woodcutter's arm to her.

'Because yours was the first door we came to,' said Patti, prettily. Judith gamely signed her name under the couple's – Simon and Patti Borkowski – despite her own heart-gutting love of Simon. Every love affair has its casualties. As they walked out of the grimy civic building, matching electric-blue velvet trouser suits, fingers entwined, man and wife, a photographer stopped them.

'Man, you two are it,' he said. 'I have to catch this.'

The poster of this beautiful, gaunt, swinging couple was tacked onto a thousand teenage bedrooms well into the seventies, yet the marriage barely lasted a month.

Their perfect suitability was superficial. Simon nursed a romantic pessimism about their situation; having lost their footing he announced that they were doomed and should bow out. He was so obliquely poetic that Patti could not tell if he was urging suicide or simply a restorative spell in the country.

She, by contrast, began to find their misfortune bracing. Patti had a rock-hard core which marked her out as a survivor. Any emotional excavation floundered against this layer of granite. She enjoyed the notion of being a tragic heroine but she lacked the necessary capacity for self-destruction. Simon was puzzled and frustrated by her lack of yielding depths. She became increasingly bored by his appetite for infinite misery.

One day she cleaned the flat thoroughly and settled down to a frank personal audit. She needed to turn her loss into profit. Her experience was raw material after all. When she presented herself for an interview at the women's desk of the *Daily Express* she was asked to produce ideas that would appeal to young women readers. She wrote, under a false name, about her experience of abortion. It was considered daring and controversial.

She pursued her gynaecological theme. During her post-op yearning period, she had read in a medical journal about a fertility doctor who had been making great strides in his field. It was too new and complex an area to have reached mainstream journalism but his fame had spread through word of mouth, and appointments had to be made months in advance. Women worshipped him for his scientific or divine skill, according to opinion, and for his black curly hair. Roberto Berluscoli was too highly strung and intellectually absorbed to be swayed by his patients' devotion. His surgery was his laboratory and he worked long hours with hysterical intensity. Outside it he was preoccupied and forgetful. He was forever retracing his steps to look for scarves, coats or, far more precious, scraps of paper with his scribbled thoughts. He could never remember to eat.

Dr Berluscoli was particularly animated on the day that Patti came to see him. Despite the high rate of failure in his work, the potential for success was tantalizingly within his grasp. He greeted Patti absent-mindedly and gestured for her to sit down. She must not think him rude if he walked up and down but he was restless.

'To tell you truthfully, I may not be able to help you now, but in five, ten, twenty years I will, I pledge this to you.'

Patti was intrigued by this luminous, darting figure. In order to secure his attention, she removed her long, military-style coat and waited expectantly for a response to her exposed figure. None came. The doctor did not even glance at the contours of her little T-shirt. He saw her as a malfunctioning receptacle with a sad, youthful face. 'You have time on your side,' he said kindly. 'Just be patient.'

Patti's pale eyes fixed onto him like cruise missiles. 'I am not a passive person,' she said. 'I have to know what I can do. Or rather what you can do. Tell me about your work, please.'

Dr Berluscoli looked at his watch. He was past his allotted consultation time, he could not let people interrupt the science. Yet he felt sorry for this strange, unhappy girl with her striking genetic history.

So he sat down and patiently told her. He explained the possibilities of IVF and he showed her his laboratory of frozen eggs.

'Where do these come from?' she asked.

'Wherever I can get them. Some women donate them, some sell them. This is very early stages. But one of these frozen eggs is going to take.'

He flung out his arms. 'We implant, eight, maybe ten embryos in the womb. One has to work, do you see what that means?'

'And the others, Dr Berluscoli?'

'Ah, they are dealt with through selective reduction.'

Patti's eyes widened. 'How do you manage that?'

'Well, my dear, I inject the foetal sacs with potassium cyanide. But let us talk of the one that takes. I think I can say, with some confidence, that we are approaching our first IVF birth. My God, this is going to change my life; your life. It is a marvellous thing for humanity. Science for the service of humanity.'

Patti was now infected with the doctor's animation. Although in her case it was eagerness to file her story rather than tackle humanity's woe. She shook the doctor's fine, slim hand and left. Dr Berluscoli had a momentary sense that something was forgotten. The strikingly sinuous girl had failed to make another appointment.

The newspaper wavered over whether or not to run the story. Not from moral scruples but because the headline would not fit and executives were unsure whether it was a news or women's feature. It was shelved for a few weeks during which time Patti was offered a job on a pioneering women's magazine called *Working Women's World*, or *WWW*. During a quiet news period it was dusted off by a keen new women's editor, who sent a team of theoretically infertile women to nail Dr Berluscoli.

Patti's new colleague, Sally, admiringly read out the headline as an example of what *WWW* should aspire to. It read: **THIS DEADLY TRADE IN HUMAN EGGS**. A snatched photograph of Dr Berluscoli leaving his house was captioned 'The Angel of Death'. It was only Patti's innate professionalism which prevented her from claiming the story. She was afraid of the implication that she had not been sufficiently thorough or persuasive to get a story into the paper. Besides, she did not want to be cast as a specialist in womb abuse. She preferred her new role as a high-kicking feminist.

Success does not happen in isolation. Every advance is accompanied by a corresponding misfortune. Simon had to go. He may have had the talent to be a great writer, but she was not responsible for the lives of others. Patti was an instinctive existentialist. Besides, weren't there too many books published already? Last she heard, he was making puppets (this said for comic effect) in Wales. Simon, for all that beauty and promise, was never going to be a winner.

Dr Berluscoli was suspended from his post, pending an enquiry. Six months later he put his head in the gas oven.

Chapter 4

Patti was unexpectedly gentle towards Alexandra when they next met at the noon conference. Alexandra seemed subdued and Patti found herself missing her ebullient comments. She had no detectable conscience but she occasionally experienced a mild emotional remorse if she had been over-zealous in crushing her adversaries. She came to bruise Alex, not to bury her. Antagonism based on simple rivalry is not as inflexible as ideological differences. There is usually a flux in human relations. Patti was peculiarly sensitive to shifts in power. And when they worked in her favour, she was gracious. When she lost ground, she fought with tooth and claw.

Alex had been working too hard, on all those hospital league tables that informed the reader that their chances of survival were twice as high if they happened to be living 300 miles away. Patti regarded the research as worthless, asking, why stop there? Why not add to people's discontent by reminding them Los Angeles or maybe parts of India had the best consultants for your particular condition? Or that it was a pity that you were going to die because the cure would be announced at an international conference days after your funeral. You had to play with the deck of cards you had been given. Play the game and leave. Patti was impatient with illness which she regarded as an unhealthy compromise between life and death. It was ugly and attention seeking.

Alexandra had stiffened at Patti's entrance into the room but could not help responding to her almost kind expression. She surveyed Patti through her thicket of black eyelashes.

Patti's expensive beauty looked slightly tarnished today. The morning light rested on the deepening crow's feet round her pale eyes and the heavy white down on her diaphanous skin (a cumulative surfeit of vitamin E creams). Patti's hair needed doing, there was a thin crescent of grey on her crown. Alex and her old flatmates Emily and Lisa always felt honour-bound to acknowledge that Patti looked amazing for her age – whatever precisely that was – but her beauty had lost its careless quality. Her magnificently pre-served face had faded and fallen. She was impressive but no longer awesome.

Alex was surprised to find herself feeling sorry for the older woman. How would Patti manage old age? She had no children. She did not appear to have any friends. These were unacceptable sacrifices so far as Alex and her contem-poraries were concerned. Work was a right and a pleasure but it was not a philosophy. Patti's single-mindedness seemed hopelessly old fashioned to Alex. Emily had pro-nounced her 'totally last century' and speculated that she wore Janet Reger lingerie for seduction purposes.

Alex felt impulsively beneficent towards Patti. She must remind her of the small, significant contentment of a rounded existence.

She would ask Patti to come round for supper at the new flat. They would have to sit on boxes and there was hardly any cutlery but that was part of the fun of it. The two women exchanged spontaneous smiles.

Sally noted Patti's sudden shaft of affection. She had once seen a wildlife documentary during which a female gorilla playfully nuzzled her young. Then the programme maker conducted an experiment. The floor beneath the gorillas was heated. At first the puzzled mother scooped up the baby in order to protect her. As the heat became unbearable, however, she threw the baby gorilla to the ground and stood on her. Patti was prepared to play with Alexandra until her own position was threatened.

The following week, surprisingly, Patti accepted the invitation to supper at Alex's Ladbroke Grove flat. The idea amused her. In turn, she issued an invitation herself. She asked Alexandra to give a talk on a fresher's view of the media at the next Women in Broadcasting meeting.

'It sounds ghastly, but I think it will be worth your while doing it,' said Patti. 'Women are just learning the value of networking, Sir David comes and so on. You will certainly get noticed.' Alexandra frenetically tucked her hair behind her ears. Then she jumped up from her chair and hugged Patti.

'God this is such an amazing day; everything is happening to me. First Sally and now you.' Patti patted her and recoiled. She sometimes expressed warmth as a strategic exercise but not as a physical impulse. She did not much like being touched, even as a child. She fought off the embraces of relatives as far back as the pram. She really did not understand non-sexual physical affection. Sally had once joked that you would have thought Patti had been physically abused, except that no one would dare.

Patti was keen to have a word with Sally and found her in the newsroom on her mobile, ordering flowers for her mother's birthday. Patti perched on a desk, waiting for her to finish. Sally had several other calls to make to plumbers, Tesco home delivery and school outfitters but she put her phone away, apologetically.

Patti gestured to her not to hurry while crossing her legs impatiently. 'Sorry, Patti, did you want to talk?' said Sally.

'Oh nothing urgent,' replied Patti. 'I just asked Alex if she would like to address WIB. I though it might be interesting.'

'Good idea,' said Sally. 'We could do with a different perspective.'

'I just wanted to check that it didn't conflict with your plans. Alex said you had already approached her; she is going to be raking it in on the lecture circuit.'

Sally glanced at Patti. 'Oh no, it was something quite different. It was just an idea I had.' Sally's phone was ringing in her bag but Patti remained motionless and expectant.

'What kind of idea?'

Sally looked defensive as she rooted in her bag to check that the number on her mobile did not match Sophie's.

'I have just asked Alex to fill in on the lunchtime news while Fiona is on maternity leave.'

Patti's pleasure in this idea was Oscar-winning. 'What a good choice. Gosh, I hadn't realized that Fiona was pregnant.

Come to think of it she has been looking like a sea lion. I asked Jenny to get her out of the studio last week because she was making me feel sick. Didn't recognize her; I thought only a member of the public could be so gross. But then I never find out about these joyful events until I read the *Hello!* spread.' She ignored Sally's sour expression. 'Anyway, I am so happy for Alex. She is a breath of fresh air, isn't she?'

'She may turn out to be better than that,' said Sally.

Piety was a deadly sin according to Patti. When did Sally suddenly become Mother bloody Superior clucking and cooing over the young. Nursing and nurturing. Pampering and potty training. Sally's smug gift for 'bringing people on' was an excuse for her own lack of talent. She had no gifts to relinquish, unless you counted administration (which Patti didn't). It was Patti who must be stripped and shorn. How easy for Sally to be generous on Patti's behalf. She lit a cigarette and stared out of the window in a white-grey haze of rage. Sally had betrayed her. Hadn't they formed an alliance based on self-interest? Is this not friendship? They were meant to be on the same side, bound by a common enemy. In the past it had been men, but men surrendered without a fight. It was pitiful how ready they were to sign up to a new world order.

Clearly the foe was now younger women, who were as grateful as King Lear's older daughters for the privileges bestowed on them. They could not wait to rid themselves of their benefactors.

Patti realized that her interpretation of a little job share might seem melodramatic, but she knew how to dress up her grievances, even to herself.

Individuals confounded isms. Feminism fragmented into

the parts of its sum. When Patti and Sally first met they appeared to have much in common. The same high-velocity hairstyles, the same defiance, a compatible sense of humour. Patti remembered showing Sally her first proofed-up feature idea – are there any disadvantages to castration? Sally had thrown back her head and laughed. But the common references were to do with youth rather than character. Sally was the more ideological but temperamentally softer. She was smaller and wider hipped. She was fundamentally maternal. Her professional talent mirrored her domestic strengths. She liked to be busy and needed. She functioned best in a team. After her years at *WWW*, Sally found a natural home at *Women's Hour*.

She bought her own flat after taking advice from a methodical, decent local solicitor called Gordon Fletcher, whom she quietly married. For a time she kept her maiden name but once Sophie was born it made sense for everybody to come under one heading. She thought about asking Patti to be godmother to her daughter but reason prevailed over sentimentality.

Patti's career took a different route. She preferred a platform for her feminism. She found Sally's circle of like-minded, earnest-natured women skin-prickingly tedious. She was more likely to thrive among men; stars can only shine in darkness. Patti also had a shrewd sense of market forces. Mrs Thatcher's power owed much to her isolation as a woman among men. She, like Patti, felt diminished by the squidgy, sympathetic presence of the sisterhood. Besides, Patti realized that every good pioneering feminist needs an indulgent male mentor. Sure enough, her dashing brand of female liberation – playing hardball in a micro skirt – proved very successful. She instinctively grasped the business school ethos that she needed to convince only one person in the organization and, happily, that was the boss. Patti was programmed to forge an exclusive intimacy with her editors and their interests coincided delightfully. Her editors wanted a glamorous but disruptive force, whom they alone could control. Patti wanted constant attention and a disproportionately high salary, guaranteed to make everyone else envious and miserable. The amiable, collegiate atmosphere of offices was shattered within weeks of her arrival. Her editors guiltily and gleefully described the new climate as creative tension.

Patti had no time for established hierarchy. She was certainly not prepared to cover drab court cases in the North of England. She despised the petty scrabbling for overnight expenses. She was not given jobs. Jobs were created for her.

An editor of a Sunday broadsheet, who had the appearance of a Cambridge spy, devised the title of a column for her. It was to be called Patti at the Barricades.

At the time, the column was praised for its spirit and originality, although a laddish magazine re-visited it with brutal irony a couple of decades later. Back then, though, men regarded it as a sporting kind of radical feminism. It was spun from a series of stunts, thought up by senior male executives. The best-loved consisted of Patti striding freely through the Garrick club wearing a Moulin Rouge costume under her raincoat. She described club members as 'choking on their pink and green ties' although in reality they merely blinked and beamed. Even the doormen gave her a cheerful wave. 'I wouldn't call it Joan of Arc,' said Sally dryly, as she read the multitude of follow-up pieces in other papers. The stunt was so successful that it was repeated, as the subheading put it 'at the ultimate men's club – the House of Commons'.

When Patti lost her way, staff politely escorted her to the debating chamber. The newspaper was so delighted with the photographs of Patti perched on the Wool Sack, dressed as a sixteenth-century serving wench, that she was promoted once again, to star writer on the magazine.

'Congratulations,' said Sally. 'Will you be dressing as a highwayman for your new job?'

Patti liked politicians and she slept with many of them after a good dinner at the Connaught. To her credit, she became less predictable in bestowing sexual favours. There was always a core constituency of extremely powerful men who required attention. 'The natives are restless,' she would tell Sally as she cancelled dinner with her, enjoying the disapproving cluck of response.

But as she became economically and professionally independent, she courted men for more varied reasons of lust and excitement. She still found that the personal and professional went hand in hand. Men were unexpectedly useful. Private rooms were opened for her, security documents disappeared from locked desks. Work was a tremendous game.

'Isn't it odd, Sal, you are a feminist but I am just a man,' she said, sipping a cup of tea in the neat garden of Sally's first marital home. Sally's husband Gordon tried to concentrate on his hedge clipping as Patti's sing-song voice regaled them with her sexual exploits. He found his wife's friend an extremely alarming presence and preferred to survey her from the safe distance of his buddleias. Patti's listed criteria in men did not include kindness or decency but she was broad enough in her sweep to encounter both qualities. For instance, there was one minister whom the press favoured as an old-fashioned English hero. John Partridge had exuberant but strictly parted hair and a square jaw. His father had been a Spitfire pilot in the second world war, and John always turned up to the Remembrance Day Service wearing a beautifully cut cashmere coat and an expression of deep pride and sorrow. He was a serial resigner, twice claiming responsibility for a junior's mistakes. He had a small personal fortune, permitting him an honourable disdain for the money grubbing scrapes of his colleagues. He was not especially bright but his conventional good looks and perceived moral seriousness carried him through the ranks. By the time he met Patti, he was tipped as a future Prime Minister.

They met through a chance encounter on his part, and weeks of planning on hers, at a political philosophy group dinner. John noticed Patti immediately, but what persuaded him to pursue her was an extraordinary series of coincidences. It turned out that she shared his admiration for an unfashionable political philosopher and she quietly, intently, quoted his best-loved poet. More remarkable, she indulged his private love of botany and longed to visit the harsh, wind-whipped Scottish islands that were especially dear to him. He was surprised but easily convinced that her metropolitanism disguised a fierce passion for nature. At the end of the evening he kissed her on both cool, satiny cheeks, slightly afraid that she would be offended by this impertinence.

The more he saw of Patti, the more mysterious she

became to him. Of course he had heard rumours of wild and cruel behaviour but he put this down to jealous gossip. John was proud of Patti's wit, even though he could not always follow it. He was dazzled by her sexuality, which he supposed he must have unleashed. He was indulgent towards her spending, which he thought innocently girlish.

He was touched by the fact that she had few friends despite her gregariousness. In short, he loved her. At times, he felt it necessary to chide her for her high spirits, which usually took the form of dares. She did not always show sufficient respect for matters of state. It was silly of her to have defaced some important departmental papers and he would rather she didn't invent spiteful nicknames for every member of the Cabinet.

There was one particular incident that he would rather forget. Patti had nagged and nagged him to show her the Cabinet rooms out of hours. One evening, he had relented. Following a series of coded telephone calls, and favours called in, he gained access.

Patti strode round it, impersonating each minister's sycophantic attempts to gain approval from the Prime Minister. John stood anxiously by the door, whispering to her that they had to leave, for the Prime Minister was returning from the Guildhall.

Extraordinarily, Patti had then lewdly laid down on the table. She told him that betrayal was the only acceptable declaration of love. John's face was contorted with horror and lust. Afterwards, he had read her the riot act. 'For God's sake, Patti, nothing like this must ever happen again. I shall have to leave you unless you can learn how to behave.'

'What a pity, I had my eye on Westminster Cathedral,' smirked Patti. John put her response down to childish bravado. He was sure that she was full of remorse.

A month later the couple married. The *Evening Standard* pronounced it the most glamorous wedding of the year: Patti in Grace Kelly white, the Wiltshire-based Partridge family out in solid force on the right-hand pews, assorted celebrities spreading out to fill the empty places on the left. There were no bridesmaids, despite Patti's endlessly professed love of children. She shrugged that she was an orphan herself and she felt it unfair to subject John's frankly pudgy nieces to the public gaze. 'Children are so sensitive at that age,' she told him, and he deferred to her emotional knowledge.

John said that with a wife like Patti he had the strength to serve his country. His house in Lord North Street was beautifully decorated and the scene of some memorable salons. Patti had an instinctive grasp of politics and sighed deeply about Britain's commitments abroad as she curled up on the sofa. But she won the hearts of her guests by her whispered compliments, doled out like party bags at the front door. 'That phrase in your speech really struck home', 'One of the whips was praising you the other day, now who was it?', 'What is the crest on your ring?', 'An actress was praising you the other day, now who was it?' John always looked forward to being alone with his wife at the end of the evening, to hearing her sharp jokes about his colleagues while he encircled her waist and kissed the back of her long downy neck. Over a short time, however, he found the bedroom light had gone out before he had locked up and Patti was breathing steadily. 'Patti?' he would call into the gloom before sitting sadly on the end of the bed and unsteadily pulling off his shoes. He came to know that Patti did not take kindly to being woken. The bed was a symbol of both invitation and rejection. Patti seemed to sleep through her marriage. He had lost her at night and more painfully he felt her retreat during the day. She walked off before he could finish his sentences. Within months she was physically absent for days at a time.

He would trudge home from the Commons after late-night debates to find the house dark. Patti skipped constituency events and forgot to turn up to a banquet at the Palace. The Prime Minister would ask him pointedly how Patti was and he would always reply, 'Top of the world.'

One evening he crept home after fluffing an important speech on defence. The opposition ripped apart his statistics and roared with laughter at his slip: 'The navy has the feet that we deserve.'

He poured himself a whisky and stared forlornly at the gas fire. There was an envelope on the mantelpiece, on which was scrawled in black fountain pen, John, please read. The letter inside said:

Dear Big Foot, I am afraid that I am leaving you. Kiss, Patti.

'That is the trouble with your generation, so PC,' said Patti to Alexandra as they stepped into the lift together. 'There is no point in you giving this speech if you cannot speak honestly. We have quite enough liberal consensus here already.'

'But I am not really qualified to say all this,' said Alexandra pressing her hands worriedly against her Starbuck coffee. 'All I know, is that people seem really nice here and it is a great team, but obviously the management hierarchy is quite male. And I just wanted to say that I hope there is room for someone like me, I mean, being a woman and, you know, ethnic.'

Alexandra was much smaller than Patti, and in her grey jacket and skirt, the shade of school uniforms, she looked like a teenager.

Patti had a sudden image of Alex emptying from her school bag defaced matt-pink exercise books and a pencil case stained with fountain pen onto a tasteful but carelessly worn kitchen table. Patti imagined herself leaning over Alex's shoulder for a second, dishcloth in hand, advising her on a perplexing piece of homework. She wanted to nurture Alex, when she was not trying to thwart her.

'You think that you are LUCKY to be here, because you are female and correctly multi-racial? Come on, really. The lucky thing is that you have, coincidentally, merit as well. You young women do not have to worry about access. But you have to make sure that you are being appointed for reasons that have nothing to do with your sex and your race. And I would say that you cannot be sure of that until you reach the age of fifty, when nobody notices what you look like.' Patti smiled dryly and ushered Alex out into the fifteenth floor.

The flowers were out in force again on Alexandra's desk. Same florist, same card. 'Good luck on your big day, love you, Adam.' Patti overwhelmed his floral offering with a vast bouquet of her own, full of strange, spiky stems.

'Oh dear, it makes me look like the wicked stepmother,'

she trilled flute-like to the floor manager. 'Who will warn Snow White not to touch them?'

Derek laughed. 'Snow White is already in make-up, you are too late.' Patti leaned back in her chair, looking at the television screen. She stretched out her legs and put her arms behind her head. A side effect of this was that her skirt rode up and her shirt opened slightly. Derek shot a wistful glance. Patti watched Alexandra walk into the studio and sit behind the desk, self-consciously sorting through the prop pages in front of her.

The reddish tints in her short hair caught the light. The studio manager slipped the microphone onto the jacket of her grey-green jacket which Patti, by screwing up her eyes, recognized as her own preferred designer label.

Patti's leg shook with exasperation. The countdown began and the theme music to the one o'clock news started. Alexandra looked intimately towards the camera and her mouth gave a little leftward pull. Another technique borrowed from Patti. 'This is the lunchtime news.'

Alexandra's debut was considered an unqualified success by the crew and by an enthusiastic Sally Fletcher who had been standing behind the camera. Patti sensed that it was not the moment to voice her own copyright reservations. Champagne was handed round in plastic cups and later the crew, the managerial staff and a large group of assorted well-wishers trooped off to the conference room to hear Alex address the Women in Broadcasting group.

Patti waited by the temporary podium in case Alexandra needed any last-minute advice. Patti had already been generous with her time, offering annotated notes to Alexandra's speech. Alexandra arrived, slightly flushed, after most of her audience had sat down. She kissed Patti on the cheek, in an absent-minded way and tripped past her. Patti coldly turned and went to take her seat.

'I have been asked to speak today about my "fresher's" view of the media. I have in fact been working in the media since university but it is only in the last couple of months that I have been in national television. At the last meeting of Women in Broadcasting, a woman, much more experienced than I, said that this organization, "the National Toss-Off Corporation" was over represented by "public school boys".' A titter from the floor. 'Well, for the record, I was educated at a London comprehensive. I would rather not talk about my sexual preferences.'

Alex was an experienced speaker at Oxford, and paused for more laughter. When none came she felt her neck grow warm. She took a breath and fixed on a spot at the back of the room above the unfamiliar rows of adult, business-like heads.

'In my view, it is the role of my generation to correct the balance of the pioneering feminists. Quite honestly, if you are female and lucky enough to have some mongrel credentials you go to the top of the list. What is hard for we newcomers is to be sure that we have been appointed for the right reasons.

'Today I made my first broadcast as a lunchtime newsreader, which was an extremely daunting experience for me although my bosses were really supportive. Thank you, Sally Fletcher.'

She cleared her throat and tucked her hair behind her ears, which were starting to sing. How could she have not noticed how banal and egotistic she sounded when she rehearsed this in the women's lavatory half an hour ago?

'Sorry I am sounding like a dim actress,' she went on with a pleading smile. 'What I meant to say was this. People were kind enough to say that I was "good on camera". I guess, that makes me think: Was I good journalistically or was I just the right image?

'Because if I am just here for the image then I can be easily replaced. Believe it or not, there are a load of telegenic Anglo-Asian women out there.' She began to speed up. 'I think it is right to raise these sort of questions here but I am confident about the answer. Call me naive, but I don't believe that was why the lunchtime programme went well. I think it worked because of the tremendous professionalism of this organization and the absolute commitment to content. The right "image" is quickly forgotten when you are dealing with real issues in front of a real audience. I know that, as a fresher, I will get up people's noses and that I will make mistakes. But I also know that we all have a common aim, which is to make the best programmes we can. And I am so grateful for the chance to do that. Thank you.'

The press office had calls from the *Daily Telegraph*, the *Guardian*, and, on edition, *Broadcast Week* within minutes of the speech ending. What was the corporation's response to their new star's astonishing claim that racially mixed presenters went 'to the top of the list'? Sally accompanied the slightly tearful Alexandra to a private room, where, over water and tissues, they and the head of the press office formulated a response.

By the end of the afternoon, a statement was issued on behalf of Alexandra Khan: 'I regret that I have been quoted out of context. The National Television Corporation does not pursue a policy of positive discrimination in any form. I believe that I have been appointed on merit as have all other members of staff who share my gender and race.' Alexandra also agreed to be interviewed by one newspaper, the *Guardian*.

Patti meanwhile had spoken off the record to *The Times*, the *Mail*, the *Telegraph* and the *Daily Mirror*. Yes, of course it was a gaffe, there had been 'an audible gasp' from the audience. It was puzzling that Alex had chosen the Women in Broadcasting group as a forum for her 'amazing attack'. Patti then begged the newspapers to 'give the girl a break'.

If it would help, Patti herself would be prepared to be interviewed about the NTC's exciting flagship autumn news show, soon to be unveiled. This offer was made only to *The Times* and the *Mail*. The *Telegraph* asked too many unauthorized questions, the *Mirror* was not her audience.

On the same day the *Guardian* ran its media interview with Alexandra, Patti's face appeared on the front pages of *The Times*, the *Mail* and on final editions of the *Express*, the *Sun* and the *Mirror*. In *The Times*, it was the Mario Testino portrait of her on the puff panel at the top of the front page, with the caption: 'Britain's top newsreader gives a rare interview'.

In the *Mail*, her picture covered most of the front page itself, with the question in bold print 'Who is the girl on the most famous sixties poster? See page three.' Inside it was revealed as 'Patti Ward, arm in arm with her American boyfriend who died tragically in a car accident. She speaks frankly and exclusively to the *Mail*'s star writer, Diana White.'

Patti Ward looks pale beneath her immaculate appearance. She may be the envy of British women, with her stunning looks, which some say are cosmetically preserved, and her high salary, said to be in the region of £250,000 a year. But she has had to pay a price for being such a high flyer.

Patti reveals for the first time the secret that has haunted her through her successful career. It is the death of a young man to whom she was extremely close.

As a teenager, Patti met and fell in love with a privately educated American young man called Huck Pelman, who was studying at Oxford University on a Rhodes Scholarship – a contemporary of the more famous Bill Clinton.

Patti and Huck made a perfect couple, so much so that a snatched photograph of them became the image of the sixties; the previously unidentified couple in the famous Athena poster, which briefly outsold the tennis player lifting her dress, was none other than Britain's most famous newsreader and her handsome fiancé.

Their romance came to a brutal end when Huck was killed in a car crash on the way to Heathrow airport.

Patti told the *Mail*: 'I don't really want to go into it too much, it is still quite raw, even after all these years. I guess you could say that Huck was the love of my life.' Asked where her fiancé was buried, Patti revealed that she had thrown his ashes into the Cherwell, the Oxford river, as he had once asked her to. She had then sold the South Kensington flat that Huck had bought for her, intending it to be their marital home. 'The memories were too painful, and I felt it was too grand for me.' Patti was born into an impoverished middle-class family. 'We did not have much money, my father was a clerk and my mother a housewife. I remember making toys out of cardboard boxes. But my parents had a strong sense of right and wrong, which I hope that I have inherited. We were always a close family.' After shining at the local grammar school, Patti made her parents proud by winning a place at Oxford University.

Despite her grief over Huck's death she was awarded a top degree and worked for a variety of papers as a writer and top political commentator before moving into television. 'I felt that I had to achieve something, for Huck's sake. I worked hard. Any spare money I had, I sent back to my parents.' Patti led an almost monastic existence until she met the English aristocrat, and MP, the Hon John Partridge, favourite of the Prime Minister.

Partridge was attracted by Patti's looks and intelligence, while she felt that he would shield her from her previous tragedy. Sadly, this safe haven of a marriage ended in divorce. Patti tells the *Mail* exclusively: 'I don't want to say anything out of turn about John. He still means a lot to me. Let's just say that he had other interests.' Many women will be surprised that this stunning, brainy beauty has had such a tragically unfulfilled love life. But it does perhaps explain her professional drive. 'I am not actually ambitious,' shrugs Patti sadly, 'but my life has taken unexpected turns.'

This is a far cry from her reputation at NTC, where colleagues describe her as 'Darwinian'. But her unluckiness in love does reveal Patti's softer side.

Will she ever find love or is Patti Ward doomed to become a career spinster? According to close friends, Patti has recently formed a close relationship with Mark Wyndham. 'You should have seen them at the Movers and Shakers party,' said a friend. 'She was all over him like a rash. We were all quite shocked.' Patti was also seen sipping champagne and sampling artichoke dips, unusual for a woman who is famously disciplined about her weight. Could it be love at this late stage which is making her so relaxed about her diet? She refuses to confirm whether her relationship with Mark Wyndham is more than platonic. 'I have much to be grateful for,' she says carefully. 'I have many friends, and nieces, nephews, godchildren. I feel very blessed in that sense. Marriage and children are of course the greatest happiness in life, and I have been denied that, but you know, I am thankful for what I have achieved.'

There are achievements still to come for this remarkable woman. Patti Ward confirms television rumours that she is being lined up for the NTC's autumn flagship news show. 'I can't say too much about that, but obviously it is very exciting.' Patti Ward has been to hell and back but now she is proving to British women that there is life after fifty.

Patti read the piece hurriedly, her lips pressed together. The fictional Huck Pelman was a persuasive creation, she was pleased with that. But then there was no such thing as a wholly sympathetic interview in British papers, however much you feed them. They would always slip in a knife somewhere. She had told Diana clearly that she was forty-eight.

The Times interviewer was a young, fashionably dressed woman with a whispery voice. She wanted to know more about Patti's Women in Broadcasting group. Her cousin was an NTC trainee, her father a governor of the board.

Patti was friendly but wary. She mused on what other connections she might have with her interviewer. She tentatively ran through the chief media dynasties and found her interviewer related to three of them. After this, she relaxed and chatted about books and their shared commitment to life/work balance. She kissed the pale, pretty girl on both cheeks and promised to look out for her at David Frost's summer party.

Patti's autobiography tended to be flexible and approximate. She was not remorseful about this. Of course one had to adjust to one's audience. It was just tiring keeping up with the latest version of the truth. At the end of her marriages, she found tangentially connected people waiting, sympathetic, heads cocked, for her to account for herself.

Patti found that a cogent narrative was bound to be untruthful. There are at least four interpretations of a marriage: the husband's, the wife's, the lover's, the child's. Not to mention in-laws, colleagues, local dry cleaner. In a way, it was more honest to decide on a plot and make the details fit.

After the day's exertions, she dialled Mark's number. 'Want to have dinner tonight?' she asked, tracing her reflection with her finger in the hall mirror. His voice was muffled by the shower running in the background. 'Darling, I'd love to, but I've got my little brother staying the night with me.'

'Half-brother!' a gruff, imperfectly pitched voice intervened in the background. 'Tristan has been on the march,' explained Mark. 'Hence his pointless belligerence.' Patti asked to speak to Tristan who made a face and delightedly shuffled over to the phone.

'How are you?' she asked softly. 'Shit,' said Tristan, unconsciously pulling at the ring in his eyebrow, deepening the concentric redness. 'I mean, sorry, yeah, I'm OK, but I have been at the march? And like the police just kept us in this pen? I think I was on TV?'

'Well let's see,' said Patti. 'I'm just going in to do the news. Want to play the game?'

'Yeah, yeah,' said Tristan. 'Could you get in the word PIGS?'

'Watch me,' said Patti. 'I'll try. Good luck at school, Tristan, come and stay with me next time.'

Tristan grabbed a beer bottle from Mark's fridge, although he did not feel much like a drink, and settled down to catch the news. Theme music, Patti's face, grave and beautiful. 'The May Day protests today closed a section of central London, and brought an estimated thousand protesters in conflict with heavily prepared police . . .' Tristan caught sight of a strip of his forehead, masked by the annoying bouncing of women protesters in front of him.

Patti moved on to various Government initiatives and then a pretty woman, much younger than Patti, did a piece to camera about the new findings on the merit or otherwise of milk.

There was only five minutes left before the sport, Patti had ducked it. 'The cases of foot-and-mouth disease are now in single figures. Three new cases were confirmed today in the North of England and we report on the case of one herd of rare sheep whose owner is resisting the cull through the courts.' A woman sniffed into a handkerchief.

The correspondent rounded off his report and handed back to Patti who, unscripted, asked him: 'Any other animals affected?' The correspondent looked puzzled. 'No, Patti, as I said, just this herd of sheep.' Patti looked ironic and composed. 'And now let's check up on the weather. Sunshine tomorrow, Karen? Or will pigs fly?' Tristan let out a high yelp. Patti was brilliant fun. He didn't know what she was doing with a dwork like his brother. He couldn't wait to tell his school friends that he was going to stay with her during half term.

Later that night, Tristan was playing championship manager on the computer in the bedroom he was sharing with
Mark. He heard voices in the hallway beneath and poked
his head down the stairs. Patti's crown of creamy blonde
hair was incandescent beneath the bulb, her arms raised up
against the door. Tristan was about to call out when he
spotted Mark pressed against Patti, his trousers round his
ankles.

God, what was he doing to her? God. Tristan crept back
to his room. Why couldn't they just do it in a bed like
everyone else. He switched the light out and stared at the
ceiling, until his over-wrought brain shut down and his
smooth hairless body gave a final involuntary shudder.

Patti was as decisive and self-sufficient about shopping as
she was in every other aspect of her life. It was a question
of first principles: how could she upstage the hundred other
women, the majority of whom were younger than she? Patti
made a swift diagnosis: the trouble with her fellow female
presenters at these award ceremonies was that they threw
their dresses at the occasion.

They did not think beyond the initial battery of lights,
whereas Patti was a strong believer in second impressions.

The way to ensure press attention was either to dress
elaborately, 'looked like a princess' or more usually to wear
almost nothing, '*that* dress'. Wholesale exposure of flesh
would get you on the front of the *Sun*, a bombardment of
taffeta on page seven of the *Telegraph*. Patti's media strategy
was long term – who she was rather than what she wore.

An elementary rule of upstaging was to dress against the

grain. If the invitation said black tie, then Patti opted for understated daywear. This evening, she wore a new silver-grey trouser suit, which emphasized her slenderness and height. An anonymous phone call to the papers had alerted them to the fact that Patti's earrings were stamped with a three-feathered crest, a present from Prince Charles.

This revelation, coupled with the fact that Patti strode up the red carpet to the Grosvenor House hotel with Sir David Leach, who was shaking with laughter at her whispered aperçu, secured her the front page of the *Daily Telegraph* along with *The Times*, the *Guardian*, the *Daily Mail* and curiously enough the *Financial Times*.

Once inside the hotel, Patti found Mark, awkward in black tie and clutching his guest list. He ran his hand through his limp hair and reeled off some names of television actresses. 'Could be my lucky night,' he shrugged. Patti grabbed the list and read it close enough for Mark to smell the aromatic fragrance of her thick blonde hair.

Once his smile became sufficiently sheepish, she led him to table three, fussily laid out with a central floral display, cutlery, name place and goody bags. As the couple shared jokes about the naff stage design and the bustling young female organizers with their headphones and name books, Sally and Gordon arrived.

Sally was wearing an unflatteringly flouncy shot silk evening dress, and a pashmina shawl.

'Hi, Sal, you look lovely, hi Gordon, so who is the babysitter?'

'Our daughter, with a bit of help from a teenager down the road!' they said simultaneously, with the same proud winces.

'Perhaps we can pay her off with this goody bag,' said Gordon, merrily brandishing some branded soap and chocolate.

Behind him, Alexandra and Adam were weaving their way to the table. Alexandra was wearing a hippyish red velvet dress that set off her strong dark colouring. Adam was paler skinned, blacker haired and slightly dishevelled in his borrowed evening jacket. He had been mistaken both by the paparazzi and the event's PAs for the star of a Sunday night classic series and a possible friend of Madonna's. Tired from a hospital night shift and overexcited by the heat and glamour of the reception room, he had already drunk too much. Gordon leaped up to shake the couple's hands, Patti kissed Alexandra on both cheeks, Mark gave a cheery wave.

He draped his arm round Patti's shoulder but she swivelled round to give Adam her full attention, she had been curious to meet him as his surname had a profound resonance for her. His contribution to Alexandra's piece on health and religion had obviously been invaluable, she said. What was it like at the coal face? She was fascinated, simply riveted to hear that his ambition was to specialize in female fertility. She knew little about this field although of course she understood the agony of childlessness. Adam's long slim fingers played with the cutlery. He was not an easy conversationalist, and found the glare of the older woman's attention overwhelming. His natural inclination was to listen and observe but he could not drag himself out of the spotlight. Eventually the older woman's probing, caressing voice seeped into him like a drug. He took several short sips from his wine glass, feeling the effects immediately on his empty stomach. He tried to deflect Patti by suggesting that television was a more exciting topic than his over-crowded, under-funded hospital. 'Don't encourage doctors to whinge,' he said, knitting his mobile black eyebrows.

Patti leaned closer to him, her voice low.

'I suppose you must need a great sense of vocation to be a doctor. Do you feel that you have it?' Adam felt suddenly, embarrassingly, close to tears.

'Not really,' he said gruffly. He glanced across the table at Alex but she was bantering gaily with Mark. Adam was sinking.

He tore at his bread and then at his hair as he poured himself a succession of drinks. He heard a voice, shockingly his own, telling Patti that he would have liked to act. Instead of dismissing this absurd statement, she closed her eyes for a moment and when she opened them again they had become a more candid blue.

'Isn't that strange?' she said shaking her head. 'I thought the second I saw you that you had a great presence, either film or stage, I can't tell which. And such emotional intelligence. How terribly hard for you to be assigned the wrong role in life.'

Adam blinked at her. There was something compelling about her detached sympathy. Her head was tilted towards him so that he addressed her in profile, the waterfall of pale hair, her straight nose and the long curve of her delicate mouth. Her drop-diamond earring was hypnotically bright. He blinked and tried to focus instead on the blonde hairs across her forearm and the glint of her thin platinum watch. Befuddled with drunken adoration he seized her wrist and held her warm, scented hand to his cheek. She waited a few seconds before sliding it down past his neck and chest and resting it on the table in front of him. There was something so sexy about her worn beauty, the slight sagging of her lower cheek, the faint rings around her neck. Sexy yet motherly. Sort of. She acknowledged his tumbling confessions with little nods, and encouraging glances. When he told her about his father and the burden of his legacy she ran her finger round the rim of his wine glass in silence.

Finally she looked at him with complete concentration. 'Would you like me to speak to your mother?' she asked. Adam felt a surge of stupid infatuation.

'God, would you do that, Patti. I am sure she would listen to you.' He did not need to be strong. He would surrender to this remarkable woman. A few words would restore his sense of purpose and direction. Adam felt loose and liberated. He was terribly pissed. Patti dropped her arm reassuringly onto Adam's thigh.

'Sure I will,' she said.

Patti had meanwhile lost control of her orchestra. Mark was watching with some anthropological interest the procession of Lycra-clad soap actresses, with their aggressively protruding breasts and sulky expressions, totter towards the lavatories. Meanwhile, the head of news had taken the chair next to Alexandra and there was an animated exchange of cultural references.

Same Oxford college, although Sebastian was five years older, same authors, same holidays. Patti had never managed to win over Sebastian so easily.

Age is the only unbridgeable chasm she supposed. Also, Sebastian, despite being openly gay, was temperamentally straight as an arrow. Patti had an instinctively lateral approach to human relations. She insinuated herself. When Sebastian had first arrived, a couple of years ago, she had dubbed him the boy wonder and fixed lunch at the Ivy.

Sebastian did not drink and looked at his watch every fifteen minutes. Worse, he batted back Patti's questions and answered her subtle, ironic expression with a direct gaze. Patti had been so unnerved by the young man's lack of animal interest in her that she had promptly booked herself into a health farm. Since then she had treated him with a feigned briskness.

Divide and rule. Patti leaned over the table and asked Gordon Fletcher if he could advise her about garden hoses. While he gave her a delighted detailed response, she traced her finger down Mark's thigh, beneath the white tablecloth. Meanwhile, she poured Adam his seventh glass of red wine. He raised his glass to her, loudly declaring her to be the most beautiful woman in the room. Sally asked Alexandra if she would accompany her to the ladies.

The taxi squealed to a stop outside Patti's house and the engine continued to chug as she stroked Mark's cheek and told him that he could not come in. Her light-hearted ''night!' echoed across the silent street as she fished in her jewelled evening bag for her door keys. Someone coughed nearby. Patti glanced round and then, seeing nobody, she opened her front gate. As she closed it behind her, under the street light, a hand squeezed hers. It belonged to a short elderly man with a veined complexion, wearing a navy blazer. Patti whipped away her hand and looked at the wheezing figure contemptuously, although her heart was thudding.

'There you are, Patti,' he said, showing stained teeth. 'You have kept me waiting.'

'Who the fuck are you?' said Patti.

'I'm Arthur, of course. We love each other.'

Patti slowly scanned him. His hands were in his pockets. It was too dark to see if he had a weapon.

'Arthur,' she said slowly, 'turn round now and go home. Go home, Arthur.'

He grabbed her arm and jutted forward his angry face, spittle collecting in the corner of his mouth.

'You whorebag.' Squeezing her wrist with one hand, he began to undo the gold buttons of his jacket with the other. Patti experienced the absolute calm of terror.

'Let me go inside to turn off the alarm,' she said. 'Then I will invite you in.' Arthur glared at her.

'Give us a kiss first,' he said. Patti looked at his foaming mouth and mossy teeth. 'Here,' she murmured, cupping his face in her hands and lifting two fingers towards his eye. She pushed until the blood trickled onto her knuckles.

As he staggered backwards, she ran up the step and turned the key, breathing hard but never emitting a sound. The old man made no noise either. Patti waited behind the locked front door. After an hour or so, she went and washed her hands in the kitchen sink.

After another hour she went upstairs and peeped out of her bedroom curtains. He was gone. Her hands were still as she took her cleanser from the bathroom cabinet and wiped her face. Her face in the mirror was pale but impassive. It was her victory, not his. She hoped that he was blind. Patti, unusually, put on a pair of pyjamas and pulled the duvet round her face. She would not phone Mark, she would not tell the police. She would fight her own battles.

She dreamed of tracking down her stalker. Inside her handbag was a kitchen knife. She hailed a taxi and when the driver turned around, his face was Arthur's. She smashed the glass with her hand and slit his throat with the shards. His eyes opened wide in appalled recognition of death and they were Mark's eyes. Patti sat up in the dark, her pyjamas clinging to her. The clock was ticking by the bedside, it was silent outside.

She looked out of the curtains again, searching for the figure under the street light. There was no one there. The clock said 3 a.m. Where was the baby's cry? It was time for the baby to wake up to feed. Could she have slept through it? Could Arthur have overridden her dreary dream sequence of the hospital ward? Patti pressed her ear against the bedroom wall. What had happened to the baby? Who had killed the baby?

Patti refused to relinquish self-control, the purpose of her being. She walked softly back to the bathroom. Her hair shone under the light, but her face looked old and frightened. Who cared for Patti? Patti had murdered love. Where was the baby?

She found some sleeping pills in the cabinet and tiptoed back to the bed, smothering her head in the pillow. When she awoke, the light was shining through the curtains and she could hear the milkman clinking the empties on the doorstep.

Her head throbbed and her shoulders were stiff. She showered and dressed, hurriedly applying lipstick and putting concealer under her eyes. Her chest ached from the deafening thuds within. Perhaps she was having a heart attack.

She would go to the gym, that would settle her. But what if she had a collapse there? Why, it had happened to an acquaintance of hers. He had fallen lifeless from the step machine. What a pathetic way to die. Please, dear God, let me die with dignity. Wasn't the phrase a misappropriation of the euthanasia argument? And yet, wasn't it perfectly expressed. It meant, surely, the right to die at a time and in the manner of your own choosing. Which did not mean slumping over a piece of gymnasium equipment.

Her heartbeat had slowed to an acceptable rhythm. Patti picked up the post from the hallway and looked for envelopes addressed to next door. Here were a couple from six months or so ago. One looked like a cervical smear recall, the other was a charity request.

She knocked on her neighbour's door, although the noise was drowned out by the renewed tempest in her chest. Her ears rang with the noise. The door was opened by Veronica, a neat blonde who completed her toilette early in readiness to be a daily asset to her investment banker husband.

'Patti, hi?'

'The postman had the wrong address,' smiled Patti looking into the hallway. 'Is everything all right?'

'Yes,' said Veronica, puzzled.

'Baby OK?' asked Patti, her mouth like dust. Veronica beamed.

'She slept through the night for the first time, I feel like a human being again.' She stepped back and lifted the fat infant from her baby bouncer. 'Didn't you, darling, say hello to Patti. No, that is not nice!'

Patti nodded coldly. 'Good, anyway, I must get off to the gym, bye.'

The gym was the great healer. Its rituals, its congregation, could not help but soothe Patti's soul. She parked her Aston Martin in its usual space and made a dash to reception, her head bent in the manner of the late Diana, Princess of Wales. The girl behind the desk was new and did a clumsy double take when she fitted Patti's signature to her face. Beyond this, guests and staff deliberately ignored Patti's celebrity. She dumped her bag and raincoat on a chair at the side of the gym and climbed onto the step machine, wearing an old sweatshirt, tracksuit bottoms and trainers.

Club members on either side of her looked resolutely ahead, a gym instructor looked over her shoulder at her computer programme, did a thumbs-up and wandered off. Patti was in splendid isolation, her preferred state. She pedalled until her body ran with sweat and her legs ached.

The greater the physical pain, the calmer her mind became. She pedalled on until she became light-headed, until she could no longer feel her limbs. She felt a breeze carry her upwards. It was either the air conditioning or the Holy Ghost.

Chapter 5

Alexandra had a day off work. She had been doing the lunchtime news for three weeks on top of her health reports for the evening slot. She had also volunteered stories for the *Today* programme and enlisted for Sunday evening main news. Sally Fletcher and Sebastian were delighted with her commitment. Patti called her 24/7 – the girl who could not say no. She said it in a nice way, fond, concerned.

Alex was enjoying the limelight. Her haircut had been named after her, like a rose, by the *Daily Mail*. The newspaper sent three volunteers to try the same cropped style and concluded that it was ideally suited to heart-shaped faces. The following week they included her in a computer-generated line up of celebrities, to demonstrate how they would all age. The *Guardian* rebuked the *Mail* for refusing to take seriously the Oxford-educated news-reader, illustrating their attack with a huge picture of her.

The *Daily Telegraph* tracked down Alex's parents to Middlesex, warmly describing them as 'a union of a first-generation Asian immigrant shopkeeper and a middle-class white school teacher, who had a shared belief in hard work and family values'. The *Daily Mirror* carried a fuzzy picture of Alexandra and Adam hugging on the steps of their new flat, with the caption: 'Doctor in the house'.

Alexandra laughed off the sudden fascination with her as harmless frivolity. She was too well anchored, too ambitious to be flattered by it. She wanted to be around in twenty years time – like Patti. Alex did not completely get Patti. She could be so attentive, giving advice, introductions, gifts, but then she would suddenly blow cold. She would pay great attention to all Alex's ideas, then, in sorrow, demolish them.

Was Patti her friend or wasn't she? She had giggled at the *Daily Mirror* piece but was grumpy about the *Mail*. 'Alexandra I hope you are not becoming vain,' she said looking at her over her reading glasses.

The week before, Sally had arranged for Alexandra to have a driver: she said that she needed one with the hours she worked. When Alex had taken the tube she had found plenty to do. She read newspapers and novels and rolled her eyes at fellow passengers when the train stopped between stations.

Recently, it had to be said, she was aware of more stares than the usual quota for pretty young women. So a driver was, well, nice, although she no longer got any work done on the journey.

Of course the drivers all wanted to talk about Patti, some of whom had ferried her around. She had her ways, they said. She always knew a faster way and blamed all traffic delays on the driver.

One Indian driver said that he had asked to be taken off Patti's rota after she had performed an obscene act on her male companion. Alexandra was horrified and spellbound. At her age! When she told Adam he shook his head in wonder. For several days afterwards he had adopted the same fleetingly aghast expression. Alexandra hoped that he was not dwelling on the image. She realized Patti dominated at least half of their discussions. She did not want to think that they were obsessing about her.

The reason that Alexandra had taken the day off was to move into their new flat. The act of purchase had sealed their relationship and been a material symbol of adulthood. They had picked up the keys from the estate agent in a state of wonder. A generation ago, she might have been carried over the threshold. But dual financial responsibility made nonsense of all that.

Instead, Alex had wandered across the empty rooms, registering electricity points, fussing over newly exposed damp patches, trying out views from the living area onto the street and the bedroom onto their small garden. She basked in the possibilities of empty spaces before they disappeared in the cheap clutter of their joint possessions. She felt a passing sadness that the personality of her environment would soon be merged into someone else's.

Alex felt the vibrations of the removal van and padded to the front door in her leopard skin pumps. Adam, in a T-shirt and sweat pants, was directing the van into the parking space, waving his arms like a conductor. 'Tighten the wheel, mate, left, left,' he called.

It was good to see him so enthused. Alex hardly had time to notice him over the last month. They had both been working so hard. Tasks were hastily shared out through text messages or shouts from the bathroom.

They had not sat down to a meal together for weeks, living more or less on hummus, tortilla crisps and breezers. Once the alcohol kicked in they fondled each other in front of the late television news but Alex either became too preoccupied by the programme or she fell asleep so they never got as far as making love.

'Did you know, Alex, that couples have more sex in their first five years together than the rest of their lives together?' Adam had said wryly, while climbing into bed the other night. Her dark head lay still on the pillow. He brushed his own head of curls against her cheek. She turned sleepily towards him.

Chapter 6

Patti wandered into the conference room. It was quiet today. Mark was out covering the election, Alexandra was off. Sally was arriving late because of some arrangement to watch Sophie's teacher take maths. Since Sally did not find it necessary to bring Sophie's teacher into a television news conference, why the other way round? thought Patti. Steve the sports editor was doodling on a piece of paper while listening to Radio Five on his headphones. Patti gave a tight smile. 'Fantasy football?' she mouthed. Steve took off his headphones.

'Patti!' he greeted her cheerfully. 'Bit of a graveyard here. Are you sticking around?' She picked up a pile of newspapers, scanning the news and diary columns. She threw them back.

'Nope.'

'Fancy a drink?' asked Steve. And began singing: 'Oh we'll drink, we'll drink, we'll drink to Lily the Pink, the Pink, the Pink . . .'

'Is there nothing more recent?' said Patti to herself, checking through her emails.

Steve stroked his beer belly thoughtfully, then jumped.

'Hey, what about: "I get knocked down, but I get up again?" . . . Nah, it is all drugs songs now. Nothing about a friendly pint. Anyway, will you do me the honour?'

Patti grimaced. She could no longer drink during the day without feeling headachy and tired. Another lost perk of youth.

'Another time. I have to go and get my hair done . . .'

'As you do,' said Steve brightly.

As Patti wandered out of the building, she felt a hand suddenly grasp her shoulder. She lashed out sobbing, 'Fucking get off me, you pervert.' Her vision was blurred with shock but it cleared once Sebastian stepped back.

'Whoa, Patti, whoa.'

She braced herself, moving the muscles of her face into a smile. 'Sebastian,' she said shaking and smiling. 'Why are you pretending to be a mugger?'

Sebastian looked as shocked as she was. 'Well I won't try to rob YOU on a dark night. Is that your normal response to human contact?' Patti felt a little dizzy. For a second she contemplated leaning against this cold young suit and begging for help. She delved in her bag for her packet of cigarettes. Her hand passed over the lumps of her mobile phone, her Filofax, her scent bottles. She started to scrabble, pulling out packets of tissues, her purse, her notepad, sleeping pills, her cheque book. Sebastian leisurely produced some cigarettes and a lighter decorated with pictures of copulating men from his pocket. 'Here, have one of these.'

Patti leaned forward, puffing at the cigarette until the end grew bright. 'Just the occasional,' she smiled thinly. 'Aren't you having one?' Sebastian shook his head and involuntarily took another step back, as if to distance himself from her neurosis. He waited a minute, looking up and around him, pulling a petulant Sebastian face.

'I was going to say that I'd like to do another pilot. Get a better sense of the shape of the programme. But maybe this isn't the time,' he said.

Patti tried to catch his eye. 'Last one no good? I wondered whether we had the right studio audience. They were a bit day-time TV weren't they?'

Sebastian was non-committal. 'I'll let you know as soon as we can fix a date. Just relax, Patti, breathe.'

Patti walked slowly to her car. She got in the back wordlessly and buried her head in a newspaper. What was that little shit up to? She was in this business when he was still poring over his exam sheets with his faggoty cigarette-lighting fingers. Was he going to take her on? Would he dare?

The car pulled up in front of the hairdressers. She had been too distracted even to argue with the driver's route. Inside the salon she glanced up at framed photographic portraits of actresses, MTV presenters and a soft-focus picture of herself. She would have to get that removed. The Prime Minister's wife was not up there, so neither should she be.

Patti's hairdresser was waiting for her, gentle and solicitous. As he guided her towards a private area, followed by sweet-smelling manicurists, masseurs and eyebrow graduates, she relaxed. These were her people.

This overhaul used to happen every six weeks, then once a month and now about twice a week. Classic cars need more maintenance Petre had told her proudly, while folding strips of silver foil onto her head. She assented, bitterly. At what point did it become uneconomical to spend so much

time in the garage? It was now about two-thirds maintenance to one-third living. How had women managed in the
past with so little help? How fortunate that cosmetics had
kept pace with medical advance. She had no doubt that she
would rather be dead than ugly.

Later, varnished and restored, Patti slid into the back of
her car and returned to the television studios. Mark must
have returned from the election battle bus by now; she
found herself increasingly interested in his movements. She
had asked for a daily itinerary of Labour's campaign, so that
she could imagine Mark in a directory of unfamiliar places
that she never wished to visit.

She mused over his ink-stained pocket, his unbuttoned
shirt and his habit of rubbing his chin to check whether he
had shaved, which was also an unconscious gesture of
creativity. She knew exactly whom he would be seeking out
in the late afternoon, the parliamentary sketch writer; his
mentor and father figure. 'I have to tell you what the Great
Man said today,' he would promise Patti when he remembered, inconsistently, to phone her. 'God, I wish I could
write like him. He knows everything. Come and join us,
darling, he'll love you.' And now Sebastian had so unsettled
her that she was not sure that the Great Man would love
her. Patti felt an unexpected flutter of longing as she strode
along the NTC corridors. She broke into a wide smile,
directed at no one as she pushed the fire doors. Good
heavens, she was almost happy.

Sally was chatting to Jenny in the conference room,
which was otherwise empty.

'Hey, where is the gang?' asked Patti, her smile now
fixed.

'Girls' night in,' said Sally. 'News writes itself. Election then straight over to foreign. So Jenny and I are debating the shade of Anne Widdecombe's toenails.'

'That is a gorgeous pink,' said Jenny, gesturing at Patti's feet.

'No Mark?' asked Patti evenly.

'He went straight to Westminster,' said Sally. 'Decided that he would do it straight from there. I tell you, this election has destroyed our reporters' homing instinct. By the way Alex phoned in, I knew she couldn't switch off. She says she has been reading an amazing writer called Ahmed Rashid who is really worked up about events on the Pakistan border. The Taliban are this monstrous threat, but the West doesn't want to know. What do you think, is it worth a proper treatment? Alex is keen to fly out there, but I don't know if Sebastian will buy it. Jenny thinks it is a good idea.'

Patti caught Jenny's eye and smirked. 'I think I would stick with Anne Widdecombe's toenails. No one could give a fuck about any country ending with "stan".'

Sally folded her arms across her roomy sale jacket. 'You are right, unfortunately, you are right.'

'Unless you want to discuss any other aspects of the Third World, Jenny,' said Patti, 'I think we had better go on with make-up.'

Despite her exquisite exterior, Patti continued to feel out of sorts. She quibbled with Jenny about the shade of eyeshadow, although Jenny protested tearfully that it was her usual colour, she asked for her chair to be changed and she complained that the autocue was no good, for she was becoming short-sighted. Only the strength of the lights could calm her. Yet, even as she gazed at the camera, she was irritably aware of the margins of her surroundings. She was not yielding, she was faking.

After the broadcast, Patti left immediately, neglecting to answer, feigning not to hear, the customary post-programme pleasantries. Sally was shaking her head over one of the exchanges.

'Well fuck you,' muttered Patti as she began to run along the corridors. 'Speak to Sebastian if you don't like it, fuck you.'

It was starting to get dark outside and Patti peered across the car park for her driver. Several indistinct figures were slumped in their seats, either asleep or determinedly unaware of anything to compete with their air-conditioned, newly upholstered interiors.

Patti punched out the mobile number and a couple of minutes later she heard a key in the ignition, and the lights of a car illuminated her pale hair.

'Hi, home please,' she said. St John's Terrace was her home, in that it contained everything she valued and it was her sanctuary. She would not call it home in the Sally sense of the word. It made no demands but it contained no love. Patti had opted for self-esteem. This had served her well and she did not want to doubt the scale of the achievement.

A fully realized relationship would have dragged her down. Instead she had reached an aesthetic Utopia. Hers was an unchained existence. She could live or die as she pleased, attractive and unfamiliar. And yet, how much would Mark impinge on her freedom? She would not have to clear much room. There were his books and his newspapers. He had a piano. Everything else was crammed into a suitcase. She loved and feared his packed case. He had a wonderful, heartbreaking lightness of being. She closed her eyes in memory of his scent and the beating heart beneath his cotton shirt. If only he were waiting inside for her, loving, amused, but ready to leave.

She clenched her key in her palm and hurried up the steps, slamming the front door behind her. Patti scooped up her post and turned on the answering machine. The phone went down twice and then she heard Mark's voice above the din of an office, not a pub. 'Patti? It's me, I'm stuck here with the Great Man and some other guys. We are just having a drink. It's, oh what time, late, too late to come round so I guess I'll hang on here. I hate to think of turning up all sweaty and disgusting, you would turn your goddess nose up at the sight of me. I know you.

'Hey, guess who I met in the constituency today? Your ex-husband. Did you know that he is fighting this hopeless seat? He asked me back to his house. Hello, Patti? Is this message still recording? I saw John Partridge today and I went back to his house.

'It is full of pictures of you. There is this little room at the back which is a shrine to you. Photos of you, paintings, there is this bronze bust, I'm not kidding. Hello? Can I keep going? So I asked him, "Sir, can I ask what your new wife thinks of all this?" Not a strictly political question, I grant you. I think he was suspicious, and I didn't have the heart to tell him that I thought, from recent memory, that the nudes were not anatomically correct. They don't do you justice. Anyway, pretty weird, eh? I'll tell you all about it tomorrow. Pats, I . . .'

The message gave out. What was the end of the sentence? Patti played it back again, then again. Could it have been? It could have been anything. Typically frustrating of Mark. Always sunny, never jealous. She sat on the bottom stair and opened the post. An invitation to an election night party from the investment banker's wife next door: 'Not that we think we have anything to celebrate!'

A note from Adam Berluscoli:

Dear Patti, it was so good to meet you the other week. But I wanted to apologize for my behaviour. As you will have noticed, I was disgustingly drunk. Alex was, rightly, appalled. I seem to remember an absurd suggestion that you should go and get me off the hook with my mother. I need to make a decision about my career but this is not your problem. You have been kind enough towards our family without getting any further embroiled. Anyway, thanks again. I would offer to buy you a drink to say sorry but it is better for both of us if I stay sober! Good luck with the new programme, I am sure it will be terrific. Yours, Adam Berluscoli.

Patti experienced a strange pin-pricking sensation which she acknowledged as shame. What a ghastly chain of events. She had meant no deliberate harm. How could she have known Adam's father would turn out to be so sensitive. She had only been thinking of herself. She shivered at the tangled wreckage of her action. This was her life's hit and run. Patti wondered if she could compensate for the past. Would a good deed go someway towards cancelling out the bad? She would find Adam's mother's address and she would visit her after all. She may have, inadvertently, destroyed Adam's father but she could save the father's son. There was a third envelope, addressed in capital letters without a frank. Her hands started to shake:

Dearest Beloved, I do apologize if there was a misunderstanding between us that night. I feel that I was not clear about my intentions. I merely wished to impart important intelligence information re the behaviour of the darkies. I can see the mosque from my window. I believe that an attack from there is imminent. I am sure that an attack is planned on her Majesty the Queen or comparable public figures. Would this make a news 'item' on your programme. The intelligence services have been very neglectful despite my proven evidence about the capacity for weapons of mass destruction. I don't know how familiar you are with the 'Internet', Patti, but I have discovered much irrefutable evidence about the plans of Islamic extremists. This is what I have been trying to tell you. Perhaps this is all too 'technical' for you. Might I take the liberty of suggesting a period of courting? I have recently acquired a full set of Morecambe and Wise tapes, including the well-known instance of Angela Rippon's dance. What a beautiful lady she is. Doubtless, she is known to you. What say you that I come to the National Television Centre for a 'tour' before further physical contact. You might introduce me to Angela. I have waited for you outside the NTC on several occasions and I also came to collect you from the hairdresser yesterday. You want me to notice, so why did you get in another car? If you do that again, I will rip out your cunt. Yours faithfully, Arthur.

Chapter 7

The weekend rush out of London was especially heavy after a searingly hot Friday. It had begun at dawn with a buzzing, soil-cracking warmth and ended with a crescendo of Mediterranean heat. The television weather forecaster tried in vain to warn of gathering storms. But the British public wanted to believe that this was the first of perhaps five summer weekends that would not end in disappointing drizzle. With the instinct of the herd, city folk dragged sacks of barbecue coal into their yards and confidently left outside overnight cushions, glasses, sweatshirts, and even children in makeshift tents. This was a night when everyone would toss and turn, luxuriously cursing the still, airless heat. That first hot Friday evening of summer was seemingly endless. Children chased each other with water cannons up and down wide dusty pavements while their exasperated parents loaded bikes, cases and Tesco carrier bags into cars until every window was blocked. The single were thronging round corner pubs, carrying spilling pints into the road. The rowdy laughter and occasional shrieks had a shimmering summery timbre.

Through meticulous planning, Sally had managed to

beat the crowds and the family were in Oxfordshire by early evening. There was no distinct moment of darkness, just a gentle eventual dimming of light, as the shadows across the lawn spread into a soft balmy dusk. Sophie and Tom disappeared into the sheep field and Sally watched from the kitchen as they bobbed in and out of view, shedding clothing and collecting large sticks. She called them in half-heartedly but they were bent over an object in the distance, which they prodded delightedly. She called them more firmly; they looked up and shook their heads. Then with great care and dignity they carried the sheep's skull towards the back door.

'Look, Mummy, what I found,' called Tom, his voice carried to her by the calm acoustics of the countryside.

'I found it,' echoed Sophie. 'Get off, Tom, let me hold it.' They glared at each other, reduced to skinny silhouettes on the sweet-smelling lawn. Then, jostling and shuffling, they laid their dirty treasure before their mother.

'It is your birthday present,' Sophie said.

'Bath time,' said Sally, bovine with happiness. Gordon was watching Tony Blair's return to Downing Street on the small, grainy sitting-room television but Sally wanted no intrusion on her domesticity. Surrounded by her family, completing her homely chores, making up the beds and preparing supper, the joy ran through her veins.

The following day, Patti also embarked on a pastoral idyll. Mark sent her ahead to his cottage in Sussex while he finished off his reports. She packed two bags, one of face creams, the other crisp light clothing wrapped in tissue paper. She picked up some champagne and cold meats from the local deli and threw them into the back seat of her

Aston Martin. She cursed the usual battery of speed cameras but her spirits were tremulously high.

When she had been twenty-three she had felt much older. Now, suddenly she was past fifty and had the heart-beat of a teenager. She retuned the radio to Classic FM and was touched by the mawkish personal requests for songs. Silver wedding anniversaries, university finals. United, decent, Albert Hall-going families with their fond banter and common interests. What music did Mark like? There were no tunes in their relationship, only news.

They had been together for two years but only in short sexual bursts. She must fill in some background colour and shapes. They would have long walks together in comfort-able silence. She needed accelerated familiarity. A weekend's intensive course to achieve decades of foundations.

Did one need a shared past in order to achieve a secure future? She had no emotional or moral credit to draw on. Did Mark need a memory of her in order to tolerate her imminent decline? Did he have to see her in the face of their children to be reminded of his love for her? She had to be adorable enough to justify the lack of any ties. She had come this far by working hard. Now she had to try harder. If she failed, then she had nothing to look forward to except the Siberian bleakness of unloved old age.

Patti swung the car into the unmade track, past the apple trees and rusting farm machinery. The small red-bricked cottage peeped out of colourful overgrown shrubs. She found the key wrapped in the honeysuckle round the squat window and let herself in. Mark's presence was imbued in the cottage through symbols. A brightly col-oured tie he must have shed on the hall table, a pair of

Timberland shoes underneath it. A bicycle. Fishing rods propped against the rustic oak cupboard. Piles of old news-papers and news magazines.

Patti wandered into the low-ceilinged sitting room with its faded furniture and cardboard boxes shoved behind the environmentally unfriendly widescreen Sony television. The boxes contained Mark's childhood history, deposited there by his mother after a vigorous spring clean. Patti knelt down and pulled out a school photograph: Mark in the prefect's row, his arms folded in a mildly subversive gesture.

He was unusually gaunt for his age, his thin face sur-rounded by collar-length brown hair. His sleepy blue eyes and girlish mouth had a familiar expression. Patti diagnosed it as sceptical, with a social conscience. You could take the liberal out of the public school . . .

She sketched the small face with her finger and smiled. Beneath the photograph were the irregular school reports, chronicling a bright but slightly non-conformist child – in the tradition of the school, in fact, where individualism was the convention. Patti found well-expressed, solicitous, let-ters home. Mark gave literate, modest, obviously edited accounts of his activities to his mother, always remembering to ask after the dogs and the garden. What comfort these must have brought.

She dug around for university photographs. Mark with his arm round his Cambridge sweetheart. Patti examined her round, large-eyed face; pretty in an unexceptional way, earnest, evidently headed for the VSO. So young looking then, and much younger than Patti still.

How could Patti insinuate herself into this easy-going life? Boarding school had given Mark good manners and an unshakeable self-sufficiency. He admired and desired Patti, obviously, but would he need her?

If he had navigated himself round women for twenty years, what would make him drift into the harbour now? She was tossed towards the shore by the prospect of old age, but Mark was still blissfully independent. Patti had been able to upturn men, until now, with her glamour and aura of drama, but she knew that she could not intimidate Mark. His quiet core of confidence could be her final rebuff.

She re-packed the box so it was how she had found it and then walked blinking into the sunny porch. Soon afterwards an undistinguished second-hand car came belting towards her. Mark's complete lack of interest in cars was a charming attribute, if you happened to love him anyway. Mark opened the car door and held out his arms to Patti.

It was an afternoon of purest contentment, recreating scenarios already rehearsed in Patti's mind. Despite Mark's reservations about taking Patti on the farm walk when she was wearing her suede Tod's shoes, they did indeed complete the circular walk, over stiles, along streams, through woodland of wild garlic and fresh greenery. Mark carried her over muddy patches and stopped to make love to her in a sun-streaked glade.

This was more awkward than the fantasy version. The ground was hard and uneven, she could not altogether dismiss the grass strains on her couture Capri pants and a party of ramblers came barging through moments after the act. Still Patti felt that she was approaching Mark's being. She was blissfully at ease with him.

When they returned to the cottage, Patti offered to make supper and Mark squeezed her gratefully. She laid the table outside with the mismatched cutlery and brought out her random choices from the delicatessen.

'Champagne?' she asked flirtatiously, brandishing the bottle.

'You know, darling, I would love a beer,' said Mark, picking at a plate of salami absent-mindedly while flicking through his current batch of weekly news magazines. 'And bread maybe?'

There was no bread, nor beer, nor milk or tea and coffee. Patti was not trained to stock fridges. But she was too old to play charmingly undomesticated.

'Damn,' she said thoughtfully. 'I saw those kids round my car. I thought they were just admiring the open top. But they've filched the shopping. Is there a shop round here?'

'Car radios and mobiles are the usual line,' said Mark humorously. 'I didn't know kids had got so homely. Maybe they were Nigella Lawson's children. Don't worry, I'll go.'

Patti turned to go inside the cottage. She heard the little car pull away. She was going to have to work on her performance. She went upstairs to unpack her bag, organizing the cascade of bath products on the little shelf above the basin. Her complexion looked a little red in the bathroom mirror. Lovemaking was good for the spirits but bad for the skin.

She applied fresh make-up, for light camouflage effect in the summer light, and doused herself in fragrance. A mobile rang out. She made a step towards her bag but the sound was coming from the floor where Mark had thrown down his overnight case. She would ignore it. No, she would answer it.

'Oh, hi, is Mark there please?' Patti recognized the voice.

'No, this is Patti Ward, can I help?'

'Oh Patti, it is me, Alex. Really sorry to disturb you. I'm reading the news tonight and I was hoping Mark could run me through the implications of the reshuffle.'

'He's not actually on duty today,' said Patti.

'Oh I know, but he is so good at explaining everything and I just didn't want to fluff it. But no, of course, I can speak to the duty reporter. Sure, sorry for disturbing you.'

'Don't worry,' said Patti. 'I'll tell Mark you called.'

She replaced the phone carefully askew on the floor and stood motionless by the window waiting for Mark's return. It was a broad truth that if someone was attractive, then they were attractive to everyone. Had Patti thought she alone perceived Mark's unassuming charm? She did not suspect Alex of scheming but the threat of unconscious attraction was just as great. Patti had been fighting her emotional Cold War for so long that she was unable to give other women the benefit of the doubt.

It was getting chilly by the time Mark re-appeared with the box of groceries and so the couple ate, after all, in the little sitting room before stretching out on the sofa for a desultory evening of television.

Mark stroked Patti's palomino-streaked hair and, with passionless tenderness, her breasts. As the variations of dusk finally merged into shadowless black and the birds fell silent, she clasped Mark tighter.

'What now, darling,' she asked in a low voice. 'What do you want to do? Shall we stick together?' Mark's head dropped to his chin. He was sleeping.

That night, they both slept in Mark's narrow bed on the sloping floor. Mark slept deeply, Patti fitfully. As the early morning light penetrated the thin floral curtains she began to dream.

First, that she was tending the herb garden at the front of the cottage when someone cleared their throat. She looked up. Alex was walking towards her in a pink polka-dot bikini. Her stomach was as tight as a board. 'I need to discuss the news with Mark,' Alex said firmly. 'Where is he?' Patti could not let Mark see this taut, youthful figure. She ran inside the cottage to find a broom and chased Alex away.

Patti awoke, both amused and appalled. How ridiculous. She stared up at the ceiling in disbelief. Her dream was so funny that she almost felt like telling Mark. But while the plot was comic, the subtext was tragic. Foolish old woman, Patti.

She drifted once more into sleep. She was back in the hospital. The slim, dark-haired nurse walked briskly towards her. She was carrying a crochet wool bundle which she handed to Patti. 'Time for feeding,' she said. Patti pulled herself up onto the pillows and opened her night-gown. The tiny, swarthy-faced infant pressed its fingers against her breast and banged its head against her until it was comfortable. Patti held the baby still and felt the sharp pressure on her nipple. She stroked the fleshy tucks of the infant's neck, her sense of awe undiminished by the pain of the sucking. When she awoke, her breasts were still swollen and sore but she was alone. Mark was downstairs cooking bacon.

Alex always liked the hot summer afternoons when London was deserted. She was woken early by the sun cascading through the curtainless window. She needed to get some blinds. And lamps. And cutlery. The trouble with her generation's reluctance to get married was that no one had wedding lists and therefore no one had 'things'.

She did not have time to do Peter Jones today. Adam had already left for his double shift on casualty and she wanted to get to work in time to mug up. Adam had muttered, when he brought her tea on his way out, that she could do with a day off if they were ever going to unpack the boxes.

Her mother and Adam's had also formed an unholy alliance to stop her working so hard.

But she loved her work, just loved it. It was the animation of her day. She had voted in the election with a heightened sense of purpose because she was now a major shareholder in life. She was the co-owner of a property, she paid 40 per cent tax, she had a pension plan, she had gravely chosen her charity schemes. It was her role to pick up the tab. She had become a materially dutiful, if slightly patronizing, daughter. Even her friends unwittingly looked to her for leadership on which restaurant to meet in or whether they all enrolled for yoga or Pilates. 'What's the decision, boss?' Emily would ask, with bright, ironic eyes.

On matters that did not directly affect them, however, such as world affairs, they accepted collegiate responsibility.

The women had known each other too long, and were too similarly educated, to allow the wrong world view to slip through their net. While they all believed in political debate, there were some subjects, such as the environment or the Palestinian question which were moral imperatives and so not up for discussion.

At some point during their girls' nights out, the conversation would always turn to Patti. Her spectre either appeared in relation to the life/work question: 'But would you really want to be Patti?' or on the level of gossip: 'But what HAS she done to her face?' or, 'Is it serious, do you think, with Mark? How much younger is he than her?' Alex always felt slightly guilty after these exchanges. Her friends' eyes burned with an excitement bordering on malice and their laughs were unpleasantly high pitched. On the other hand it would be pious not to join in and, furthermore, she felt that it redressed the balance of power, which was sharply in Patti's favour, if she and her friends could safely poke fun at her. It was usually Emily who went the furthest, using sunglasses as a prop for her ageing movie star impersonation. Alex objected with pleasure.

Plus Patti was an imperfect feminist role model. She was too capricious and ungenerous. She was blatantly indifferent to environmental issues. Emily had asked at the end of a meal whether Patti was pre-sisterhood, which had brought gales of laughter from the others: 'What pre-suffragette? She is not THAT old,' Lisa had said. In response Alex had quoted Sally's rare conspiratorial observation that Patti was too unrepresentative to feel empathy for the sisterhood.

'Her beauty defines her more than anything else,' Sally had said. 'Beauty skews everything, you immediately lose any common denominator.' She had not said this bitterly, but reflectively. Part of her friendship with Patti was based on the simple aesthetic pleasure in regarding her. She took the same pleasure in the soft, clear skin of her daughter and her daughter's friends.

Alex had no investment in teenagers at her age, although she took a polite interest in Sally's proud if slightly rambling anecdotes about her children. But Alex had a reflexively cooing regard for babies. She would pucker her lips in the street when she passed a pram, and give Adam's arm a squeeze. Adam did not wear his parental instinct on his sleeve in the same way, and he would tease Alex about her lack of realism.

'I am afraid that you can't get round the biological act,' he said. 'Something has to happen for you to get pregnant.'

Alex took his reproach in good spirit. When she was properly established, she would stop being so tired and she would have more sex. Procreative sex. At the moment there was fat chance of any kind of sex.

Alex pulled on a pair of combat trousers, a T-shirt and trainers. She felt much more herself out of the silky, tailored suits she had bought for television. She looked too telephone sales in them. Sally had said something about Alex needing to find her own style. Had Patti complained? The thought made Alex blush.

The day passed quickly, mostly on the phone. She started to feel nervously excited about the programme. She would phone Mark. He was so good at all this, so funny. Maybe she could have a cup of coffee with him and pick his brains.

As soon as the voice answered she recognized it as Patti's. Better plough on.

'Is Mark there?' Of course Patti knew it was Alex and responded with her own brand of rude politeness.

Alex felt at sea with Patti. She so wanted to please her, but increasingly she seemed to get on her nerves. She had once broached this with Sally who sighed, rolled her eyes and said nothing. Alex had worked out that her fault was presumptuousness, however unintended. Any favours or kindness from Patti could only be a matter of grace.

Chapter 8

Patti returned to London to find twenty messages on her answering machine and one from Sebastian. 'Patti, hi, it's Sebastian. I can't get you on your mobile. Can you give me a ring about the pilot? I've got a window at the end of this week. Let me know which times you are comfortable with.'

Patti cursed him violently and rang him back. She could hear Mozart in the background, muffled by voices and laughter. There was a tapping of shoes on a wood floor, the ting of glasses and a more distant cluster of conversation. She could almost describe the drinks on the balcony. Television women in transparent skirts and beaded cardigans. Bobbed hair and little handbags. Crowding round the minority of heterosexual men. 'Sebastian, it sounds as if you are busy. It's Patti,' she said. She hoped to convey relief in being elsewhere as well as reproach at not being invited. Being both proud and forlorn was a delicate balancing act. Sebastian was insensitive to her artful nuances.

'Hello, Patti, thanks for phoning back. I am sorry for disturbing your weekend. Alex gave me the number for the cottage, but you had left by then. Patti, do you mind if we speak in the morning, I have a few friends round right now. I hope we can work something out. I have a few guests in mind, though I am having trouble raising the Tories. They want to keep the powder dry I guess. Let me know if anyone occurs to you. *Ciao*, Patti. Sorry, Fred, I'm just coming.'

Patti put down the phone. So who gave Alex the number of the cottage?

She calculated that Mark must have reached home by now. She had invited him to stay the night with her, but he said that he needed to pick up his post and iron some shirts for the week. Patti toyed with the idea of confiding in Mark; she could tell him that she was afraid Sebastian was immune to her, that he was deliberately delaying the decision to give her the show.

Patti could seek reassurance from Mark, about her talent and attractiveness. He would be indignant and protective of her. He would be nonplussed as to how Alex had got hold of his number. Touched by Patti's vulnerability and still able to smell her perfume on his clothes, he might blurt out that he loved her and wanted to marry her.

On the other hand, he might not. Patti had distanced herself from men in the past in order to avoid the tedium of their naked emotion. Now it would be wise to remove herself to prevent her own rejection. Her strength lay in the fact that she did not ask others for reassurance or advice, or rather only in a flattering sense. 'Tell me what YOU think. I would love YOUR opinion on this.' She must be her own protector. She lay back on the wide, cream sofa and assessed the risk. Need was a form of defeat. And yet, wasn't it also a bridge in human relations? Could it possibly strengthen the bond rather than weaken it? Her instinct told her not but, against her better judgement, she grabbed the phone and tapped in (from memory) Mark's number. It rang and rang without answer, metallically, indifferently. She was superstitious enough to take this as the answer.

Who else could she phone? She considered her lack of options without self-pity. It had been her choice to discourage friendships. They were really not necessary. She had company, through work and her work-related social life. Confidences could be employed against her. Much of her success had been achieved by operating alone. Her rivals were unable to use psychology against her.

By the structured phasing of her life, her acquaintances could not cross check. Angie, her school friend had tried a few times with calls to the duty desk but Patti had relied on the screening process to shield her. There had been that woman, Judith Walker, who had jumped out at the Tate, but she had managed to lose her. Only Sally had been too long on the voyage. And, unsurprisingly, they liked each less the longer they knew each other. It was a great failing in human nature for people to believe that the more deeply they were understood, the more they would be loved. The opposite seemed far more likely. Patti had known many public figures who had been deluded into thinking that one more interview, a further confession, would bring the public round. Almost always, first prejudices were simply confirmed.

The exception to the law of diminishing likeability was Mark. Perhaps because he was no more tangible now than when she had first met him. This was not the moment to fall in love. The tide of success, which had carried Patti this far, had abated. Several elements were against her, Sebastian, Alex, most of all age. She had to rely on force of will, on pure concentration, to speed her on.

First, ritual. Patti shut the bathroom door behind her, even though she was alone. Then she ran the bath to the brim. She applied mud to her face and nut oil to her hair. She soaked herself in a cocktail of scents and took a cocktail of pills to help her sleep. Her last thoughts before wrapping herself in silk beneath linen sheets were of career strategy. She could die prematurely, inciting hysterical remorse, or she could battle on. Death was a romantic option but she could not stand the thought of the gossip and the pity. Not yet.

By the time Sebastian arrived at work, pouting and holding a bottle of mineral water, Patti had produced the elusive Tory. You could count John Partridge's majority on one hand. He would speak for the battered Conservative Party. Mark, who had dropped into the party during the early hours but had a more robust constitution than Sebastian, shook his head in amusement at the guest line-up. If they had been a jury, they would have been dismissed.

'Are you looking for a contribution from Alex?' asked Patti, in order to draw attention to her absence. 'Because I think she'll be looking for some time off after all that filling in.'

Sebastian turned to speak to Mark. 'Oh, she's not taking time off. You got her so enthusiastic about the grey vote last night, that she is going to do a special for me about long-term residential care. She is out with the oldies this week.'

'So why do they want another pilot?' asked Jenny loyally, as she brushed bronze blusher across Patti's face. 'I thought the last one was really good.'

Patti addressed herself in the mirror, her face bright and rested beneath her ivory hair. 'I wasn't happy with it, sweetie. There was a problem with the direction, but I think Sebastian is more in control now.'

'I just made up John Partridge,' said Jenny. 'He is quite a fan of yours. But weren't you married to him? I was dying to ask him but I wouldn't do anything without your permission. Obviously. But what happened, can I ask?' Patti thought for a moment.

'I couldn't see the point of him. One's own life is futile enough without confronting the pathos of somebody else's. All their boring self-delusion and vanity and vulnerability. The terrible burden of it. I never could connect.'

Jenny carefully packed away her brushes. 'I think other people are really interesting,' she said faintly.

'But they're not,' Patti said loudly. 'People are terribly disappointing. Torture. I keep telling you that you are better off with your cats.'

'Yeah right, well I'd like the chance to find out about that,' muttered Jenny. Patti surveyed her impassively, as beautiful as a statue. Then she shook herself.

'OK, I think we're there,' said Patti. 'Root for me, Jenny, will you?'

'You look a million dollars,' said Jenny. 'Honestly, you're amazing.' Patti squeezed Jenny's arm.

'Thanks, pal. When this is over, I want the whole low-down on Tim. I have had some further thoughts. Right, here we go.'

The studio had been refurbished by sub-contracted

designers. The colours signalled warmth. The sofa was soft and curvaceous, making it hard for Patti to maintain her rod-like deportment. She perched on the end of it while John Partridge floundered in its sinking centre.

'So, John,' Patti asked, her eyes as blue-white as an iceberg, her mouth a cold bell curve: 'Is Conservatism dead?' John Partridge obeyed every choreographed move. His answers were controversial enough to be newsworthy while helplessly following Patti's lead.

She provided the concept, he the inferior execution. He stumbled back to the green room, to be ushered out of the building by a researcher. Patti went on to interview the lead singer of a boy band, recommended by Mark's half-brother, Tristan.

The singer was charmingly inarticulate and painfully besotted by the interviewer. The charity worker from UNICEF was recommended by Sebastian. Patti's eyes widened, suggesting bottomless sorrow and sympathy.

'What can each of us do?' she begged. The charity worker reeled off a number of initiatives and described in detail a project in the Sudan.

'As you must know, Patti, this is the forgotten war.'

Patti nodded. What fucking war? She was told this was going to be about Montserrat. Mark was to appear in denouement, so that she could question him on the Government's attitude to the island's demands. She had Clare Short's quotes about wanting 'golden elephants' in front of her. She knew fuck all about the Sudan.

'It is a complicated situation, isn't it?' she asked. 'Rather different in the north than the south?' The UNICEF worker became angry. 'I can assure you it is very simple. People are dying, whatever you think about the politics.'

But what were the politics? And what was the British involvement? None, that she could think of. Patti looked enigmatically into the middle distance of the invited audience.

'I wonder if the audience has any opinions on this?' A hand went up. Patti located it beyond the circle of light. 'Yes, you, sir.'

'Why should we help these darkies when we have pensioners here who were given a derisory seventy-five pence increase by Gordon Brown? It is an absolute disgrace.' The delay timer whirred into operation at the word 'darkie'. Patti looked at the speaker through the camera. He was an elderly man, with a vein-threaded face, made more scarlet by the stitching across his eyes. It was Arthur.

Patti felt her body temperature plunge. She attempted a wry retort to the unwelcome party guest but her mouth was powdery and nauseous. Jenny was moving towards her with a moist puff. Patti could not bear to be touched; she leaped from her sofa, pulled at her microphone and stumbled out of the studio.

Patti could not leave the building, because he would be waiting for her. She could not go home, for he would be there. If she stayed in the building, he would find her. She went to the green room, seeking safety in the cordon of researchers and other marginalized studio staff. There, she curled up like a sea urchin in an armchair and tightly shut her eyes.

When she opened them again, she saw Sally and Sebastian sitting watching her. Sally seemed concerned, her soil-coloured eyes blinking in her round face. Sebastian was quizzical, one arm outstretched on the sofa.

'Feeling better?' he asked, managing to sound both

sympathetic and bored. 'Spot of nerves from our thorough-bred. We can screen those audiences for balance, but not for vulgarity, I am afraid.'

'Perhaps you weren't feeling so well,' suggested Sally tactfully. 'There is a bug going round.' Patti stood up, her height being her only available weapon against Sebastian.

'I am absolutely fine. Shall we resume? Where is Mark?'

Sebastian shook his head: 'His pager went off. He's got an interview with the new candidate for the Tory leadership. Let's leave it for now, I've told them to strike the set. I need to do some thinking. Why don't you take a rest, Patti.' Indignity piled upon indignity. At least Patti had lost all fear of her stalker, faced with a far greater fiend. As she walked out, Sally bustled after her.

'Patti, I am taking you to lunch. No, I am afraid that I won't take no for an answer.'

They went to Giolotti's, a friendly, dingy haunt of NTC staff. Patti felt diminished by Sally's gesture of friendship but she had nowhere else to go and she needed a drink. Sally greedily searched the menu, while Patti ordered a bottle of wine and a packet of cigarettes.

'Still smoking?' asked Sally, momentarily distracted from the pasta dishes. 'I'd have thought you would have given up by now.'

'I haven't decided,' answered Patti looking around her. She despised addiction and disliked the clubbishness of smokers. If a colleague ever cried: 'Thank goodness another smoker!' she would automatically stub hers out. Neither would she be as predictable as to 'give up'. It implied age as well as dependence. Sometimes she smoked and some-times she didn't.

'Aha, so you still do!' exclaimed Sally with friendly

disapproval. 'I remember when you used to smoke those cheroots,' she continued cosily. 'I always think of you, tipping back your chair at your typewriter and smoking those foul-smelling things.' She patted her hand on the table, her wedding ring tight on her swollen finger. 'Yes, yes, I can remember exactly what you were wearing. You had those beige sort of jodhpurs, think they were, and that beautiful patterned shirt. Bill Blass, wasn't it?'

Patti lit up and shook away the match. 'Yup, nice fashion history. Can you remember what I was writing?'

Sally made a kindly grimace. 'Journalism doesn't last, Patti. It is only for the present. I have made the mistake with Alex of referring to pieces we wrote, great stories we covered. She puts on this terribly polite expression – it is absolutely meaningless to her. Funny, isn't it? You know the story she loves though. It is the one about you storming El Vino's and ordering two Scotches on the rocks. I hated the stuff, but we had to down it before being asked to leave. It is unthinkable now, isn't it? Imagine a woman barred for wearing trousers. Alex wouldn't believe me when I told her.'

Patti, who had begun to relax, flinched.

'Tell me, have you actually signed the adoption papers for Alex yet? Or is it a broader-based NTC initiative to sponsor a child? Why do people talk about her the whole time?'

Sally shook her head, sternly. 'I just don't see Alex as a rival, Patti. I enjoy her youth. It is a great privilege to nurture talent in someone, and so rewarding.' Patti drew hard on her cigarette and exhaled up towards the ceiling. Sally softened. 'Do you know, in a funny way, Alex reminds me of you when I first knew you. She is more straightforward, but that is partly the context. Women don't need to be an underground resistance any more. Alex has your drive and some of your star quality. Plus, she's nice. I want to see her get on, I really do.'

Patti stubbed out her cigarette.

'But where can she get to, Sally? She gets to be me? And what am I supposed to do? I am not supposed to retire for another fifteen years. But my life has to be split into two parts as if it were Hollywood. The role of the young Patti Ward will be played by Alexandra Khan. I ask you, is this fair, Sally, is this feminist? I work hard to be the best. I get to the top of my particular summit. But I can't rest for a moment. I see all the men around me sunning themselves and enjoying the respite but I get pushed down in some kind of landslide. No room for me. Did it ever occur to you, Sally, that your infatuation with younger women is something of a betrayal?'

Patti was reduced to an angry hiss because Sally's food had arrived. Patti's perfectionism as a performer made her uneasy about eating in public. The noise, the tomato-splattered mouth, worse, the possible greasy stains down her front.

'You tuck in,' she said to Sally unpleasantly, while lighting another cigarette. Sally nodded, her mouth full of pasta.

The two middle-aged women surveyed each other. Patti, fastidious about her colleague's tendency towards dumpiness, accentuated by an ugly tent-like shift dress. She was ashamed of her contemporary. Sally thought Patti looked slightly mad, thin and over stylized. They both smiled.

Sally cleared her throat: 'No one is pushing you, Patti.

But on camera work is bound to be ephemeral. We have all got one trick. One-trick ponies. But after a while audiences want something different. Not better, just new. Fashion isn't fair. Had you ever considered radio? You have a lovely voice.'

Patti was now icy. 'A lovely voice for television, a great face for radio. Or I could do more charity work, couldn't I?'

Sally missed the irony. 'Well, that would be marvellous, Patti, to put something back. I think it would give you a real purpose in life.' She tailed off in the blast of Patti's wintry expression.

'Charity is where the old go to die,' said Patti. 'It is interesting. You think that you are so concerned about other people but it is only ever from your perspective.'

'And what is that exactly?' asked Sally, both cross with her friend and keen for the rare opportunity to talk about herself.

'From the perspective of a mother,' said Patti quietly. 'From someone who has children and spends their life patronizing those who don't.'

'That is not true,' said Sally in amazement.

'Of course it is true,' said Patti, her china-doll eyes fixed on Sally's warm alarmed hazel ones. 'Mother hen, mother earth, mother courage. Clucking over everyone at work, talking about their children, pushing the subject round to yours. Building bloody nests everywhere. Can your muddled, maternal brain comprehend what it is like for those of us without children? We who don't measure time by the annual school photograph. Who can't seek comfort in the past or the future. We who are trapped in the present, with hearts so charred with grief that we wish they would stop beating? And all around us are soft-focus yielding shapes of parents and children, totally at ease, wholly exclusive. And you dare laugh at us for being awkward or self-conscious because we don't know how to hold children or to talk to them. And we must bear your pity and your ridicule. Because the only role you will allow us is humble, perverted witness to your infinite love and pleasure. Your moral superiority. Which is just nature's greed. It is repulsive, it is wicked.'

Sally dissolved into heavy globular tears. She put her hand over her face, stretching and rubbing in shock over the violence of the assault. A waiter uncertainly offered her a napkin and office workers at adjoining tables glanced sideways in curiosity. Patti watched Sally's flesh colour and shake, her shoulders slump in misery, then she blew her nose noisily and gave a little whistle.

'Well, you know how to strike, Patti. You do.'

'You hit first,' said Patti. 'But I hit harder.' The accuracy of her aim surprised her. She thought she had been rather melodramatic. But there was no doubt about it, mother hen had fallen calamitously from her perch.

Alexandra was on her third old people's home and beginning to wilt in the suffocatingly dry central heating. The layouts were uniform; a common room in which ugly brown seventies-style chairs formed a circle as if to begin a game of pass the parcel. The thin brown carpets were heavily hoovered. There was an overwhelming sense of inactivity. Alex was used to streets and offices where people in dark clothing click-clacked past each other impatiently. There was perpetual movement, and chatter, most of it into mobile phones. Here, people sat and stared at nothing in particular. The centrepiece of the room was a bulky television, decorated by a lace doily, on which sat a marigold plant in a flowerpot. A trolley of stewed tea and custard cream biscuits was parked next to the over-bright screen. The television which was always on, and sometimes watched, was showing a sly couple talking about their squalid, complex relationships. The woman hiccoughed in excited grief and the man smirked in staged remorse but the high drama washed over the residents of Rose Hill elderly care centre. The bent figures in the chairs drifted in and out of sleep with little starts. Life passed slowly, in a fug of indoor warmth and memories. Their stories had nothing in common with the day-time talk shows. They did not understand such greedy and explicit self-gratification. A few standard phrases covered their condition. 'Mustn't grumble', 'She's a martyr to her digestion', 'I am expecting visitors', 'My visitors have been delayed', 'It was a smashing funeral'.

An unexpected interruption to their lives of quiet dread, came in the form of an animated young woman, barely older than a school girl, accompanying Mrs Linton on her rounds. Alexandra shook the tortoise-like hands with loose-limbed ease and plonked herself on the plywood coffee table, stretching out her legs encased in black woolly tights and ballet pumps with diamanté buckles.

'So, hi, everyone.' She bobbed her head in collective acknowledgement. 'Sorry to burst in on you like this, Don and I would like to do a bit of filming, have a bit of a chat. OK with you guys?'

The women glanced at each other, unsure whether guys was a term that included them. On the other hand, Rose

Hill women outnumbered men by ten to one so it would be rash of this pretty girl to discount them entirely. The residents were all rather startled by the attention. They were used to their existences being erased from public display. They were not young, or beautiful or famous. So they were of no interest to politicians, except during elections, and were shunned by television and newspapers, except during sudden campaigns to lend the brand some warmth and integrity. Every ancient face was a circulation loss. Alex was far more indignant about this than they were. They protested that they too wanted to see the young, the 'up to date'.

They were more likely to see the young on screen than in the flesh. There was one irreconcilable difference between the young and the old. The former were busy and the latter were not.

The regret among the old people in the homes was that they had to be lumped together because of the one common denominator. The loss of individuality, which amounted to loss of dignity, was hardest to bear. Snobbishness was therefore rampant. 'What do I have in common with them,' was the complaint whispered to Alexandra. The old folk were good neighbours but bad cohabiters. It was the other way round with the young.

Rose Hill care centre was a pleasant Victorian house set back from the road in a London suburb. The chief executive of the private nursing home was a former primary school teacher who found the work more profitable and her charges more respectful. Otherwise, the rules and conditions were the same.

'We aren't making a mess in here are we?' she asked, striding through the common area. Two old women who were house monitors looked mortified as they struggled to their feet and moved the coffee mugs into a straight line on the table.

'Alexandra is here from NTC to see how well we are all doing,' the chief executive announced to the room. She had a headmistress' eagle awareness of any dissident activity. She noticed at a glance dropped tissues or fidgeting or fading pulses.

'That's exciting, isn't it?'

A gaunt-looking woman in her nineties with haphazardly silver and violently red hair swivelled her head round the formed semi-circle of guests.

'Why are we on the television? Is it because of the Queen Mother?' Another woman answered above the piercing note of her hearing aid, 'It must be a golden wedding anniversary, is it Kenneth's golden?'

'Don't be silly, his wife is dead,' said the first woman. 'Your wife is dead, isn't she, Kenneth?'

A dapper, upright man in the opposite corner of the room, made a non-committal gesture with his hands. He was embarrassed by being the constant centre of attention as the only male of the group. Alexandra took her cue.

'Do you mind if I sit here? I am a reporter from NTC, and I am trying to get a picture of what goes on here. This is my cameraman Don. Are you OK about a quick interview for television?'

The old man adjusted his necktie and nodded.

'What is it you want to know, Alexandra?' He had a handsome, hawkish face with heavily creased grey eyes. Alex was so used to her special status of being professionally outnumbered by men that she almost laughed to see the hunted demeanour of a man encircled by women.

'I bet you are popular round here,' she said flirtatiously. Kenneth met her stare with wonder.

'Oh, my dear, you reminded me so much of my daughter.'

Alex was touched by the seriousness of his tone. He was not a member of the public to be indulged and patronized by a television presenter on the make. He was a proper person.

She blushed and said respectfully, 'That sounds like a compliment to me. How nice of you. Where does your daughter live?'

'Oh not too far away,' nodded Kenneth vaguely.

'Are you very close?' asked Alex, signalling to Don that this was a preliminary chat, unsuitable for interview. Kenneth smiled and said nothing.

'Do you have grandchildren?' asked Alex. He smiled again. Maybe she needed to find some other characters. Silence was bad television.

'Perhaps you know her?' asked Kenneth thoughtfully. 'She is on your channel.' Alex gave a warm grimace.

'Gosh, you know we employ so many people. I don't even know who they all are. I am quite new. Do you know which department she works in?'

'Oh yes,' said Kenneth. 'She reads the news like you do. She is called Patti Ward.'

It was one of those coincidences that are a drug to journalists. Reporters sift through fragments looking for the connecting piece. Here it was, of all places. Alex's senses were concentrated.

'You are Patti's dad? I can't believe it, I know Patti really well, I mean I work with her. She never told me. I suppose it never came up. Gosh she'll be so surprised when I tell her who I have been with . . . does she see a lot of you, I bet she does, a nice man like you?'

Kenneth put a square, trembling hand to his cheek. He shied away from the inquisitive roomful of women. Alex had a more refined sense of taste than many of her trade and she was embarrassed by her shrill intrusiveness. She waved the cameraman away; and reached instinctively for the old man's hands.

'I'm sorry,' she whispered. 'I didn't mean to be crass. Families are private things aren't they?'

Kenneth Ward's grey eyes were filmy.

'I haven't seen Patti for thirty years,' he whispered back. 'Forgive me, I am a silly old fool, do forgive me.' Alex delved in her black backpack for some tissues. She could only find torn lavatory paper, used to wipe off her lipstick. The old man reached in his breast pocket and brought out a large, white, initialled handkerchief. He was about to give the military trumpet blow of his generation when he caught sight of Alexandra's watery eyelashes.

'Here you are, my dear,' he said. Alex dabbed at her eye make-up in disbelief.

'Wow, sorry, this is ridiculous. What kind of interviewer am I? It's just the idea of a dad not seeing his daughter for that long; it is so, so sad.' Kenneth responded with forced jollity.

'Don't think they'll be sending you to the next earthquake.'

'But why, Kenneth?' asked Alex, turning her blotchy face towards him. 'What happened? I mean, where is Patti's mother? What happened?'

'Nothing happened,' said Kenneth hopelessly. 'Patti left home and then time passed. I wrote to her at the television address but she didn't reply. She never tried to contact us.'

'Maybe she didn't get your letters, maybe she doesn't know where you are,' said Alex eagerly.

Kenneth shook his head: 'She knows. Mrs Linton got through the switchboard, actually spoke to her. She asked her if she would like to visit, asked her without telling me, d'you know. Patti told her to mind her own, "b" word business. Edith over there heard the conversation. There is a bit of eavesdropping goes on here among the women. Patti isn't interested in the past, d'you see?'

Don was setting up his equipment in the centre of the room. The old folk could not decide whether he or Kenneth were most worthy of attention and swivelled their heads as if at a tennis match. Kenneth, pricklingly aware of the eyes upon him, picked up his Patrick O'Brian novel to signal the end of the conversation but Alex could not stop her questions. Her nature was part social worker, part journalist and her head throbbed with injustice and curiosity.

'Mr Ward, Kenneth, I am sorry, but I have to ask you. Did Patti have a terrible childhood?'

He looked thoughtful. 'About in the middle I'd say. She was an only child, so that may have irritated her. We had a rather nice house, detached, and holidays, that sort of thing. She had pets. I bought her a guinea pig, then a cat, then a marvellous spaniel called Floppy who was a bit of a handful. I think I ended up looking after all of them, like most parents, ha!

'She was a rum one. Liked to play on her own, but that would be on account of having no brothers or sisters. There was a chestnut tree at the side of the road, and she would climb in it to watch me come home from the station. She would jump out at me and I would give her a piggyback home. Not a bad childhood, Miss Khan, no. An ordinary childhood.'

Alexandra frowned. 'What about later? What about when Patti got older?'

Kenneth looked tired and cautious.

'My wife, Mary, was a teacher. She was used to exercising control over children. But Patti defeated her. She was so damn wilful. And lies, terrible lies. Told her headmistress that there was violence in the home. Fortunately, in those days, schools listened to the parents. I would say: "Patti, why can't you tell the truth?" And she would look and look at me, holding her breath until I became frightfully worried. She was . . . a funny little thing. Not very kind. I remember one time Mary came across Patti looking at herself in the mirror in her bedroom. Mary told her that she shouldn't look at herself so much, that she was a bit vain. Which she was, she was.

'Patti started to pray out loud for us to die. I think that upset Mary. Patti started to do it at table, she never forgave Mary for throwing out the darned television. Patti always loved television. Anyway, Patti would press her fingers together and say, "Please God may my mother die so I can have interesting parents." Well, I got jolly fed up with it because it was very distressing to Mary. I ordered Patti upstairs, and I spanked her with one of my slippers. She was a proud girl, didn't cry, just stared.'

The old man's breathing was sounding trapped and his complexion was tinged grey. Alex drew back in concern.

'You know, let's not talk about that stuff. It's over, right? Every family goes through a bad patch. I bet things got better once Patti was at Oxford. And she has done so well since. Real credit to you.'

Kenneth picked up Alex's optimistic tone. 'Oh yes, I am sure Patti became happier. But she wasn't at Oxford. Wouldn't settle for all that, though she was frightfully bright.'

'Not at Oxford?'

'No,' said Kenneth, 'she couldn't wait for all that. She went to London. I am afraid that she worked in some fairly unsavoury bars.'

'What about your wife?' asked Alex, against her natural sense of fair play. 'Is your wife dead?' Kenneth pulled at his jacket lapels and cleared his throat.

'Mary passed away and I was brought here.' He put his hand up. 'Now don't keep apologizing, you aren't the first to start asking me questions. The second this month, in fact.' Alex folded her arms in surprise and, curiously, irritation. This may not be a professional encounter, but it was still her story. No reporter likes trespassers. Kenneth fumbled in his pocket.

'I got this letter from some chap on the Anthony Clare programme. Said he was "in conversation" with Patti about doing something.'

'Patti do Anthony Clare?' cried Alex, wrinkling her face in disbelief. 'Why would she do that?' Kenneth looked a smokier grey.

'Can't tell what she might be up to. Can't read my own daughter. Patti is a marvellous woman but she is a damn liar. Just you be careful with her.' His brittle limbs were beginning to tremble. Mrs Linton strode over.

'Don't exhaust Kenneth, Alexandra, he is the only man

we have got round here, aren't you, dear?' The room tittered. Kenneth grasped the arms of the chair.

'We've been having a bit of a chinwag, Mrs Linton, that's all. Merely passing the time of day. But I am sure this young woman has more interesting things to do, and if you don't mind, I would like to get back to reading my book.' Don was moving across the room, trying out different angles, pushing furniture and papery residents into different formations.

'Alex, can we start filming now? Are we recording this conversation?' Alex assumed television's false brightness. 'Sure, yeah, I'll do this to camera.'

'I'm here to see what the residents of Rose Hill hospice, sorry, shit, edit, edit. I'm here to see what the residents of Rose Hill elderly care centre think about the Government's initiatives on long-term care. And these ladies are going to tell me what THEY think about society's view of familial duty and the current rate of tax on savings. Edith, let's start with you. Edith is a youthful eighty-seven and she has plenty to say about what needs to be done . . .'

Don gave Alex a lift back to the NTC. The suburban A roads were choked with traffic, the car fumes mingling with the sunshine into a throat-itching gauze. Don hooted and cursed and made U-turns into back roads, which were also gridlocked. No one was going anywhere. Alex was opening and shutting her window in sharp degrees, in an attempt to let in the air but not the smog. Don gave a whistly smoker's laugh.

'I can see you doing one of those little dances at

Gothenburg. Nice.' Alex managed a token laugh through her nose, which she then rubbed ruefully.

'The thing is, Don, I do really mind about the environment. We have got to do something. I guess I should start cycling again.' She waved at a scruffy, slouching, group of school children waiting at a crossing. 'These are the innocent victims of President Bush,' said Alex passionately. 'Don't they have a right to get home without being poisoned?' The gang sauntered in front of them, one of the girls in an unbuttoned shirt and loose, low, tie, insolently thumping the bonnet as she passed. 'Get off my car, you little shits,' Don shouted.

Alex went back to examining the pile of colour-coded cards in her lap. She had yet to create the flat in her own image. She seemed to lack execution. The East European decorators who had arrived without ever needing to be asked, on her doorstep, suggested that she tried out sample colours on the walls without committing to them. But there was no time for rehearsals. Everything in Alex's life had to go live at the moment. And of course she was punished for her haste by finding that the gentle blues on the side of the pot looked like a public swimming pool over a large area. Adam treated her Little Woman mistakes with gentle humour, but Alex was cross. Deep down she believed in her Martha Stewart instincts. She felt she should narrow her eyes, point at some skirting and say without absolute conviction, 'I want this.' She had read in one of her secret horde of home-making magazines that a good interior decorator would move a table a couple of centimetres or hang a mirror just so and a room was newly created. Alex noticed a distinct lack of melting cohesion in the flat. She

swung from fretting enthusiasm about this to complete
forgetfulness. She hummed and held up the colour to the
windscreen light to suggest professional critical appreciation. Should she go African hot or Tuscany burnished, or
Nordic cool? What would Emily say, who had great taste
although no domestic inclination.

'What colour do you think Patti has her walls?' she
asked Don dreamily.

He smirked: 'I think I can answer that. Sort of creamy.
Expensive-looking, like the lady herself.'

'Have you been to her house then?' asked Alex.

'Patti and I have been around a long time,' said Don.

Alex looked at him with fresh curiosity. He was weath-
ered-looking with tough, creased skin but his eyes were still
cornflower blue and his hair thick and dark with only
random grey hairs. She supposed he must have been attractive, in a Mick Jagger kind of way. Blimey, that was another
detail to relate to Adam. They joined a long queue of cars
trying to turn right.

'Do you mind if I hop out to the newsagent's?' asked
Alex. She darted into the shop, her floaty ethnic scarf
wrapped round her mouth to counter the pollution. Her
legs were sweating under her tights. She looked round and
rapidly rolled them down as if changing for gym. She cut
an eccentric figure. Alex pulled a couple of bottles of
mineral water from the refrigerated glass cabinet in the shop
and spontaneously grabbed a postcard of a Beefeater from
a shelf next to it. Shielding her eyes from the glare outside
she looked up and down the road for the car. Don hooted;
the car had barely moved. Alex climbed back in and balanced the card on her lap.

Sarah Sands

Dear Mum and Dad, she wrote. *Here is a postcard from the glamorous A4. Sorry I have been too busy to ring. Will very soon. Lots and lots of love, Alex. 4, The Drive, Greenford, Middlesex.*

She slipped the card into her bag among her colour charts.

The sun had set by the time they reached the television centre. She had not explicitly decided to seek out Patti but the old man's features were fresh in her mind and she burned with righteous anger. Patti could, and did, trample over those younger than her but she had no right to make the elderly miserable. Alex had a profound respect for the family. For the sake of her own parents, she would make Patti acknowledge Kenneth. She clamped her jaw, tensed her hands and strode towards the make-up room. As the opportunity grew nearer the notion became far less plausible. She hovered outside the door, wondering how to frame the words. She started to walk away then took a breath and returned. That anguished, elderly face was photographically clear in her mind. Patti had gone adrift and Alex felt an impulse – a moral duty – to tow her back to her father.

She took several more breaths and walked into the make-up room. Patti was alone, flicking through the evening's running order. Her hair fell like a veil over her shoulders which were silky bare. Alex felt as if she had caught Patti at prayer and sniffed nervously to indicate her presence. Patti looked up and surveyed her wryly.

'Well, it's Florence Nightingale. What news from the wards?' Alex perched against a jutting surface and unconsciously started chewing at her fingernails.

'I wasn't at a hospital. It was, like, an old people's home?' Patti nodded, and stared. Was her expression sympathetic or disdainful or just bored? Alex couldn't tell. Patti's beautiful eyes were impenetrable. The safest thing to do was to shut up and go. Wish Patti goodnight. Comment on the weather, or the traffic and leave. But a fresh wave of anger welled up.

'I met your dad,' she said in a trembling voice.

Patti continued to stare, her expression altered only by subtle degree. Her half smile grew fainter, her pupils darker. She was quite still. Her lack of marked response forbade any further exchange. But Alex rushed onwards:

'Patti, he looks so bewildered. He is a dear man and everybody at Rose Hill dotes on him. But he misses his daughter, it is so clear. And with Mary dead, you do know that your mother is dead, you are all he has. For God's sake, Patti, he is your father.' Still, Patti said nothing but continued to stare as if in a trance.

'Well, it is your bloody loss,' choked Alex, her face dissolving. She snatched her backpack and fell clumsily towards the door. As she glanced back she caught the last wintry rays. Patti was still watching her, but her expression had lots its ambivalence. It was pure hatred.

Alex did her walk/run down the corridor, a skippy movement she had perfected from her school days in order to scrape within the St Catherine's rule. The light was on in Sebastian's office but she was too frightened to look in. She held on to the radiatingly comforting image of Adam waiting for her at their home. He would be watching the footy on television, his newspaper crossword balanced on his knee. He would stretch, showing a patch of gristly stomach beneath his T-shirt. Then his head would tilt back onto the boulder of the sofa and he would fold his muscular hairy arms over his chest. Adam slept beautifully, his well-drawn, unshaven face quite still. After half an hour or so, his eyes would flicker and his anemone lashes would part. This was the state in which Alex longed to find him – she wanted to nestle into his strong, warm chest, for him to stroke her head and massage her shoulders and pour her a drink. This was the bliss of his companionship.

As she left the NTC building and walked towards the garishly lit car park, she noticed a short, elderly man dressed in a tweed jacket and a flat cap. She assumed that he was something to do with the racing commentary. She smiled to herself at the unseasonal formality of his clothes, reminded of her peculiar pre-dawn decision to put on woolly tights under her summer dress. The man smiled broadly back, displaying a non-televisual row of broken discoloured teeth.

'I'm waiting for Patti Ward,' he volunteered. He looked seedy close up, with rivulets of veins across his face and black stitches over his eye. She supposed that he must be Patti's relief driver.

'Goodnight,' Alex said, sidestepping him to hail a taxi. She fleetingly wondered if he was a victim of the last recession. Drivers did not usually carry heavy tomes on the clash of cultures between East and West.

The windows to the flat were wide open. Adam was not emerging from sleep as she had pictured him. Instead, he was perkily leaning out of the living-room window watering Alex's newly acquired window boxes. Alex's spirits rose at the sight of his familiar, muscular form and his sweet smile.

He looked so healthy and capable. She was not alone in her admiration of him. Occupants of the surrounding flats were waving and shouting encouragement. It was like some opening scene to a musical. Adam made friends easily; people trusted him and confided. Being a doctor was his genetic disposition.

Alexandra let herself in with her shiny new key. The place was a mess, although many of the cardboard boxes had been flattened and furniture moved into position, including the large sofa, where she had imagined herself in Adam's arms. She resolved once more to take some time off. She wanted a domestic haven, with proper, cooked food and tidy/comfortable rooms, but this swallowed so much time for so little showy reward. But you could not be permanently dashing out of homes. They showed neglect as quickly as people did.

Alex's wobbly conversion to domesticity was partly pragmatic. Fiona Liddle had been in the office yesterday showing off her new baby to Sebastian and Jenny. She had told her rapt audience that it had changed her life and taught her the meaning of joy.

'I realize that there is something so much more important than me,' she said, beaming into the blanket. Nevertheless, she was extremely keen to get back to work and had spent the second week of her baby's eclipsing life interviewing nannies to look after him.

To demonstrate the intense bond between her child and the studio, she had asked Sebastian to be godfather. He had relayed this to Alex with pride. It was his eighth godchild, drawn from the spectrum of breakfast, day-time and evening women television presenters whose careers depended on him. Alex felt that it would have been crass for her to mention the knock-on effect of her own redundancy as a newsreader. She was surprised and cross at her mean-spirited response. There were plenty more health scandals for her to cover; the subject was hotting up politically. She might even influence Government policy. This had always been her intention at journalism college. The current show business and royal reporters had, of course, all said the same.

Adam came down the stairs and hugged her.

'Hi, poor tired mouse. Would you like me to make you an omelette or something?' She nodded silently. She was dirty and tired and had ended up having a horrible day.

'It's just Patti,' she sobbed, burying her head in his T-shirt, reaching for the warm pulse of his skin.

One thing to be said for Patti Ward. She was very good at snakes and ladders. She knew that she had just slid down a long one. Alexandra's encounter with Patti's father was a nasty piece of misfortune. The odds against such an encroachment were enormous. Patti had developed a low view of investigative journalism. She found that offering pre-emptive information usually stalled inquiries. But she could not insure herself against freakish chance. In these unhappy circumstances she must defend herself by attack. When her driver picked her up outside the door to the main building, she was wearing dark glasses and a headscarf, a signal that she was in no mood for conversation. Someone knocked on the window but she turned away. The traffic had lightened during the evening and she reached her house swiftly. The road was empty – children in these houses had large playrooms or even indoor swimming pools so did not tend to spill out onto the street. The quietness was the privilege of the rich. There was no pub on the corner, no rat-run route for cars. Local commerce was interior decorators or top-of-the-market estate agents who shut up shop by four or even earlier on Fridays. Residents knew of each other through the social pages of magazines and tended to meet at formal events rather than in each others' homes. Any domestic activity was the preserve of the staff. Patti pinged the gate shut behind her and touched the leaves of the bay trees on either side of the wide door. Their dampness satisfied her that her housekeeper had done a day's work. Once inside she shoved the post into her handbag and picked up her luxuriously packed dry-cleaning from the hall table. It rustled against the banisters as she headed for the bedroom. The master, or rather mistress, bedroom was dusted and polished and expectant. The only occupied room in the house. Patti threw down the dry-cleaning on the linen chair covers and kicked off her shoes. Then she stretched out on her plumped and creaseless bed and held a strategy meeting.

Her dispassionate assessment of her situation was this: the problem – diminishment of the brand due to market forces and excessive human resources. Negative associations of the brand – not relevant, out of touch, no longer has the confidence of the management. Non-familial. The solution – Radical re-think. Move on. Attract the interest of rival, leading to renewed interest from own management. Play to strengths rather than weakness. Extremely well-known brand, inspiring confidence in an unstable market. High personal value. Quote audience figures. Quote authoritative newspaper survey on men's preference for beautiful older women over less attractive younger ones. Quote women's preference for older women on grounds of self-interest. Quote European directives on discrimination at work. Drag Sebastian before an industrial tribunal if necessary. Tip off the press pack to follow her to work for dramatic confrontation with Sebastian. Ensure the howls of support from ageing women newspaper columnists.

Patti switched on the light, pulled a pen and an envelope from her bag and wrote down: *Phone Mike Thomas at Pegasus News, open negotiation.*

She noticed the envelope was addressed in tangled, unformed handwriting. She opened it and pulled out the A4 sheet of lined paper.

Dear Patti, I hope you don't mind me writing to you at short notice. The head of the army was meant to come to our speech day but he doesn't want to come anymore (because he is worried the sixth form are too hard, Mr Reynolds says!). Anyhow, the Head asked if we know any celebrities and I said I knew you really well. But I have lost your phone number. Rob and Chris say like I know you in my dreams. I bet that you are really busy and you probably have a celebrity event to go to and wouldn't want to come to this hole. But could you come and do the prizes next weekend? Have enclosed the programme and a map of how to find this place. Do you think you'll be driving the Aston Martin? That would be so cool. I phoned Mark to ask him to ask you but he says he hasn't been in touch? I really hope you guys aren't splitting, although I can't see what you see in Mark (only kidding!). Anyway, could you phone me on my mobile? Or text me? Mr Reynolds says I can keep it switched on in class in case you phone. We all watched you on the news about that Bulger case. I reckon those boys will end up being on the Internet. If I met them, I would beat them up. James Bulger was just a little kid. We are going to see a film tonight. It is only a fifteen though.

I really hope that you can come to the speech day. Lots a love,
Tristan.

The problem: Mark was slipping from her grasp. Not in
any deliberate, decisive sense, he was too easy-going for
that. But days would pass, then weeks, then he would pitch
up at some party with a girl in tow. Alex? Patti needed to
regain his attention. Solution: Tristan.

The problem: Alex and her busybody breakthrough.
How should Patti re-establish her filial credentials? Adam's
mother? How should Patti re-establish primacy over Alex?
Adam? Patti made no note of these last two sub-strategies.
Instead she ran herself a deep, scented, candlelit bath and
prepared for the morning.

Patti was at the gym by 7 a.m. The car park was already half
full with expensive two-seater sports cars, this year's
bonuses for the City traders. There was a testosterone pace
and purpose to these early gym hours before the mothers
arrived, dawdling and indecisive, blocking the stairs and
fumbling for their cards and crying, 'Hi! how are you?' into
their mobile phones as if they had been separated at birth
from their lunch dates. The traders barked 'Hey!' into their
phones treating the flashing chrome like a weapon rather
than a garden fence. She took her place on the smooth
black machines alongside the exhaling, aggressively fit figures of the money-makers. She liked these members of the
boot camp regime so much more than the soft flexible yoga
crowd who would show up in an hour or so, with their
slow gentle voices and watery blue eyes and fleeces to pop
on during the relaxation period. This was better, pounding

away on the StairMaster, a towel covering the arduousness of the graph. She punched in the time, the level and her body weight. She hesitated over the indifferent directive, specify your age. Forty. The machine whirred into life, rising to a piercingly higher pitch. Patti watched the sweat collecting on her inside elbows, felt it trickling down the back of her neck. She ran on, until she was blinded by the salt. A muscular American man in his twenties took up her rhythm on the machine next to her. They exchanged exhilarated competitive glances. Twenty minutes on he whistled under his breath and slowed down. Patti accelerated into her final stretch, her long, damp body weightless with adrenalin.

Afterwards she kick-boxed and trembled under crushingly heavy weights. By the time she threw her white towel over the shower glass she felt unpleasantly faint. Even her formidable will could not conquer her age. Her body had its limits.

Patti emptied her bag of its laboratory of vitamin supplements, mild steroids and HRT. Her strength returned with a jolt as the club beautician conditioned and blow dried her hair.

'Such a beautiful colour,' said the girl. 'Where do you have it done?' A shade of blonde this natural, had to be artificial.

Patti roared out of the club in her Aston Martin just as the first housewives were parking diagonally, on their way back from the school run. She guessed that they would discuss her over cappuccinos with their tennis coaches. They would manage to sound both admiring and pitying.

'I don't think she can be happy,' she had once overheard

a woman observe, impertinently. 'It is a very selfish kind of life.'

So resentful, so self-righteous. Well Patti might not give anything beyond her Atlas-like tax support of the social services but she did not take anything either. Whereas, she thought, these women grew like ivy around their husbands, sucking every penny out of them with their greedy, needy wiles. And what did they do in return? One school run. Thank you, but Patti would not be taking any lessons from these women. Looking Scandinavian and an interest in interior decorating did not entitle you to pass judgement on women who worked for a living. Patti turned to face her flustered accuser. 'I can assure you,' she said coldly, 'that I am very happy.'

The rest of the time, she took no notice. She knew her appeal lay with men. Women were too harsh and fickle an audience. Of course it was women who were the bulk of her viewers but she performed for her qualitative audience of men.

At 9.31 she telephoned Mike Thomas's office. A happy consequence of her fame was that senior executives were not in meetings or 'with somebody'. They did not call her back. They answered her phone. Executives are not in fact very busy. They are selectively occupied.

'I'll see if he is in. I'll put you through.' It was as easy as that.

'Patti, good to hear you. What can I do for you?' Patti was momentarily startled. She had developed scales over the last days which prepared her for rebuffs. Kindness made her squirm. Perhaps after all it was Sebastian who was out of line. She had attached herself to the wrong man.

'I'd like to see you, soon. I have a proposal that may interest you.' See how the bureaucratic waters parted.

'Sure, you want a cup of coffee? I could do eleven fifteen?' Patti pressed her lips against the phone.

'Yup, that's cool, I'll call in.'

She fed the meter in Knightsbridge. Her knowledge of time and distance was exact. Forty minutes window shopping in Sloane Street, enough to be busy without looking sweaty. Two cappuccinos. An easy drive south of the river, unusually allowing other cars to turn into her lane. She arrived five minutes early and slouched wryly in the primary-coloured body-shaped chair. She was surrounded by gigantic posters of weekend comedy shows. Patti, whose visual strength was her sublime gravity of expression in the event of world disasters, felt the awkward juxtaposition.

The receptionist, pretty, self-confident, ironic about her temporarily lowly position, called across to her,

'Are you OK there, Patti? Mike will be with you just now.' Patti smiled glacially. Could people sense the drifting balance of power? Was it not clear that it was she who was granting the favour?

Fortunately, Mike appeared through the pipe-shaped archway – doors had been dispensed with resulting in a time-consuming and expensive tussle between architects and planning officers. He was a slight, tense figure, always on the look out for a newer thing. He responded better to screens than people.

'Good to see you, hi, hi, you got coffee? Good, let's talk, right up this step.'

His office was in fact an apartment, corporately equipped with more chairs-cum-bouncy castles, and framed photographs of him back slapping comedians at television award ceremonies. He ushered Patti onto one of the rubber sofas and almost bounced her off it by settling into the other side of it.

'So, what is the zeitgeist at NTC? You've had some good audience figures. Nice programming scheduling. What is the buzz about Sebastian?'

Patti attempted an upright position by holding in her stomach and craning her neck. She sighed thoughtfully. 'I think he is feeling his way, actually I get on with him quite well, people should really try to give him a chance.'

Mike's expression was one of disinterested concentration. 'Are other people critical of what he is doing?'

Patti sighed again and frowned. She looked as if she were anxious to be fair.

'I'm not sure about general morale, you know. But I wonder if he knows where he is going?'

Mike nodded. 'What about this big autumn show, what is happening there?'

Patti gave a modest shrug. 'Oh we are getting there slowly.' She hesitated, 'But I am beginning to wonder, absolutely confidentially, whether Sebastian really knows what he is doing. I mean, I just wonder whether he has the right commercial instincts. He's not like you, Mike, you have this great sense of what you want, that is why your shows are so great. You just understand the television audience.'

Mike poured himself a glass of water. Patti wrestled with the next thought.

'You know, I am happy enough at NTC, they treat me very well, I am very well paid, blah, blah, blah. But I feel like a challenge. I'm getting itchy. I think, for me, it might be the right time to change companies. It would be a big shock for NTC and the newspapers would go crazy, but it is just my instinct, you know?'

Mike sipped from his glass.

'I hear what you are saying, Patti. And I think that you are talent, I have no doubt about that.

'But my advice is that you are totally identified with NTC. You are great for them. We are a new company, we should be experimenting. We need to be seen to be creating our own stars. I'm just not into all that poaching shit. It doesn't work. We have tried it, taking people on at the top of their professions, if you don't mind me saying so, at the pinnacle of their salaries. Then there is a backlash from our shareholders wanting to know why we are spending so much money.

'The press are right on our backs about your greed and our lack of creativity. And somehow, when you remove stars from their natural context, the audiences don't like it. They should follow but they just get pissed off. We are in graveyard territory.'

Patti felt herself sinking helplessly into the rubber. 'Listen, my salary isn't that important, I am single, I can make bold choices.'

'Nah,' said Mike, 'if you accept less money then you look as if you are on the way out. I told you, the thing doesn't work. I gave a talk at the Westminster conference last week and clearly outlined why poaching was not part of my vision for Pegasus. To be honest, we want to look at the little known. I am in touch with one of your junior colleagues, who I think could make a big noise here.'

'May I ask who?' said Patti, although her acidic stomach already offered the answer.

'Well, confidentially, it is the lunchtime fill-in girl, Alexandra Khan. You know her? She is very much the image we want to project here right now. But so far she says she is not interested, so we'll see. I mean, Christ, if you could lean on her a bit. You are the role model for all those girls.'

Patti rose. 'I have a meeting with David Leach at twelve so I had better go. Thank you for clarifying things for me. Sometimes you take the greatest place for granted and I wanted something to compare it with. I could never leave NTC, no matter what else was offered. I realize that now. God, it is like falling in love with your husband all over again.'

She offered a hand to the sprawling Mike Thomas and left before he could see her out. She would dispute his version of this meeting in the High Court, before God, if necessary. Why was he so interested in Sebastian? Professional rivalry or gay network? More snakes than ladders ahead.

Patti arrived at work, after an extended shopping break, late afternoon. Her colleagues were gathered, sitting or standing around the largest television screen.

'What's happening?' asked Patti.

Mark sprung up and offered her his chair next to Alex. 'Henman has lost the set to Federer, my sweet.'

Alex was peeping through her fingers. 'I can't bear it, come on, Henman, come on.'

'No drama in the inevitable, is there?' said Patti.

Sally, who was perched on a desk top, groaned. 'Don't put the Patti Ward curse on him. Henman has been playing flawlessly.'

'Apart from all those double faults,' said Mark, changing sides tactfully.

'When did you all become the bloody experts?' said

Steve irritably. 'How come I am not allowed to have a view on *Question Time* but you all take over as soon as it is July. Fair-weather punters.'

The Wimbledon crowd swayed with vicarious energy. Tim Henman made a small stiffening gesture with his forearm and served a double fault. He looked flustered, anxious. His opponent was expressionless but his body formed a line of powerful relaxation.

'Wow, watch him go,' said Patti. For a few minutes the Swiss man played with quiet, psychotic brilliance. Henman's experience then prevailed. Pity. Killer instinct was so much more interesting than mere technique.

Alex jumped up and hugged Sally.

'He did it, he did it.' Sally had nipped out earlier to Tesco for Pimm's ingredients which she now served from a jug into NTC merchandise mugs.

'Sorry, no glasses.'

'Sally, you are a heroine,' said Alex.

'Gosh, I am exhausted. What a match.'

Mark brushed a finger over the back of Patti's neck. 'What have you been up to?'

Had Patti been fifteen years younger she would have flung herself at him. But age must stand on dignity, the only defence against foolishness.

'I've been tied up,' she said hardening her longing glance into a glare. Mark had a fluid nature; he flowed over the wounds.

'Shall we do something next weekend?'

Patti was stung by his lightness. Why didn't he say this evening? Today, tomorrow, next month. It was all the same to him.

'I am afraid that I have a date with Tristan this weekend.'

Mark gave a surprised laugh. 'What have you two cooked up?'

'I'm giving the prizes away at his speech day,' said Patti.

'What? You never told me?'

'Do I have to?' asked Patti archly. Sally joined them jovially.

'Patti doing a school prize-giving? Christ, that is putting the fox with the chickens isn't it?'

'Have you met Sally, one of my oldest and most loyal friends,' drawled Patti.

Alex looked shyly over. 'They will all fall in love with you, Patti, I wish we had had someone as glamorous as you at our prize-givings instead of those lady mayors who looked liked buses.' Patti gave a slight smile. What a graceful compliment, managing unconsciously to draw attention to the yawning difference of age. Steve puffed out his chest, exposed through his unbuttoned shirt.

'If I dressed as a school boy would I have more chance of a date, Patti?' he said.

'Get back to your tennis players,' said Patti with flirtatious severity. 'Ask them if it has sunk in yet.'

'Oh, you are so patronizing,' said Steve. 'Okey-dokey, let's get this side-show on the road.'

'Patti,' gestured Mark. 'Your public awaits you.' His hand lingered in hers and she felt another stab of desire. But he slipped through her hands, as he always would.

'Are you staying?' she asked casually.

'I have to get back to the Commons vote,' he said. 'I said I'd take Alex, she's very keen to see how the whole thing works. I said I'd introduce her to the Great Man. He likes pretty young women for some reason.' Alex materialized wearing a leather jacket and a shoulder bag. Dressed for the back of Mark's scooter.

'I told her women have no business being in the Commons,' Mark said cheerfully. 'Ten minutes there and she'll be demanding crèches and netball pitches.'

'Excuse me?' laughed Alex. Patti felt tired and sad and old. She wanted to sleep in Mark's arms. But she must fight on.

Chapter 9

Pleasures are mostly associated with novelty. Because Patti was accustomed to being driven, she was slightly thrilled to twist her key in the ignition, to catch the flattering glimpse of her face in the wing mirror – which reflected her colouring rather than the detail of her disintegration – and to hear the muffled, constrained roar of the engine. Above all she enjoyed being alone, with an aloneness that stretched before her. There was no need to ward off conversation by holding up a newspaper or playing with her cellphone. She quite understood that one had to pay for one's pleasures and consequently every long-distance trip was followed by a hail of speeding tickets, although still fewer than strictly warranted, so well worth the risk. The car drew many admiring glances which she absorbed rather than witnessed. The Aston Martin had no independent existence, it was another aspect of her unobtainable loveliness. Patti accelerated happily out of the suburbs along a decent stretch of motorway. She passed families squashed into over-loaded vehicles with bike racks, she overtook cocky young men without the engine power to live up to their reckless spirits. Finally she roared up a drive to a large Victorian house surrounded by playing fields. Pupils of Benedicts School, fashion fighting with dress code, formed into hunched groups, dividing naturally according to their attractiveness and popularity. Breaking away from the crowd who were the most experimental with uniform – and whose hair was slime green following unsuccessful attempts to find the antidote to banned orange – came Tristan. His unsmiling swagger gave way to an excited trot as he reached the car. He banged the roof proprietorially and peered through the window, his handsome features only slightly marred by the angry row of spots along his hairline.

'Patti! So cool that you've come. I knew you'd be in your Aston Martin. Can I park it?' Patti leaned out of the window and kissed him on both hot cheeks.

'We'll go for a drive afterwards. I don't think it would look too good for you to plough into the building before we've started, eh?'

'Hey,' yelped Tristan delightedly, 'I'm a really good driver. Shall I take you to the marquee? Or would you like to, um, freshen up, beforehand?'

Patti slung her bag over her shoulder and pushed her sunglasses over her head. Tristan was almost her height now, and she easily slipped her arm through his. His blushes were almost disguised by the sporty glow of his face. He pursed his lips to prevent a smirk and pushed up his gelled hair into the cockatoo style of his peers. No master was going to make him comb it down while he had a famous blonde on his arm. He could hear the envious muttering of his mates behind him.

'The graduate, the graduate,' Rob was calling from a safe distance. Tristan broke into a grin. Patti turned and raised a withering eyebrow.

'Oh shit, she heard,' yelped Rob, diving behind Chris's back. Patti and Tristan dipped their heads together to get though the flap of the vast airless tent. Then Tristan solicitously and self-importantly guided her to the foot of the platform where the headmaster was rubbing his hands together with the congeniality he reserved for parents' days. Acknowledging the envious or curious glances from the school, Tristan made his way back, hands in pockets, to the lower-sixth row of wooden fold-up chairs, which were barely big enough to support the boys' heavy sporting frames. He devotedly watched Patti shaking hands with women in flowery dresses and men in suits and navy blue ties.

As Patti took her seat, the audience of pupils before her took on individually distinctive shapes. The children were of comically extreme sizes, some of settled looks and some frantically disorganized. The handful of extremely pretty girls had already acquired their own self-consciousness. They eyed Patti with the critical fascination of rivals. The rest with open-faced admiration. Patti looked at them with a small conspiratorial smile. No one quite dared to smile back. The practised darting eyes of teachers used for class control defied any pupil to move unduly. The headmaster spoke of the school's wish to produce rounded human beings and the dangers of a materialistic society. Patti adopted her grave, riots in Bradford expression. Then it was her turn to stand by the large, ugly table and dispense books and trophies for effort, achievement and, oh to keep a straight face, for kindness and consideration. She held each diffident, clammy hand and whispered 'well done' with delighted irony.

After a while, however, she began to tire of her unfamiliar role as good citizen and role model. As she rose for the school hymn she brushed open her shirt a little while holding up her prayer book. It was a tiny but distinct signal to the more developed girls in the back rows that she was still ahead of the game. Tristan was waiting for her outside the marquee surrounded by a large crowd of his peers. The least proud thrust exercise books, magazines and limbs encased in plaster for Patti to sign.

'God, my friends are so embarrassing,' smirked Tristan.

'Haven't you ever met anyone from television before?' Patti winked at him and a few minutes later gestured that the session was over. It was mostly girls who were left. Tristan piled his bags and rackets into the boot of the car and climbed into the passenger seat. No one could have missed him getting into an Aston Martin with a telly blonde. He was living *FHM* magazine.

'Wicked.' He grinned at Patti as she accelerated out of the school gates. 'Thanks a lot, Patti, sorry my friends are such losers.'

They drove through the country lanes to dislocatingly harsh urban rap music. Patti glanced at Tristan. He was very like Mark in profile, but without the wear and tear. Mark, was a man of boyish looks. Tristan was a boy who looked like a man. The safeguard of maternal instinct was not present in Patti. Her only fleeting calculation was whether it would look bad in print. No one would dare, too libellous. She pulled into a rough track.

'Want to try a little drive?' she asked. Tristan ecstatically changed seats. The car jolted several times and then sped forward.

'Hey, calm down,' laughed Patti putting her hand over his as he fumbled for the gears. 'Let's start from the beginning, shall we?' Tristan glanced slyly at her. He found it extraordinarily difficult to read signals correctly but he wondered if Patti was touching him in the right way. As she slid down, his mind burst into kaleidoscope-coloured fragments.

'What the fuck . . .'

As Patti pulled into a parking space outside her house, she saw a figure waiting for her on the steps. It was Mark, his head buried in a pile of flapping newspapers.

'There is your guardian,' she murmured. Tristan's colour was alarmingly high and his expression dazed. Patti was irritated. It was written all over him. Stupid little boy.

'You won't say anything to your big brother?' she said with fond menace.

'I, I don't think I can speak to him,' said Tristan in a strange falsetto voice. 'I mean, if he thinks that I have been having sex with his girlfriend.' Patti turned to him, her face pinched with fury.

'Shut up, Tristan, shut up. You never mention this to anyone.' Tristan looked frightened and miserable. Mark waved at them and collected up his papers.

'You want to do this again?' asked Patti in a new, wheedling tone, her eyes fixed on Mark's approaching figure. 'If you play your cards right and say NOTHING, we can do it again.' Tristan nodded. Mark opened Patti's door for her.

'Hello, temptress, I bet you have knocked the boys dead. Tristan, you look as if you have been through the wars. I hope you have thanked Patti. It is extremely kind of her to give up her day to you snotty-nosed lot. Where are your bags?'

The sun was hot and the pavements dusty as Mark draped an arm round Patti and led her to the front door. In his ignorance of the source of Patti's sexuality he felt only desire for her and protective goodwill towards his annoying little brother.

'Come on, my family,' he said closing the door behind them. 'Tell me all about it.'

Sally had also spent the day at a school open day. It was her daughter Sophie's final year before leaving for grammar school. Sally had always shouldered her duties towards the school, making costumes, baking cakes, persuading minor television personalities to come and talk about corpsing before the camera. Steve, the sports editor, had to be talked out of his seventh appearance at the school. He said he would do anything for the kids but Sally felt that even the nine year olds' unconditional admiration of any form of celebrity was beginning to wane.

'I don't mean to sound ungrateful, but who is benefiting whom here?' she had muttered to Sebastian as Steve had scanned the local paper for his name. Sally's only regret was that work had prevented her from being a school governor; she would have liked to have had some influence over the running of the school and Gordon always said that navy blue suited her. The pull of respectability had surprised her. She had thought of herself as a sceptic but in truth she was a doer. She was both exasperated and pleased when Gordon and the children looked to her for administrative direction. Her greatest gift turned out to be planning. Her life motto was not, as she once boasted, go with the flow, but be prepared. At the end of each family expedition, every school calendar, or news programme, she would ask herself: Did it all go to plan? At the end of each day, when the house was locked up and the children asleep, she would nod and smile as she ticked off the final item on the day's list.

This did not make Sally a bureaucrat. She was not thrown by the unexpected, rather she was braced for it. Illness or misfortune was all part of the plan and space was required for it. Life's natural rhythm was accommodating. As her children required her less, she prepared to nurse her ageing parents. As her husband's practice dwindled, she took on extra work. 'When do you have time for yourself?' Patti had asked her. But this was herself. She was most present in other people.

Gordon followed the line of cars into the school field, glaring unnoticed at the drivers who overtook him in a circular path, creating deep tyre marks on the soft grass. Sophie and Tom climbed out, assuming the wary posture of siblings pretending not to know each other. Sophie pulled her jersey sleeves over her hands and looked in one direction. Tom sucked at his brace and faced the other way. Sally stayed where she was, seat belt still on, applying lipstick and eyeshadow with the guidance of a small compact mirror. She pressed and rolled her lips together as her generation always did. She rubbed the excess powder from her matt Roman nose, which she considered her best feature. Gordon waited patiently, long familiar with his wife's routines. He in turn checked the windscreen fluid, double-checked the handbrake and turned round to see if the inside light was on, although the children were too old to fiddle with it. His checklists were not as long or as wide ranging as Sally's but they had also become part of his character. Sophie disappeared into a little of cluster of friends who screamed and hugged her, partly because of the rising hysteria of their last day and partly to show off in front of Tom who stuck his thumbs into his belt and scowled. Both sister and brother threw loving, discouraging looks at the fussy figures that they called their parents.

Just as Sally found it hard to remember the substance of their children at earlier ages, and was always taken back by the sheer infancy of past photographs, so Tom and Sophie had no mental record of having youthful parents. There were childhood episodes; picnics on windswept beaches, their darker-haired mother holding their hands as she delivered them to their first teachers. The rare scary days when their mother stayed in bed and instructed them feverishly on how to make tea. Their parents' friends who sat drinking on the patio and apologized for bad language 'in front of the children'. The kaleidoscope of the past, where it was mostly summer and the family was broadly cheerful and playing garden rounders, was impressionistic about personalities. Because they were only perceived in relation to their children, Gordon and Sally had no existence before their children's memories, and so were trapped in perpetual middle age. Tom and Sophie could not confidently answer biographical questions about their parents. They knew almost nothing about their internal life. This was what made the family dynamic so successful. Asked by an enthusiastic English teacher to describe what made Sally and Gordon 'special' Tom had answered sincerely, 'Nothing at all.' They were just parents. He added obligingly that his mother knew some famous people.

Sally passed the day on a plane of contentment. Most of her friends were parents of her children's classmates. They exchanged proud grimaces about school achievements and a brimming sympathy for the pitfalls. The year one exclamations: 'What will become of us all?' were answered over time. The statistically unlucky parents suffered cancer, the freakishly tragic children died in banal accidents, the rest howled with shared anguish and plodded on. Another generation of school children collected their prizes and passed on. Sally knew that her greatest preparation was still to come. Her children, who had already surpassed her in height, would outgrow her emotionally in the blink of the decade. Like the headmistress, she would remind them of the values they had learned and urge them to become good citizens in life. They had finished with her. She mimed the pompous, Victorian words of the school hymn, overcome with fear and love.

Patti stretched out in her newly laundered sheets. The scent of jasmine reached her from the window, where it had wound itself around her drainpipe. It had been planted by Veronica next door but inclined longingly towards Patti's house. This was only Patti's due. She opened and shut her eyes. A faint, urban breeze tickled her face. It was going to be another lovely day. Patti unfolded her long limbs across the bed. Generosity of space was the privilege of the single. It made up for the alternative scenario; a creak on the stair, the door pushed open with an elbow and Mark appearing with tea and the newspapers, to be read together companionably in bed. Patti had insisted on sleeping alone for two reasons. First she no longer wanted Mark to see her without make-up. Second, she could not rely on Tristan to behave rationally if she offered him the spare bedroom. She enjoyed intrigue so long as she was in control of it. But last night there had been a jutting edge to the atmosphere. Tristan had grown sullen and goading, interrupting his half-brother's attempts to talk about the new Government with drunken aggression:

'Like, no one cares Mark, it is so not relevant, it is just politicians jerking off.'

Mark had become increasingly exasperated by Tristan's moodiness.

'Do you have to be quite so moronic?' he asked, as Tristan recited the most violent gangsta rap lyrics he knew during a discussion on gun control. Tristan lunged ostensibly at Mark's packet of Pringles crisps but hit his brother in the groin.

'For Christ's sake,' shouted Mark, 'what is the matter with you?'

Patti refilled their glasses, turning her back on Tristan. She felt awkward. This was not a twinge of conscience but the result of rapid risk assessment. She had expected Tristan to be mute and doting, but he was perilously highly strung. When Mark stood in front of Patti, massaging her shoulders, Tristan had shot her mad signals with his eyebrows. Youth was not wasted on the young but sex was, in her opinion. She upturned a final bottle into Tristan's glass then shrugged sympathetically to Mark that he had better take his half-brother home. She was too weary to deal with teenage drunkenness. Mark crossly dragged Tristan into the street to look for a taxi, bumping into an elderly, red-faced man on the corner of the street, scattering his cargo of leaflets which read: 'The threat from Central Asia! Ignore at your peril!!!'

Despite the discordant doubts about Tristan's reliability, Patti was broadly confident that she had done the right thing. Mark had been tender and attentive towards her. Gratitude could be close to a loving impulse. Mark was evidently deeply paternal towards the boy and so he proved himself capable of commitment. If only she could bind Mark to her using those family ties. She was practically an orphan herself. She could be both mother and child. She rose from the bed and planted her feet on the floor. Her left ankle was sore, possibly arthritic. Another little indignity of age that she must bear. Her bedside radio was automatically tuned to Radio 4. She particularly disliked the regional folksiness of Sunday broadcasting. Some sop was imitating the sound of a thrush. Patti limped to the bathroom to soak her face in creams and brush her teeth at sonic length. She felt so much more clear-headed when she was clean and moisturized. She hopped back to the bed and pushed away the copies of *Vogue*, the *Spectator*, the *New Yorker*, *Time*, *Newsweek* and the literary supplements. She kept abreast of book reviews but did not read books. They felt so padded out to her, she was especially bored by description and feelings. Life was so much simpler than novelists pretended. Birth, getting what you wanted, not getting what you wanted, death. Simple.

Underneath all this unrecycled material was her letter from Adam. Patti thought that this was a good day to telephone his mother. Sunday had a pastoral feel to it although she usually spent it in the gym, or in the shops, or at work, much like any other day. She glanced at the radio clock. It was 9 a.m., gruesomely early in medialand. But she knew from hearsay that good women were usually early risers. It was picked up after a couple of rings. A small, clear, accented voice read back the number, a sure sign of someone who lived alone. Patti's voice was sympathetic and low.

'Mrs Berluscoli? My name is Patti Ward, Adam asked me to give you a ring. I wonder if I could drop by for a cup of coffee this morning?'

The woman hesitated. 'Why, that is very nice of you. Adam asked you to did he? He's all right, is he? The thing is I will be at church this morning and I am sure that you are very busy.' Stupid not to have thought of that.

'Oh, of course I meant after church. Perhaps for a sherry? I have a lunch appointment so obviously I can't stay.'

Mrs Berluscoli cleared her throat. 'Yes, I have some sherry somewhere. Well, if it isn't an imposition for you, I can be free at twelve. Will it last long? It's about Adam is it? Nothing has happened has it?'

Patti cooed reassurance. 'Adam is absolutely fine. He just thought that we should meet. We have so much in common. But Mrs Berluscoli. I don't want to impose on you, of course I don't. And as I said, I have to be somewhere at one. So we'll say twelve shall we?'

Patti was strict about her Sunday observance. She got to the gym by 10 a.m. on the dot. The City boys would not arrive until later, finally worn down by drink and different time zones. It was a period for single women who fretted about leaving their stomach muscles untested for a day. Patti went for cat-like stretches and showcase suppleness on this occasion. She did not want to look aggressively worked out for her appointment. Plus she wished to make clear to her fellow gym toilers that she was having sex, while they demonstrably weren't, so she sighed, spread out her limbs on the mat, rolled over to one side and played contentedly with her bouncy hair in front of the mirror.

She noticed in the reflection a woman of similar height, build and blondeness to her monopolizing the Cybex thigh-stretching apparatus. She wriggled closer to the mirror. Oh, but there was a difference. The woman's skin was tighter on her arms, her breasts were high and pointy beneath a grey T-shirt. She was performing the exercise in a desultory, intermittent manner while burying herself in a newspaper. She was taut in flesh rather than manner. Patti experienced a wave of sadness. Then she rolled her eyes, lifted herself up and headed for the exit, hobbling slightly. As she left she whispered to the instructor that the woman in grey on the leg machine had exceeded her fifteen minutes. She just thought he should know. She drove home, showered and applied a body lotion of lavender and eucalyptus to enhance her soothing, health visitor image. She chose a demure outfit of trousers, a vaguely academic-looking cardigan and flat shoes. Her proud touch was an Alice band. Now, what could be threatening about that? Patti arrived at Mrs Berluscoli's first-floor flat in Marylebone at 11.55. She pressed the buzzer and announced her name in the soft, charity worker's voice she reserved for hopeless human interest items towards the middle of the news.

As she padded up the one flight of worn carpet, the door opened a fraction and Mrs Berluscoli peered out, a small, neat figure, with black hair theatrically streaked with white bands.

'How do you do, Miss Ward,' she said politely.

Patti gave her long, scented hand and looked into her large black eyes. 'Hello, Mrs Berluscoli, thank you for inviting me.'

The flat was very small, but immaculate, almost clinically so. As Patti glanced round the living room, Mrs Berluscoli waved a small hand apologetically.

'I'm afraid it is not very welcoming. I live alone here, my husband died, so there's no one to try to please but me. I was a nurse, I can't see a room without scrubbing it.'

'Oh, I love clean homes too, I'm the same. Never happier than on my hands and knees,' said Patti gaily, sliding her silken hands into her cardigan pockets. 'Now, let me guess, that must be Adam's room.'

There were two rooms off the living room and open kitchen. The door to one was closed, the other wide open, revealing a brightly painted wardrobe, a brass bed and walls entirely covered with photographs.

'Can I peep?' asked Patti, judging that she had permission from Mrs Berluscoli's ecstatically proud expression.

Every nuance of Adam's childhood was documented here. The chubby, night-eyed toddler crammed into a plastic car, the leaner school boy in a neat tie and v-necked jersey, the changing hairstyles, and sudden growth spurts. Adam on the rugby field, Adam emerging from the sea, then Adam at medical school, twenty photographs of the same wistful smile and white coat. One photograph was blown up far beyond its reproductive capacity. Alongside the blurred poster-size shot, was a small photograph of his father staring animatedly from his surgery.

'This is Adam's father,' said his widow, needlessly.

Patti looked from one to the other. 'Marvellous, Mrs Berluscoli. In their different ways.'

The wife and mother gazed at the photographs. 'Not different, Miss Ward, the same. I never lost him.'

Patti touched the woman's arm, hoping that the eucalyptus' properties would serve as a substitute for human sympathy. 'How about some coffee?' she asked.

Mrs Berluscoli flinched. She lived only for her son, but she retained Pavlovian responses to social correctness. If she was not hospitable then she was letting down her household gods in their photograph frames.

'Please, sit down, let me fetch you some coffee.'

Patti stretched out her legs on the sofa and let the non-decaf coffee that was duly handed to her grow cold.

'Mrs Berluscoli, I want to speak to you from the heart.' She reached for the approximate position beneath her cardigan. 'You love your son and you want what is best for him. I know him to be a remarkable young man. But he is remarkable in his own way. He is unique.'

Mrs Berluscoli held up her hand in delighted modesty. 'Thank you, Miss Ward, coming from you especially.'

'Mrs Berluscoli, Jessica, I don't know what it is to be a mother, I wish I did. But my detachment, my tragic detachment as it were, from your position, may give me some insight. I don't think Adam is a doctor. I think he may be a very brilliant actor.' Patti waited to be contradicted, but Jessica looked back at her silently, with her son's innocence.

'Oh do you think so, Miss Ward? Well that is a strange thing. I wanted to go on stage myself but I thought I would be more . . . useful, as a nurse. Why did Adam never mention it?'

'He thought you would be disappointed.'

'Disappointed? That he took after me rather than his father?' Jessica buried her face in her hands. 'Sorry, oh forgive me. I wanted him to keep alive his father's memory. But if it is me who lives on in him, oh, that is a greater thing for me. My son, my son, my son.'

Patti was puzzled and alarmed by this strange twist in the woman's Mediterranean intensity. Mrs Pepperpot was becoming Diana Rigg. She breathed in the cooler scent of lavender. 'Goodness, is that the time? I would love to talk about all this further, but I must go. I am so pleased for you, for Adam. What a misunderstanding.'

'I must go to Adam?' asked Jessica, with a smile of wonder.

'Let me talk to him,' said Patti firmly. 'Then he will come to you. Keep the coffee brewing!'

'Would you like to look at Adam's school reports?' breathed Mrs Berluscoli ardently. 'I have kept everything, all his drawings, everything. He was a little dreamer, plenty of ability, but I told him crossing the road is important too, Adam! He's a good boy, nice manners, kind to his mother. I am so grateful to you, Miss Ward, for taking an interest. You know, if someone is good to your son, you are so happy, so deliciously warm inside.'

Patti nodded vigorously while backing towards the door.

'But you have no children?' asked the woman, garrulous with maternal love. 'You see my husband lived to help women like you. That was the purpose of his being. It broke his heart when he could do nothing. He always felt that science was behind him, that he was waiting for medicine to catch up and then, oh then, he could make women happy. It is a good ideal, isn't it, Miss Ward, to bring women fulfilment?'

Patti dryly assumed that this was not up for discussion. It was a rhetorical wish on a par with being on the side of world peace, or kindness to animals.

'But you know, Miss Ward, I would also say to him, these women are being tested by God and maybe they will rise to the test. All that love will be dispersed in different ways. As with you, Miss Ward, you are being kind, you are being maternal, towards my son. I feel that we are mothers together.'

Patti was pressed against the door. She could not bear any more of this. Mrs Berluscoli stopped and held her hands to her cheeks.

'Oh dear, listen to me. Sometimes I forget that I am English now. This is not very English is it?' She folded her arms into her lap, assuming the studied pose of an Edwardian gentlewoman. 'May I say, Miss Ward, that I have always admired you on the news. You are a little bit regal. Do you mind me making personal remarks? I've told Alexandra, she is very pretty and I suppose she is popular with younger viewers but she doesn't have your posture. She will slouch. They all do these days. Anyway, she is a good girl.'

'Isn't she,' said Patti signing off. 'And she needn't worry about standing to attention just yet, I still get to do the state occasions.' She smiled winningly at the dignified little woman and let herself out of the door. As it happened, she was wanted at the television studios to rehearse the Queen Mother obituary. Posture is destiny. As she drove home to change, her thoughts assembled in no particular running order. Could she remember the names of the Queen Mother's corgis? Had Tristan talked to Mark? How was her funeral chic? Dress versus a suit, pearls? Too Jenny. Must check her highlights.

What an amusing morning it had been. How little we all know about each other. What would Adam's reaction be? She was uncertain of the net effect of her visit. Is a good deed of inherent value, regardless of motive? Or does every good deed have the capacity for badness? She wondered if her self-awareness prevented her from being wholly good or absolutely bad. Did she actively wish other people ill? Or was it simply that she had a heightened sense of self and a correspondingly shadowy sense of others? Was she, in other words, more true to nature than she gave herself credit for? The death of Dr Berluscoli was an unavoidable accident of her character. Of course, of course, she regretted it. She had not sought it. But she could not have acted otherwise. Her self-preservation did not produce the state of isolation she desired. It meant she lacked antennae, the road sense, to know when she had hit someone. And now the relatives were producing their claims. It was awful. What did she feel for other people? Less, apparently, than those around her. But perhaps she was simply more honest. Of course she did not mind if the Queen Mother died. How could she? She did not know her. It was of mild historical interest but it had nothing to do with her. But whom did she know? In her heart, would she mind if Sally died? She would be sorry but she would have the same sense of disconnection. Mark, she thought she would mind about. Sad for herself. Wasn't that the key? It was only empathy if you felt sad for yourself. She would wear black stockings if the Queen Mother died. And that is what she hoped the public would remember. Patti in black stockings. As she turned into her street, weary of self-analysis, she saw a figure hunched outside her door. Tristan waved his arms, how like Mark, and bounded up to the car. Patti got out gingerly.

'Hi, Tristan.'

'Hi, Patti, I thought I'd come round.' He smelled of particularly noxious aftershave.

'Tristan, I have to go to work, I'm just getting changed then I have to go. I can't ask you in,' Patti felt mildly panic stricken.

'Oh right,' said Tristan, crestfallen and still. 'I was just going to ask you if you wanted to come to something with me.' Patti locked the car door smiling.

'What, a date?'

'It's the Newquay surfing championship on Saturday and, like, I'm in it?'

Patti burst into laughter. Tristan drove his hand frantically through heavily gelled and spiky hair.

'Yeah, I know, it's not Glyndebourne, right? But Mark said he'd come and I reckoned you might if he did. I mean not for me but for him.' Patti stared at the hectic, muscled, childish figure.

'Why not?' she said. 'Sure, why not.'

Tristan gulped and nodded. 'Right. I had to let the organizers know who I was bringing so I, like, had to know straight away. You going to work now?'

Patti nodded. 'Yup, in a minute. Sorry I can't offer you coffee.'

'No, that's cool, I'm meeting some friends, anyhow. See you then.' He lunged at her cheek and hit her nose instead. 'Sorry, God, am I tosser or what?' He grinned unhappily and loped off down the street, a jiggling mass of hormones.

Patti shook her head fractionally and hurried towards her front door. After showering again, in order to produce a slightly altered aroma of lime and jasmine, changing into a charcoal grey suit, and ostentatiously dumping five unopened envelopes, covered in spidery writing and strange pictorial symbols, into the dustbin (her wars were on several fronts) she drove to the studios. Sally was already in, photocopying list lines and making tea for the languid royal biographer on hand. At the magazine Sally had written a rousing piece entitled WOMEN WHO GET TO THE TOP DON'T MAKE TEA. Later on in her career she had revised her opinion. Someone had to make it. She made it very well. And in the choice between mother or minx, the only categories available in the office, she chose the first. Steve turned up proudly in a black tie in order to announce which sporting events were to be cancelled. Conscious of the faux gravity of the circumstances, he burst into a chorus of 'Black, black, my world is black, I can't get Patti into the sack,' sung at regular intervals. Sebastian popped his head round the door, yelped as he saw Patti and hurried back into his office. Patti looked at Sally dryly.

'Is Sebastian feeling all right?' Sally made a strange, jowly grimace. Then Mark arrived, his head down, flicking through some newspaper cuttings. *Et tu*, Mark? He looked up, his soft blue eyes meeting Patti. There were no secrets there, just his usual abstraction.

'Hi, sweetheart,' he said kissing her on the cheek.

'Hi, darling,' chuckled Steve.

'OK,' said Sally. 'Let's start with nation in shock. Then we'll go through the procedure, the family, the sense of duty, the war years.'

'The overdraft!' said Steve.

'Steve, isn't there a cartoon you could be watching?' asked Patti.

'I know,' said Steve contentedly. 'I'm just a big kid.'

'Is Alex coming?' Mark asked Sally, his chin in his hand. Patti's stomach dropped a fraction. 'I mean the old lady's health is part of the story, no?'

Sally patted his arm indulgently. 'You are right, of course, I own up, I told Alex to take a day off. She needs to do a bit of nesting at her flat. She told me she and Adam no longer recognize each other in the street.'

'Hey, my Sunday football team don't recognize me in the street, can't I have some time off?' said Steve. Patti grinned at him conspiratorially.

'OK, Mother Superior,' she said. 'We little band of misfits better get on with it, eh?' Ignoring Mark, she recited her first sonorous line:

'A short time ago, Buckingham Palace made an important announcement . . .'

Alexandra was woken by a cacophony of car alarms and the shuddering gears of lorries regretting the short cut through her street. She lay still, looking at the ceiling. She guessed it was early afternoon. The comforting sense of sleeping through the day reminded her of minor childhood illnesses. She wanted to reach for the Lucozade and Capital Radio. But her forehead was cool and her mother was not hoovering downstairs. She smiled and stretched out her foot, feeling for Adam. He sleepily thrust himself towards her. His hair was inky against the sheets and she felt his warm, stale breath close to hers. She raised her arm to stroke his face.

'Darling,' she whispered. 'You are meant to be at work.' Adam leaped out of bed and pulled his shorts on. Alex, wrapping herself in the sheet, stood up and tugged him back.

'Joking.'

It was nearly 3 p.m. when they ate stale, crumbling croissants in the kitchen. The answering machine was flashing seven messages.

'Let's just hide here and make love,' said Adam wiping the crumbs tenderly from Alex's lips.

'Actually, let's go to Sainsbury's Homebase,' she wheedled.

Still full of sleep and sex they caught the tube to the local centre and pushed the trolley around, the shelves of hardware and paints and lavatory accessories serving as a set for the greatest love scene of their lives.

'I am so happy doing this,' whispered Alex, reaching up to kiss him.

'I want to marry you,' said Adam. They lifted the plants and compost from the trolley and lugged them back to the flat for more playful home-making. Then they took the papers to the nearest brasserie for a combination of breakfast, lunch and supper.

'I want to marry you too,' said Alex. It was an intense exchange of affection rather than a statement of intent. Marriage was not a social or moral imperative, nor even a pleasurable conclusion to their relationship. The act itself seemed anachronistic, the vows quaint. But they liked to discuss it, for its courtly overtones. They meant only to say, with grander rhetoric, that they cared for each other deeply. That night, in bed, Alex clutched Adam's back and whispered into his rough, angular jaw that she wanted his baby. She meant exactly that.

The ebb and flows of emotion surprised Alex. The thrilling adoration of the last day had come from nowhere. The daily familiarity was not at all the same as this ecstatic intimacy. He had burst into her just when their relationship was flagging. Yes, she loved Adam but recently this had not been her priority. She could relax, fall into step with him, but mostly she had not had the time. She found herself consulting him less, and she no longer felt the need to play her day back verbatim, so that Adam could share her indignation over slights and pride in her triumphs. She no longer telephoned him anxiously to make sure that he had recorded her on television. In fact she preferred him not to watch her now. His responses were too loyal and elementary. Alex needed an expert and the number she dialled most was Mark's. To be honest, she sometimes preferred Mark's company as well. They had rapidly built a foundation of shared references and jokes, a shorthand. She felt that she sparkled more in Mark's company. She would play back their banter in her head, finding her lips moving and her eyes flashing. Adam would look at her oddly when this happened. He was always interested in her work and would quiz her about colleagues and stories. She tried not to respond impatiently, but increasingly she edited her responses. For time reasons, as the American networks say. But today the liquid intensity of her love was restored. Alex felt both at peace and tripping with energy. By awkward, exhilarating coincidence, her career also entered a new phase. Perhaps this too could be attributed to her magnetic state. On the quiet Sunday in which their relationship was renewed, Alex received a phone call which changed her professional expectations and by extension herself.

Leaving Adam dozing, his limbs thrown across the bed in post-coital peacefulness, she had padded naked into the kitchen to check the answering machine messages. There were messages from her mother, a couple from Emily and Lisa and five from Sebastian. He wanted her to drop her plans for Monday and Tuesday. He needed her on a project. By the last message, his enthusiasm overcame his obliqueness.

'Hi, Alex, Sebastian again. Have you run off to join a convent or something? Look, basically I've had a flash of inspiration. I want to do a pilot for *The Hour*. This is all D-notice stuff OK, but I've booked the studio and everything so I need to know that you'll be there. Only Sal knows, so for goodness sake keep it under your hat. Isn't that a weird expression? Phone me, OK? Any time tonight.'

Alex felt a wave of euphoria followed by dread. If Patti found out she would kill her. Was it just too shitty? She'd fall on her face and nobody would want to employ her. She just didn't have the experience for this kind of thing, it would be a disaster. And it wasn't fair on Patti. She would telephone Sebastian and say that she just wasn't ready for it. Alex crouched by the answering machine, biting her nails. She went and took a bottle of beer from the fridge. The oven clock said 22.10. Maybe it was too late to phone now. Any time tonight. Should she go and wake Adam? What would he say. And he had to be up for an early shift, let him sleep. She desperately wanted to telephone Mark. He would give her the best advice, but he was the one person she couldn't phone. She filled up a glass of water and tipped it over her new orchid plant. Her brain was buzzing. She had not sought this. She wanted to get on and yet be liked. But her rise was necessarily someone's else's fall. There was no such thing as a vacant position. Patti would understand that, she of all people. She would be angry but she would understand it. She would be bloody angry. Sebastian had said it was a secret. It was an experiment, it would never work and no one would know. How could she say no? Alex's heart thumped inside her slender frame as she dialled Sebastian's number. He answered rapidly in his light, tenor voice.

'Hi, I'm sorry to ring so late, it's Alex Khan,' she said professionally.

'Alex, you tease, where have you been?' chuckled Sebastian. 'You got the message about tomorrow?'

'Yeah, wow,' said Alex. 'I mean, thanks very much for giving me the chance. Is this going to be cool with everyone?'

'Well it may put one or two noses out of joint, but I've got this gut feeling about you. And we have to take risks to stay ahead. Let's just give it a go.'

'Right,' said Alex, a shimmer of excitement in her voice. 'So where do I go, what time?'

'Eight a.m. I've hired a studio in town, it's the one in Soho Square where we did the OB with the dissident doctor during the election, do you remember?'

'Yup, I'll just write that down,' said Alex tracing invisibly with her finger on the tiled floor. 'Eight a.m. See you there.'

'Sleep well,' said Sebastian.

Alex shivered. It was getting cold. She went softly back to bed and slid under the sheet next to Adam. His arm flopped sleepily over her. She gave it a kiss and pushed it away. She lay on her side, her eyes bright in the darkness, her mind dancing like a firefly. Eventually her eyelids closed. When she awoke at 6.30 a.m., Adam had already left. You could tell he was a doctor by his quiet movements. He was incapable of jerking open drawers or dropping shoes. He even managed to turn the shower into restful background music. Alex felt a little sad. She could still smell him on the sheets, the most acute reminder of his presence. She should have told him; he would have been interested and supportive. On the other hand this was something only she could do. She felt she concentrated better if she did not discuss it. Also, Adam would innocently ask about Patti, of course he would, and that would make her cross and defensive.

Alex and Adam agreed that Patti was fundamentally a bad thing. Adam had been shocked to hear about Kenneth's sorrow although he disagreed with Alex about the solution, being more accustomed to the hard mystery of human relations. He had told her that the most complicated section of the hospital forms to fill in was next of kin. One could never assume. Family breakdown was endemic and emotive, often manifesting itself in the illness which required hospital treatment. 'It is impossible to resolve from the outside,' he had told Alex. 'You can't start meddling in people's souls.' Adam's tolerance and sympathy was an uncomfortable wisdom. He would cast Patti in a new light and Alex would not be able to look him in the eye. There was only any point in telling him about the pilot show when she had something concrete to confess. Why be hanged for a hunch? She performed a few edited Pilates exercises then showered, towelling her short hair dry. She flicked through her work clothes on the rail. The slithering silk suits now gave her the creeps. Instead she slipped a plain red cotton dress over her head, with suede beige pumps. A car was waiting for her. Who would have thought it, she giggled to herself as she jumped into the back. She arrived in Soho at the same time as Sebastian and the crew. There was immediately a search for coffee and croissants and no one settled much before 9.30 a.m. Two well-known figures wandered in, one a sportsman, the other a television actress. The chance of talking about themselves, even for a dummy show, was irresistible. Alex felt herself become more austere as she took the chair. One eyebrow was raised and her lips became ironic. Sebastian clambered up to her in his Bob the Builder T-shirt and leather trousers.

'Alex,' he said, gravely. 'Do me a favour. Drop the Patti act. I want you to be yourself.' Alex nodded anxiously. Herself wasn't a professional persona. It certainly wasn't charismatic. The best that could be said was that she was friendly. Right. Do friendly. She flashed a grin at the camera. She wriggled into a more comfortable slouch on the chair. Her voice became less stagy, more colloquial.

'Hello and welcome to *The Hour*. My name is Alex Khan and I will be trying to look at the news with a little more depth than we usually have time for. But first, our top stories . . .'

Sally had slipped into the studio, delayed by the tube and carrying a rain-sodden supply of croissants. She put the collapsing paper bag in the corner with her umbrella, quietly unbuttoned her raincoat and went to stand next to the fidgety Sebastian.

'How is she doing?' she whispered, peering at a television monitor to the side of her. Sebastian gave a thumbs-up sign.

'She's a natural,' he whispered back. 'Intelligent, but

kind of sweet. See the way she cocks her head to one side, like she really wants to know the answers. Nothing grande dame about her.' Sally nodded.

'Don't you think she makes Patti look rather RSC?' added Sebastian.

Sally glanced sideways at his merry features. The star system was a brutal one but there was no doubt that Patti was extremely well known and popular with viewers. Gordon had grunted the other evening that he did not understand the fanfare about Alex when Patti seemed jolly good at what she did. Wasn't there supposed to be a fashion for the Catherine Deneuve types? Patti's fame irritated the very executives who benefited from her appeal. Sebastian had never grasped the point of Patti and now seemed determined to be rid of her. Sally was wholly realistic about Patti, but she felt awkward about Sebastian's gloating high spirits. Whatever Patti's faults – and God knows they were legion – she had given her best at work. Sally wondered if a man would be so capriciously dumped. Well, well, this was the way of the world.

Thank goodness her family life obeyed different rules. She thought of Tom and Sophie who were being taken to Thorpe Park today with their cousins. She hoped the weather would be better for them.

'Sally?' said Sebastian, waving a hand in front of her. 'You can come out of hypnosis now.' Sally gave an embarrassed laugh.

'I was just thinking of tonight's programme. I better whiz over to the NTC. You have all done jolly well.' Picking up Gordon's golfing umbrella, but forgetting her raincoat, she hurried out into the rain.

'Cut,' said Sebastian.

Alex turned her oak-coloured eyes towards him and grinned at the reaction. Then she screwed up her face into witch-like distortion and said, 'Or should I do it like this?'

It was the weak humour of relief. Her legs were still trembling. She thanked the crew and guests and ate several soggy croissants. As everyone picked up their belongings and went out into the strong, clean, post-rain sunlight she felt a rush of excitement. One could not exactly class it as happiness. It was too adrenalin-driven and one-dimensional for that. It was the muscular pleasure of self-confidence. She tried Adam's mobile but it was switched off. But she felt guilty at keeping this from him, so phoned the answer machine at home and left a message.

'Hi, Biscuit, it's me. Guess what, I've just done a pilot for *The Hour* and it went really, really well. I can't wait to tell you all about it. I hope your day went well too.' She tried to remember the name of the old woman with Alzheimer's that Adam had told her about yesterday. 'I hope that old lady is, er, OK. Love you, see you later.'

Alex regretted the crassness of the remark, which recorded would sound worse. She did not want her career to become a self-obsession. She absolutely wasn't going to be changed by any of this. But her career was the cuckoo in the nest, pushing out those who had rightful demands on her. Lack of time was becoming an excuse for selfishness. Maybe it was the same thing; lack of time was the greatest corrupter. She stopped at the newspaper booth and bought a couple of postcards and stamps. Then she sat down on the park bench in the little square, next to some seraphically stoned down and outs.

On the first card she wrote:

Dear Mum, I know that you are familiar with London buses but it was that or a picture of Princess Diana and you still have mixed feelings about her. I'm working on a new show which will be beyond cool if it pans out. I hope you are looking after yourself and Dad. I'll try to come down at the weekend, don't bother to cook, though, I want to take you out to that fancy new restaurant you told me about. All love, Alex.

On the second postcard she wrote:

Dear Mr Ward, it was a great pleasure to meet you the other week. I don't know when the news item is going out, I think they have cut it back for space reasons. Patti was pleased, crossed out, *Patti thinks about you, I know. I hope we meet again, very best wishes, Alexandra Khan.*

She looked at her watch. She still had hours to kill; it would be too weird going into the NTC and anyway she was officially off. She phoned Mark's mobile.

'Yup, Mark speaking.'

'Oh, hi, it's Alex. I'm in Soho, I wondered if you fancied meeting for coffee?'

'Oh hi, let me see, I'm in Piccadilly kitting my baby brother out in some horrible, but nevertheless expensive, surfing gear. Why don't we meet you at the Groucho Club in half an hour or so?'

Alex saw the resemblance immediately. They were of similar height and build, the brother more muscular and with a youthfully vacant expression. He was carrying a case too large to be for a guitar, and several bags. She gestured them to her table.

'Where shall I put the surfboard?' asked Tristan, before turning to Alex and introducing himself.

'So you like surfing?' asked Alex encouragingly.

'Yeah, I do,' nodded Tristan and looked around him. Alex and Mark exchanged smiles.

'Oh, yeah, Mark, you are coming to Newquay, aren't you, cos Patti is?'

'Is she?' said Mark. Tristan looked sullen.

'I told you, honestly you are such a dickhead.'

'Tristan,' said Mark sharply. 'Dickheads don't spend two hundred quid on surfing gear. Or rather they do, but it means you have to be nice to them.'

'I didn't know Patti was a surfing fan,' smiled Alex.

'She just wants to see my muscles,' said Tristan slyly, taking a large swig of Coke.

'In your dreams,' said Mark. 'Now drink up, I've got to get to the Ministry of Agriculture.'

'I need a slash,' said Tristan scraping back his chair and sloping off in the wrong direction, then giving an embarrassed glance back as he found the right door.

'He's nice,' said Alex, although truth to tell she was close enough in age to Tristan to lack indulgence towards teenage charmlessness. 'What's the deal, does he live with you?'

'Our mother is a bit of a bolter,' said Mark, his eyes creasing. 'She left Tristan's dad last year for a game-show host in Tel Aviv. My stepfather, Tristan's dad, made a counter move with a Palestinian air hostess. They are both too entranced by the plots of their own lives to bother much with Tristan. He wrote to me last autumn to ask if I would come to parents evening. He gave me coaching about the right things to say: "I am worried that Tristan is

179

not achieving his potential in chemistry." It made me so sad. He can be a total pain in the butt of course, but what can I do? I can't be another adult who betrays him.'

'It sounds as if Patti is a big hit with him,' said Alex. 'An ideal stepmother figure.'

'She's been amazing,' said Mark wonderingly. 'She went to his prize-giving and everything. I am really so grateful to her.'

'To who?' said Tristan re-appearing.

'I was just saying how nice of Patti it was to go all the way to your prize-giving,' said Mark, putting some money under his plate and getting up.

'She wanted to,' said Tristan angrily. 'She didn't have to.'

Alex shook hands with Tristan and kissed Mark on both cheeks and then left. She turned on her mobile. Three new messages and a text from Adam. Patti coming to dinner tonight. Your invite. Are you mad? What is this about the show? Alex cursed the phone. That was ages ago. Long before Kenneth had cropped up. Maybe Patti wanted a reconciliation. But, Alex sighed crossly, she was too busy now. Well busy was a relative term. She had just wanted time with Adam. Now she couldn't talk to him about it until he was so tired he would be past caring. And it would sound stupidly self-important all stored up like that. Plus, she would have to lie about where she had been. Oh yeah, I've been recording your show and having coffee with your boyfriend, Patti. Didn't her dad once say that you should never do anything that you would mind people knowing about? But what if it didn't lead to anything? It was up to her, right? She had self-determination. She could stop everything right here.

Alex felt a stab of self-pity as if she had already

renounced her future success. It was a shame that she had worked so hard at school, exhilarated by the promise of reward. Then there was the question of redesigning the flat and the ambitious holiday with which she planned to surprise Adam (the plan was just a few seconds old, but it immediately acquired an irresistible clarity). Come to think of it, she had also intended to bestow small life-enhancing gifts on her parents – membership of the National Trust and of the Royal Academy. Perhaps a weekend in Paris. What exactly would it achieve to erect a false ceiling? Wasn't it unworthy of her to take the timid course of action? When her feminist headmistress had painted the motto 'Aim high' above the assembly hall stage, she had not added 'with due consideration to older colleagues and without becoming single-minded'. Only the cuckoo fulfilled its potential. Alex called up Sally's mobile number and regretted it as soon as she heard the even, commonsensical tones.

'Alex, I'm going down the tube escalator, I'll turn round, hang on.' Alex felt melancholy at the thought of Sally trooping back the wrong way, probably attracting contemptuous stares from other passengers.

'Don't worry, Sally, listen it's not important. OK, yes, I'll hang on.'

'There we are,' said Sally. 'I'm going up to the pavement. Go ahead.' Alex cleared her throat.

'I was just thinking about that pilot, you know, the fact that it had to be so surreptitious. Maybe it isn't right for me. You've all been so nice to me, but maybe it isn't right. I mean I'm really grateful, I really loved doing it, it felt totally natural. It was fantastic to have that opportunity.'

'So what is the problem?' asked Sally briskly. Alex felt that she could not mention Patti's name. She was a friend of Sally's, right? Maybe Sally wasn't too comfortable with this. It could sway the argument the wrong way. She didn't want a debate, she wanted reassurance.

'I just wanted to say that I hoped you weren't doing this out of kindness, you know. I don't want Sebastian to feel he can't hurt my feelings if it was shit.'

'I wouldn't patronize Sebastian,' said Sally coolly, the roar of traffic behind her. 'There is no such thing as professional kindness. It is an oxymoron.' Alex tore at her little fingernail.

'Sorry, Sally, I feel like a total prat. I just suddenly panicked.'

Sally softened. 'I haven't seen the tape, but from watching you briefly, I thought you were great, Alex. Now, I do have to get to work.'

'Of course you do, Sally,' said Alex humbly. 'Sorry, one pilot and I start behaving like Anthea Turner. Yuk. I'll see you tomorrow, yeah?' She switched off her phone. The least she could do is to cook a decent Last Supper. She bought recipe books by Nigella Lawson, Jamie Oliver and the River Cafe on her way home and chose a medley of dishes from each, repeatedly losing the flour-stained page and flicking through the whole book with one hand while stirring with the other. The ghost of techniques returned to her as she remembered how her mother had broken eggs and thickened sauces. Alex was enjoying herself. This was largely because it was play-acting, but who says your heart and soul has to go into cooking? The dishes tended to bunch towards the end of the afternoon and the casserole seemed to require around five stages by which time both she and it were worn out. Also, she quickly ran short of bowls and plates. But the chocolate puddings, adorned with a mint leaf looked pretty in the fridge and the summer soup looked astonishingly like the picture.

It was humid and thundery outside and Alex hesitated over the need to water the plants. She did so, despite the drops of rain, because she loved this simple sense of nurturing. Then she showered, towel-dried her hair and read the newspapers on the bed dressed in a tracksuit and holding a bottle of beer. This was a period of contentment, although, like any good hostess, she could not help craning her neck to check the clock every few minutes and jumping up to finish forgotten chores in the kitchen. And in final readiness, changed into baggy trousers and a brightly coloured, patch-work silk top, Lahore chic. Then she waited a further hour, trying not to stir the simmering casserole in case it crumbled beneath the spoon, and running to the front of the flat to look crossly out of the living-room window.

Patti arrived before Adam. Alex recognized her light stride up the steps and slightly ironic pressure on the bell. Patti was wearing her trademark grey trouser suit, her hair tied back in a black bow. She held Alex at arms' length, close enough to convey her insinuating fragrance.

'Hi, sweetie, I hope you don't mind me arriving like this. Adam was so sweet to me on the phone that it almost felt like family. Hmm what a lovely domestic smell.' Patti made it sound as if she could have been referring to the lavatories as much as the kitchen. Alex smiled reluctantly as Patti handed her a magnum of champagne.

'It's nothing,' shrugged Patti. 'Sir David left it for me in the studios. I shall be bathing in it by the time the Queen Mother actually dies. Now do show me round.' Alex surrendered helplessly to the older woman's social experience and even started to enjoy herself as they chatted in the kitchen. Patti perched on the stool with a glass of wine, exclaiming over details of Alex's kitchen colour scheme and ruminating on the therapeutic effects of gardening. As Alex became loquacious under Patti's light grey gaze she twice stopped herself from revealing the morning's events. The door banged and Adam's shoes clunked over the wooden floor. Patti tilted her face.

'George Clooney back from the office.' She directed her gaze back towards Alex, to whom Adam gave a surreptitious wink.

'Who needs a drink?' he asked, and poured himself a large one. There was a bubble of tension in the air that he was eager to dispel. After a couple of large glasses and delightful witticisms from Patti he felt the atmosphere lift. Alex scraped a spoon round the casserole dish. How quickly the glow of domesticity could turn to resentment. Here she was, young, pretty and capable. She had mastered the art of the casserole while stealing away the older woman's job. And the price of this chutzpah was invisibility. Unfortunately, she could not draw attention to the irony just now. Instead she regained attention only thanks to Patti's patronizing tact.

'Thank you, Adam,' murmured Patti humbly. 'Hasn't Alex done brilliantly?' Adam gave Alex a dazed glance.

'I am afraid it is nothing grand. We get by on hospital food here really don't we, Alex?' Alex was content to make jokes herself about clay feet in the kitchen but could have slapped Adam for his lumberingly humorous insult. Usually he was pathetically grateful for the eleven-minute pasta slapped down in front of him. Why did he have to pick the rare occasion when she had adopted a new role; a womanly modesty which contrasted pleasingly with her sheer bloody high poweredness. She would remember this for another time.

'Let's eat!' she said in an off-pitch, sing-song voice. Adam and Patti crouched round the kitchen table. Patti asked Adam what he thought about patients seeking treatment abroad. She begged his opinion on the working hours of junior doctors. She wondered who he considered the best candidate to run the National Theatre. And, once Alex had retired to bed, defeated by exhaustion and exclusion, she told Adam about her visit to his mother. His drunken expansiveness subsided as he watched Patti intensely.

'Oh dear, I wanted Alex to hear this,' said Patti looking up at the ceiling in studied conflict. There was a responding belch of plumbing noises and then silence.

'Shall I get her?' asked Adam rising unsteadily to his feet.

'Poor girl is so tired,' said Patti hurriedly. 'With all her cooking and so on. Make sure you tell her first thing in the morning.'

'Tell her what?' asked Adam, grabbing Patti's wrist. She looked at his hand, at the black hairs springing from their rough pores. She stroked it, not altogether maternally.

'I felt that I had to go and see your mother. It was so important. She is . . . brave, isn't she?' Sentimental tears lined Adam's eyes. 'Your mother wants what is best for you, and I only had to convince her that this means being true to yourself. You have your father's gifts and I dare say some of your mother's character. But we are not merely products of our genes. What makes you unique is your talent as an actor.'

'Did you tell my mother this? Oh my God, did you tell her?'

Patti puckered the pencil line of her mouth. 'Sssh, darling. I told your mother. It was hard for her to accept but I just kept talking, must have been for an hour. And finally she said, "Patti, I have never thought about this but now you have explained it all to me, I accept it. I will accept Adam's decision."' Naturally, Adam began to cry at this point, hoarse, youthful, tired and drunken sobs. And it fell to Patti to comfort him as she knew best. Alex's candles flickered into a messy pool of wax as the couple moved onto the sofa, Patti's velvet bow falling to the floor.

Upstairs, Alex had fallen into a dry, fitful sleep. Lamplight shone sharply through the window onto her flickering eyelids but it was the thunderous rain that woke her. She looked wide eyed at the clock – it was one in the morning. Alex stretched her arm across the empty bed. Adam must have fallen asleep downstairs. She gulped down the glass of stale water by her bedside and swung herself onto the floor. Illuminated and naked she pattered to the bedroom door but stopped. There were voices in the kitchen. Patti must still be here. She hesitated, shivering. She would have to get dressed. And what was her reason for returning? It would be humiliating to appear, white faced and wheedling because her boyfriend had not responded to her sulky withdrawal. But she hated those lowered voices. What was happening in there? She was being absurdly fanciful. This was a distinguished, older colleague. Adam was already making a fool of himself. Alex would certainly not make a fool of herself. Now there was silence. Oh God, it tore through Alex's stomach. Please, dear God, don't let them be, not in her home. The voices started up again. Alex retreated, listening through the crack to Patti gathering up her things, to the kiss at the door, ten beats too long, to the door shut and the sound of a car engine.

Alex lay frozen in bed as Adam clumsily threw down his shoes, pulled off his clothes and pulled the sheets around him in a determinedly isolationist manner. The language of the bed is unchallengeable. Alex turned to her side, a warm tear sneaking down her cheek and onto the pillow. The silence between them had hardened by the morning. Alex had assumed the pinched righteousness of the wronged while Adam acquired the angry self-pity of the perpetrator. The fact was that both were in deep shock. The events of last night had taken on a nightmarish quality; each sought reassurance but were unable to offer it. They lay side by side, blinking. Alex laid her arm close enough to Adam to angrily withdraw if he touched it. Adam was too acutely spatially aware to do any such thing. Finally Alex said tensely:

'Do you want to use the bathroom?'

'You go,' said Adam. Alex got out of bed and, for the first time coy about her nakedness, pulled a T-shirt from her drawer and held it against her as she stalked towards the bathroom door. Having reached it, she turned and walked back. She felt deadly cold.

'By the way, what time did Patti leave?' Adam shuddered and looked as if he might cry. Alex wanted very much to touch him but it was the last thing in the world she could do.

'It was late,' said Adam reaching up to grab at Alex's thigh. It was the gesture she was waiting for.

'Don't you dare,' she said shrilly. 'You treat me like your bloody housekeeper and then you, then you, what, Adam?'

He crouched back on the bed, so that she could see the line of his muscular arms, the tiny creases of his stomach and the line of black hair reaching his genitals. She was panic stricken with hatred and desire. Adam blinked hard and spoke slowly.

'Look, Patti squared it with Mum. I didn't want her to but she went anyway and somehow she persuaded her and everything has changed. I can give up medicine.' He opened his bleary red eyes wide. Carefully holding up her T-shirt Alex sat on the end of the bed.

'My God, if you could hear yourself.' She lispingly mimicked him. 'Patti asked Mummy if it would be OK for me to be an actor. Now Mummy says I can, whoopee.' Adam glared at her but Alex continued, in a hysterical rage.

'Couldn't you have decided for yourself? I can't believe that you would be so fucking wet. So Patti says it is OK and now you are Jude Law all of a sudden. Just another crappy actor giving huffy little interviews about whether or not you will move to LA. Is that all that you aspire to? Because if it is, you don't want to be with me.' Adam stared ahead of him and said nothing.

'We are definitely finished,' said Alex, her voice breaking. 'And by the way it is a great moment for change because I am going to be doing my own show. About world events. So I really don't want you turning up to the studio in leg warmers and a fucking bandanna. Arsehole.' She waited a moment, then flounced off to the bathroom. Both were anxious to be dressed and away from each other. Alex heard the front door close before she could make her exit.

Her heart was gyrating angrily. Her blood pressure rose when she confronted the uncleared remains of dinner.

Plates half-heartedly piled, candle wax all over the table, rows of empty wine glasses. She began washing and wiping in methodical fury. She scoured the blackened casserole dish and cleaned out the oven, covering the cuffs of her white cotton shirt in grime. The hidden kitchen clock clicked along with her scrubbing. She could not bear it when she had finished. She even refused to listen to the radio, wanting nothing to distract from her victimhood. When there was no more she could do, she dragged a broom from piles of boxes, yanking at it with a breathless whimper. She was sweating with dirt as she pushed it behind the sofa. She pulled out a bundle of dust, some sweet wrappers and a black satin ribbon. Alex's face crumpled. The pain spread through her like sciatica and she curled up helplessly in response. As usual when people confront uncomfortable truths, Alex fastened on the particular expression of treachery, as if one form of infidelity was any more palatable than another. How could Adam have betrayed her on such an important day for her? In the place they had decided to make their home? After she had spent so much time on the casserole? As tears wound their way down her face she remembered a childhood phrase she had used when her brothers had been rough with her or she had been tripped up maliciously in the playground. 'I am not crying because of the pain,' she had shouted. 'I am crying because I am angry.' Where had that come from? Her father must have taught it to her. She desperately wanted to phone her parents, she wanted to return to the small familiarity of her bedroom with its assembled furniture and hoovered carpet. She wanted the view from her bedroom of the quiet suburban street. She wanted to go back to life's warm shallows. But

Sarah Sands

pride forbade her. And loyalty. She did not want others to judge Adam badly.

Her aimless misery was interrupted by the key in the door followed by careful, remorseful footsteps. Alex hugged herself, winding the satin ribbon round her hand until her flesh turned white. Adam stopped in front of her, his face taut, his eyes wide.

'I got you a coffee,' he said putting the paper cup next to her on the floor. Then he sank down next to her, holding her close enough for her to feel his rapid heartbeat. 'You'll stop your circulation,' he whispered, removing the ribbon from her hands like cats cradle.

'What are you, a doctor?' sniffed Alex, wiping her nose with her arm.

'Yes I am actually,' said Adam, stroking her hair, her neck. 'I lost my senses, darling. Of course I want to be a doctor and I want to be with you. I love you so much.' His lips were pale with shock as he kissed her forehead. Alex nodded and pushed her face into his neck.

'I'm only crying because I am angry,' she said with a muffled sob. Adam pressed her closer. 'I'm crying because I love you,' he said.

So they entered a hurt and tender phase of their relationship. Over the next few weeks they telephoned each other constantly when apart, afraid of the damage of an hour's separation. When Alex was away from Adam the nausea of betrayal shook her frame. She wanted to kick and scratch him, to smash things, to howl.

'I hate you for what you have done,' she sobbed into her cellphone, ignoring the interested glances of passers-by. 'How can I forgive you?' Adam gave no defence, just a soothing repeated murmur.

'I am so sorry, I love you so much, I am so sorry.' Alex felt more loving and less safe. After a while she wondered if her emotional rawness was hormonal. She wasn't crying because of the pain but because she was pregnant.

Chapter 10

It was the fag end of summer. The roads to the South West were no longer paralysed by caravans, although Patti still swore at the cars carrying bicycles, like headdresses, on their roofs, slowing her down to as little as 70 miles per hour. She treated her trip to watch Tristan's surfing competition like any other professional appointment. Mark was playful and chatty in between warning Patti about 30 mph signs or police cars on the bridges.

'Why do you need to go so fast anyway?' he asked mildly. 'Why is it that everyone is happy to drive at a normal speed in America but here we are so competitive on the roads?' Patti adjusted her sunglasses.

'Maybe because we have less space so we know that distance is obtainable. Maybe we just like driving fast.' Television was the modern diplomatic status. Policemen were merely viewers, although the sodding speed cameras could not be charmed so easily.

They reached the stretch of Cornish beach at midday. (Four hours door to door; Patti may have been on the wrong side of road safety campaigners but motorists would salute her.) The headquarters of the international competition was a hut at the top of the rocky path down to the beach and the organizers were searching on their hands and knees for the key to it. Meanwhile, the competitors were bobbing up and down behind patterned vans; fiddling with wetsuit zips, checking surf boards, comparing packaging to make sure they had the unofficially recognized brands of clothing, watches and marketing accessories from the correct, overwhelmingly urban branches. Patti identified Tristan among the surfeit of muscular, fair-haired teenage boys and drove her car playfully at him. Delighted, he jumped up on to the bonnet and peered through the window with a broad, boulder teeth grin. Mark was slightly irritated when his brother proceeded to slap Patti on the bottom as she got out of the car. 'Have some bloody respect,' he muttered crossly. 'What do they teach you in school?'

Patti was dressed casually, which did not of course mean thoughtlessly. She had wandered into a selection of snow/rock/surfing shops so conveniently on her route to work and found some of them were flatteringly cut in surprisingly Armani colours. She also had a Salome-style attraction to layers. As the day wore on she wriggled out of her ski pants to show a swimming costume accessorized with a fleece and Puffa jacket. The only article she never removed was her sunglasses. This sportingly incoherent look, she mentally dubbed Cornish chic. The practical purpose of it was to cope with the strangely combined heat and chill of English weather, depending on the sun's capricious appearances. A side effect was to show off her long, straight thighs mercifully free from cellulite in case any passing amateur photographer chose to pass on the film to a news desk. Mark naively marvelled at his girlfriend's effortless outdoor style, while splashing his chinos at the water's edge. It is a magazine cliché that men require mistresses in the bedroom and mothers in the kitchen. This is too narrow. They also yearn for sisters in proper walking shoes to horse around with and Girl Guides to produce camp fires. Patti's beach barbecue was shop-prepared but the effect was natural and windswept. As man and boy tore at their charcoal sausages and grilled fish they competed for Patti's favour. While Mark trudged along the beach to find a bin, Tristan helped Patti pack up the car. The sun fleetingly emerged from behind a cloud and Patti opportunistically whipped off her top. Tristan gave a convoluted groan 'Ohmygod-Pattiyouareso . . .' and lunged at her. She leaned back against the car and allowed him to kiss her. She was not attracted to him in the least but the sun warmed up the alcohol levels and made her generally sexually benign. The curious thing about sex was how it fed upon itself. Kissing Adam had made her think of Mark and that in turn made her receptive to Tristan. If she had to justify herself, (and why on earth would she?) Patti would say that she simply sought sex without consequence but this would not be true. The risk – the game – was all in the consequence; it was what made men distinctive. Tristan lurched and fumbled then leaped back again as Mark approached.

It was not quite *Jules et Jim* as they sped back to London. Mark was engrossed in a local newspaper he had picked up on the beach, while Tristan sulked at having to sit in the back despite being taller and heavier than his half-brother. His angry jabs at the back of Mark's seat further pricked any residual romance in the air. Patti added to the climate of belligerence by tuning into a pirate garage station in order to prevent Mark reading. Mark finally threatened to get out and walk, while Tristan made delighted thumbs-up signs to Patti's rear view mirror. She was relieved to drop them both off. The day's changes of temperature and diet of meat and alcohol made her head ache. She wanted the cool, white sanctuary of her bedroom. She walked lightly up her front steps, ignoring her waving neighbour Veronica. She pushed her key into the lock, but it jammed there. She tried again, manipulating it more gently. The lock finally yielded. From the scratches and dents around it, there had been an earlier failed attempt. Patti turned round to see Veronica hanging over the railings.

'Is everything all right?' she called out in an anxious tinny voice. 'Someone was trying to get in earlier, but his key didn't work. I didn't know if it was one your builders?' Patti looked at her coolly. 'Or a courier or something? Anyway his key didn't work and he went away. Should I have said something?'

Patti shook her head. 'He is a . . . picture restorer. Retired.'

Veronica looked puzzled. 'He didn't look . . .'

But Patti had closed the front door firmly behind her. Once out of view, she took several short violent breaths.

'Oh stop,' she whispered to herself, her face puckering with fear. 'Come on, Patti, pull yourself together. It's OK. It's OK.'

Sally sniffed the air as she took the dustbin bags outside. She loved the first scent of autumn and all it implied. Others may feel a cycle of decay, but to her it meant the beginning of the school year. Plastic bags full of named school socks, a sense of purpose. Of course there were also the autumn schedules but they paled beside the school calendar. This was the true order; homework, restored bedtimes and a new choice of musical instrument. The last family meal of the holidays was a particular treat as she turned to each child and said her set piece about effort preceding reward and the importance of establishing a relationship with new teachers. Dark evenings were biased in favour of families. They meant homework and board games. It was not a good time to be working flat out on a new programme but when would it ever be? Each stage of child development had its unique and pressing demands. She doled out her partially successful home-made Indian and wallowed in the banal chatter around her.

'So who do you think your new teacher will be, Tom?'

'Dunno. I bet she'll have a moustache.'

'Why do you think that, Tom?'

'Because you never get fit women teachers. If women are fit they go on TV.'

'Mum, that is so sexist, why don't you tell Tom off?' squeaked Sophie. Sally turned patiently to her son.

'That is a silly attitude, Tom. It is the kind of attitude that is producing a shortage of teachers. Teachers deserve respect.'

'I would respect them if they were fit,' said Tom. Sally looked grave and patient, ready to embark on a rehearsed speech about shallow MTV values which had corrupted all human relationships. But by now her children were fighting over the poppadoms and the lyrics to rap songs.

'You are so sad, Soph, you don't even know the real words,' yelled Tom.

'I do, I do, you loon,' shouted Sophie. 'Listen this is it.'

'No, it's not,' cried Tom, leaping up from the table.

'It's meant to be about drugs, since when was there a drug called Lorraine?'

'Sit down!' cried Sally. 'Really I can't believe I am hearing this. The sooner we ban television in this house the better as far as I am concerned. Don't you agree, Gordon?'

'Well it's your fault,' chorused Tom and Sophie. 'You do TV.'

'Not that kind of TV,' said Sally grandly. 'I do television that teaches you . . . about the world.'

'So does MTV,' said Tom. 'That tells you about drugs. That is more about the world than boring politicians.'

Sally turned to Gordon who was wandering out of the kitchen with his plate to watch the golf on the sports channel. Sally had fondly imagined family life centred round a piano rather than the television. But Tom had ditched the piano for the drums, which were unbearable, and Sophie now point-blank refused to read out loud in front of her sniggering brother. Somehow, television was the common ground in the household however much Sally resisted it. You could not enforce rules if you were not always there. Maybe the next generation was a lost cause anyway. Family life did not stand up to public display. But she was content to manage its decline, speaking up for a folk memory while secretly glad that her children were 'normal'. For all the haste of family meal times and the unenlightened conversation around her, the walls were strong and the hearts were good. She always felt a little skip inside when she heard her husband or children refer to a collective experience or use the loving phrase to outsiders 'our family'. As she wiped a J-cloth over its familiar orbital route around the sink she noticed the phone hanging off the hook opposite her.

'Why can't you kids replace the receiver?' she called out as she moved towards it.

'Oh yeah, sorry, Mum, it was for you,' said Sophie. Sure enough a plaintive sing-song voice was coming from the receiver.

'Hellooo? Could someone answer? Helloo?' Sally snatched at it.

'Oh, Sebastian, I do apologize. Our bloody family is a nightmare.' Sebastian did not contradict her.

'I've been editing through *The Hour*. God, Alex is so much the business, Sal. No offence to Patti, but she is like a silent bloody movie star compared to this. Alex is like, like a speckled hen's egg. Fresh enough to eat.' Sally groaned.

'That is a terrible simile, Sebastian. Truly terrible.' Sebastian chuckled.

'I want you to come and have a look tomorrow morning. I want to get everything signed and sealed now the top brass are back from the South of France, or the Hamptons or wherever they all go. Can you make it for nine?' Sally grimaced at Gordon who was watching her suspiciously from his armchair.

'Yes, sure,' she said lightly. 'We were meant to have lunch with my in-laws, but Gordon will manage without me.' She turned her back to avoid Gordon's downcast face. 'I guess you want me to tell Patti?'

'I don't do bad news, never could,' said Sebastian. 'That is definitely a job for matron.'

When Sally was anxious she went into domestic overdrive. She changed the sheets on the children's beds despite the late hour and violently tackled a pile of ironing. The two videos carefully chosen for family consumption went unwatched as the children gave up waiting and played computer games in the bedrooms instead. The following morning Sally embarked on a disorienting weekday regime, leaving the family watching television in their pyjamas and the breakfast things unwashed as she, blinkered, left the house in a smart suit and jumped into the ordered car carrying an armful of papers. The roads were empty and she arrived early enough at the NTC to re-trace her route as far as the coffee house. She brought Sebastian a tall latte and a muffin. He had bought her a cappuccino and a croissant.

'Don't you love office marriages?' he said camply as they settled in front of the screen. Alex did indeed look gap-year fresh and chaired the discussion with sweetness and authority, the more so once her hesitations and mispronunciations had been edited. Sebastian had artfully kept in one fluffed line in order to display Alex's youthful giggle, suppressed by her hand clamped to her mouth.

'I think she's great,' said Sally. 'But you know people will miss Patti. Remember we have an ageing population. There is some value in glamorous older women who know what they are doing.'

'I've thought about that,' said Sebastian, munching on his muffin. 'What do older people talk about? Their children, or even their grandchildren. They are endlessly proud and curious about their children, aren't they? They want to see them doing well. Apart from anything else, it is in their interest. It is their children who are going to decide whether or not they get turfed out into old people's homes. Now, does Alex look like someone who would put her old mum and dad into a nursing home? No, Sally, she does not. Her message is that the world may be a rough old place, but she will take care of everything. She is a good girl. I feel quite choked just thinking about it.'

'Oh shut up, Sebastian,' smiled Sally. 'Apart from her appeal to the grey pound, how do you think she will make out as a journalist? It is a long time on air. Any cracks are going to show.'

'It ain't rocket science, Sal. Alex is very bright but you know all she has to do is ask some questions. And read the papers. Where's the problem?'

Sally looked at her watch. She had told Gordon that she would be back in a couple of hours but it was already midday. He would probably have already left. It would only complicate matters if she telephoned now. Guiltily and with pleasure she planned an afternoon alone. She could have a really good clear up at home. Or she could take up Sebastian's offer to go shopping. Well, Sally, what the hell?

Patti had already returned from the shops by midday and was laying out her purchases on her bed. The two suits, unfolded from their tissue paper were draped over the white bed cover. It was only the Jimmy Choo boots that she wanted to try on. She clicked contentedly up and down the polished floor. More lovely armour. The front doorbell rang. Patti stood still. Who now? She had told Mark that she was out for the day. Tristan had mumbled something about going to a football match. She had no friends and was not expecting any deliveries. The bell rang again. If it was one of those poor Northern people with badges selling dishcloths she would slam the door in their face. In fact she wouldn't answer. The bell rang once more. Carefully, she sidled to the edge of the window and peered out. A tall woman had moved back from the door and was staring up at her. It was Jenny. What on earth did she want? Patti gingerly raised her arm in response. She would have to answer. She flung on a dressing gown and opened the door as if she were an elderly person and it were the middle of the night.

'Jenny!' she said through the crack. Jenny was clutching a holdall. Was that make-up or something more permanent?

'Patti, I'm so sorry,' said Jenny, unprofessionally bare-faced and shaking. 'I've had this terrible row with Tim, I . . . can I come in?'

'Of course,' said Patti, her anger tinged with curiosity. She ushered her into the drawing room, declining to open the curtains or introduce homely touches such as coffee. Jenny plonked herself on a chair and started to sob convulsively. Patti admired her boots sticking out from beneath her nightwear.

'I just didn't know, know, know where to go,' hiccoughed Jenny. 'Tim was so, so hor, hor, horrible. He said I was like a pair of old slippers he wanted to throw out.' Patti silently agreed that this was an appropriate choice of footwear to describe Jenny.

'And, and, I thought, Patti has always been so kind to me. You warned me about Tim. I should have listened to you. It is just he was my last chance, Patti.' Jenny raised her patchy red face and Patti instantly assumed a concerned expression. 'I wondered if I could stay here, until he . . . until we decide what to do.' Patti's features became regretful.

'Oh I wish that you could, Jenny. But unfortunately I

have my niece and nephew arriving this evening to stay with me for the week. I just haven't any other room.'

'Oh, I didn't know that you had nephews and nieces. Aren't they back at school this week?' asked Jenny with wretched cunning.

'They have learning difficulties,' said Patti, unsatisfactorily but confidently. Jenny sniffed sympathetically. 'But listen you must definitely stay here this afternoon. I want you to treat this place like your own. Only Jenny, you can't run away from problems. You need to confront them. I suggest that you wash your face and . . . get your hair cut. I can find someone to do it. Stay here and get a makeover. That'll be such fun.' Jenny blinked at her with her shrunken, red eyes.

'Thanks so much. Sorry to be any trouble.'

'No trouble at all,' said Patti rubbing her hands. 'I am going to dress you as me. You can lead my life for a day. Lots of face cream, lots of sex, though I am afraid you may get murdered by my stalker . . .'

'Are you joking?' asked Jenny stolidly.

'About the sex? No,' quipped Patti, already summoning her retinue of personal groomers on her mobile phone.

This was as close as Patti got to charity. It amused her to see Jenny obediently squeezing herself into last season's clothes. 'You are about my size,' Patti would say encouragingly, which was as true as saying a hippo is roughly the same size as a cheetah. Patti's hairstylist arrived, politely tickled by the conspiracy. As he chopped and highlighted Jenny's naturally coarse ginger hair he further emphasized the physical distinction between the women. Patti was by now losing interest in the project and cancelled her manicurist and eyebrow expert.

'Do you know,' she said to the excited half-finished creature before her, 'I preferred you before. Now why don't you go and tell Tim that you have been having an affair with a sex god. That'll shake him up. I have to go and fetch the children from the station.' Jenny jumped up pulling bits of silver foil from her hair.

'Of course, I'll go straight away, don't worry I can walk to the tube from here. I can't thank you enough. Sorry for spoiling your day.'

'Jenny,' said Patti sternly, 'you are a very special person. For many reasons. Now please hold your head high, in the prescribed Pilates manner. And if Tim underestimates you ever again, he will have me to answer to.' The two women hugged and Jenny departed noisily. Once she had gone, Patti felt quite fond of her.

Alex had arranged to meet Emily at their favourite coffee shop, in Holland Park. Their modest, although increasingly disparate, incomes were highly disposable and they usually ate out. Alex had made a resolution to spend more time with friends and family and Emily was an easy starting point because she had her own fast, busy life as a junior feature writer on the *Guardian*, so Alex did not have to do any tactful translation. They had the off-duty dress code of their tribe, little tops, baggy trousers and short tousled hair. They were both solemn about world debt and skittish about sex and fashion. Mostly they discussed work.

'Wait, I've something to show you,' said Emily delving into her rucksack, which matched Alex's. She fished out a pile of battered, ink-stained business cards. 'See, they have got my email address and everything. Has to mean the paper will renew my contract, don't you think?' Alex grinned at her old friend.

'It's highly significant, I agree. Who do you give them out to though? I mean, presumably the people you are interviewing know who you work for. How hard is it to find you at the *Guardian*? It isn't as if you are employed by some Internet start-up. I had a pile but I couldn't see the point of them. And I notice all the top people at work don't bother. Like they don't wear watches. Sir David Leach doesn't even know how to use a mobile phone.'

'Thanks for that put down,' said Emily crossly. 'I forget you are in such swanky company now. Well, I was going to discuss today's *Daily Mail* with you but you are probably too grand. Want a cigarette?' Alex shook her head.

'I'm trying to give up. Adam goes all British Medical Association on me. What's in the *Mail*? I haven't had time to read it.'

'Yeah,' sighed Emily, 'I only glanced at it while I was waiting for you, after I had read *The Economist* from cover to cover, you know.'

'Stop it,' pleaded Alex. 'I know I deserve to be beaten up and I'm grateful but I'm not feeling too strong today.'

'Hangover?' asked Emily sympathetically. 'You do look quite washed out now you mention it. OK, our prepared text for today is page three. What does our panel think?' There was a large picture of Patti getting into an Aston Martin and beside it a blurred photograph of a large-boned woman in her early forties. The headline was: PATTI, THE GOOD SAMARITAN. Underneath, the copy read:

An unlikely friendship has blossomed between the celebrated news presenter Patti Ward and her make-up artist, Jenny Lot.

According to NTC sources, Jenny arrived on Patti's doorstep in a distressed state last weekend. She is believed to have had a row with her boyfriend, estate agent Tim Leonard, thirty-eight. The glamorous presenter, fifty-two, whose salary exceeds six figures, immediately invited Jenny to stay with her as long as she wished until she sorted out her troubles. A neighbour said: 'Patti lives alone and may have been keen on the company. I must say it is a turn up for the books to see a woman going into that house rather than a man.' In a gesture which will strike a chord with women, Patti also allegedly offered Jenny the run of her wardrobe. The presenter, whose clothes bill is said to rival that of the late Princess of Wales, perhaps saw this as a way of building the jilted woman's self-esteem. Even more remarkable, she called in her hairdresser, whose other clients include the Prime Minister's wife and several screen actresses.

Patti Ward would not comment on her act of kindness yesterday, although she did not deny it. Jenny Lot, on her way into work on Monday said, 'Patti has been very kind to me. I respect her privacy too much to say more than that.' See Features, page eleven, women helping women; Fashion, page fourteen, the secrets of the celebrity wardrobe; Raj Persaud, page fifteen, writes on the psychology of the makeover.

'So, pretty obvious who the source of the story is, wouldn't you say?' sniffed Emily, folding away the paper.

'Not Patti?' asked Alex. 'She wouldn't speak to the papers?'

'Not much,' said Emily. 'I have a friend on the *Mail* who says you can't get her off the phone. The editor is always being hauled out of conferences to take her call on a private line. I mean, who emerges with credit from this story? Jenny? Total humiliation. Patti? Good and beautiful. Though she's older than I thought, probably older than she thought. What is she actually like?' continued Emily chattily, pulling out a packet of Silk Cut. 'Vain monster, or quite nice?' She bent her head over a match. Alex leaned away from the smoke and bit the nail of her index finger. She made a face.

'Oh, you know, very impressive,' said Alex, shakily, 'total cow.' Emily hooted with laughter.

'But she's a friend of yours, right? God what do you say about me?' Alex hesitated for a moment, torn between professional distance and urgent, angry tears. 'There is no comparison, Emily. For a start I trust you. Patti has her own philosophy about friendship. She is pretty nice to me but she also sleeps with Adam.'

Emily started. 'Are you joking?'

Alex shook her head frantically. 'Well, it is a joke in a way, but am I telling the truth? Yes I am.' Emily stared at her with her wide green eyes.

'Oh my darling. You are so upset aren't you, well of course you are.' Alex blinked and nodded. 'Do you want to tell me?' asked Emily, reaching out a thin, freckled arm. Alex dug in her cotton trousers for a tissue and gave a little whistle.

'Not the details of it really, no. It's fine now with me and Adam, or is it I and Adam? I can never remember.'

Emily wrinkled her nose. 'Fine with me, can't be fine with I.'

'Whatever,' sniffed Alex.

'What a bastard. How can you even speak to him? I mean honestly, Al, if you need a place, we have kept your old bed.' Alex was annoyed with Emily and with herself. The trouble with revealing private misfortune is that friends leap to good intentions. She had already decided to excuse Adam despite the sour anger that reared up daily, and she needed endorsement. She did not wish to justify herself. The flux in human relations is too intricate for loyal intervention. As Alex and her friends grew older they learned a wiser, platitudinous approach to each other's relationships, for situations were rarely constant. But Emily did not yet understand this better course.

'Sorry, Al, have I said something wrong? I am just so angry. When I think how gorgeous you are, honestly, he doesn't deserve you.' Alex assumed a dignified Pilates posture.

'Adam made a really bad mistake and he knows it. But you don't know Patti. She is a snake, she just cast a disgusting spell on him.'

Emily was emotionally bright enough to change sides. 'How vile of her. You are right, Adam must have been intimidated. And she is so old. I bet it gives him the creeps now to think of that wrinkly, snaky flesh.'

Alex felt immediately better. 'Yeah, I can only tell you this but I think he is seriously freaked out. He keeps stroking me and saying how my skin feels so firm.' It was a sweetly vengeful revelation.

'Have you blitzed Patti about it?' asked Emily. 'I mean you have to confront her. Tell her that Adam feels sick,'

'Shhh, you are shouting,' said Alex looking around her. 'I can't say anything, how can I? She did it to destabilize everything, I know she did. If I confront her, then I have to take action against Adam and I know it sounds pathetic and not very feminist, but I don't want to. Anyway, if I blow out Adam then she has succeeded, hasn't she?'

Emily winced. 'So if it is a war of attrition, what are you going to do? Why don't you sleep with her guy, Mark Wyndham?'

'I can't,' said Alex. 'Not now, I can't.'

Emily took some sharp puffs of her cigarette and stubbed it out.

'Look, she slept with Adam to get to you. Why? Because you are a threat. How? Because she thinks you may get her job, right? It is personal because it is professional, isn't that it?' Alex nodded cautiously. 'God,' said Emily. 'When will women stop being so Third World about their situation? Does a man have to sleep with a younger man's wife in order to stop his promotion?'

'No,' said Alex sorrowfully. 'He'd sleep with her for other reasons. Like to show what a stud he is.' Both women laughed nervously. Emily lit another cigarette. 'I wonder what would happen to Patti without the support of the *Daily Mail*. I mean investigations into television personalities isn't really the *Guardian*'s thing, but say we fed the *Daily Mail* with some stuff? I've got these pretty good contacts. The older men are all in Patti's pocket, I've seen them drooling over her at one of those Park Lane bashes. But the younger ones want to make their name if we can get them some decent lines.'

'You can't mention Adam,' said Alex horrified.

'No, of course not,' said Emily. 'But there has to be enough without that. I mean she's had loads of husbands hasn't she? We just need to start looking.'

'I met her dad,' said Alex shyly. 'But I can't turn him over.'

'Alex,' said Emily gravely. 'This is a fight for survival. She uses the press to fight her battles, right? I bet it was she that told them about your speech to her woman's group. She or her?' Alex flushed at the memory.

'God, Em, I wonder if it was her. I bet it bloody was.'

'Now don't tell anyone, this is going to be our project,' said Emily, putting her packet of cigarettes back in her small red rucksack. 'I want you to report back to me in a week or so.'

'There is something else,' said Alex hurriedly. 'This is absolutely top secret but I think they are going to give me *The Hour*. Patti'll go berserk.'

'Wow,' said Emily. 'Really, that's amazing. Can I be your PA?' Alex looked embarrassed and pleased.

'Oh, shut up. We know it doesn't mean anything. It just makes me feel more worried and vulnerable, that's all. I need your help, Em.'

Emily nodded loyally, too nice to ponder why it is that successful people instinctively put their friends into service. She believed that friendship gave you instant credit, which was paid back in lumps when you could afford it. At the moment, Alex's fortunes seemed low. What was the point of success when you were watching your back all the time and even your boyfriend betrayed you? Emily frowned to herself as she walked quickly towards the tube station. But it was not in her nature to be melancholy for long. As she ran across the road, dodging taxis and motorbikes, her face resumed its youthful eagerness. Television was odious but life was still a lark.

Sebastian asked Sally to come in early again on a bright Tuesday morning in September. He was not afraid of Patti but it would be an unpleasant business. He swallowed some vitamin tablets and some herbal calming pills. Yes, he was afraid of Patti.

'I think it is important that we are singing from the same hymn sheet,' he told Sally once she was sitting on his sofa in her heavy overcoat.

'So which hymn would that be?' asked Sally innocently. 'We should avoid the Easter hymns, because we don't want much about crucifixion or betrayal do we? And nativity hymns don't really suit Patti. What about the "Lord is my Shepherd"?' Sebastian fiddled with the PC on his desk irritably.

'I thought you agreed with me that this was the right decision, Sally? I am afraid television is about hard choices. It is a very competitive industry.'

'Oh please,' said Sally throwing down her pile of newspapers. 'I'm not arguing with you about this, Sebastian, I just think Patti deserves a little respect. I don't see why I can't just take her out to lunch and tell her, as we discussed. Just summoning her into your office to talk about growth and new directions is going to piss her off.'

'It is about management,' said Sebastian petulantly. 'There is a prescribed procedure. If we don't follow it then we'll end up shelling out millions and we'll look ridiculous. We have to offer her an alternative that we know is unacceptable. We have to say that she is unsuited to the requirements of this particular job. And we have to have personnel on hand if she takes it badly.' Sally shrugged. She had nagging toothache and was worried about Sophie's refusal to eat breakfast. Sally was terrified about anorexia which had claimed one pupil in Sophie's class. And now she was to see one of her fellow travellers shafted. Patti was not a good nor a kind person but she was the same generation as Sally, and was thus owed some allegiance.

'OK,' she said, 'I'll be in the editing room if you want me.' Sebastian intended to strike while the iron was hot, but a series of distracting phone calls and the arrival at reception of a graduate he had encouraged and then forgotten about swallowed up the morning. His stomach became increasingly unsettled and his shoulders became painfully tense so he went for a workout in his lunch hour. By 2 p.m. he was resolute. He took the back lift to his office, there were too many people running around the floors. It must be the post-holiday rush to look busy. He buzzed for Sally but there was no sign of her. Annoyed and doubly determined he called in Patti. She arrived within minutes, looking tall and purposeful, in fact uncomfortably taller than Sebastian who rapidly sat down.

'Ah, Patti, thank you for popping in.' She said nothing but looked intent. 'Won't you sit down?'

'No, I'm fine,' she answered impatiently.

'Patti, I have some plans for the early evening which I want to tell you about. My priority must be what is best for this company.'

Patti was tapping a flat suede shoe. 'Of course. But doesn't everyone need to know your plans? It is pretty chaotic out there.'

'Well, my plans particularly concern you,' said Sebastian advancing his prepared text. Then he paused. 'Why do you think it is chaotic?' Patti widened her glowing grey blue eyes sarcastically.

'Because there has been a terrorist attack on the World Trade Center, sir. Two planes hit, the buildings are ablaze.

It's all happening live.' Sebastian yelped and rushed past her to the door. Patti sauntered after him, her face ravishingly triumphant.

The following weeks were hectic at NTC. There was no more talk of autumn schedules. The order went out to get the heavyweights on screen. Audiences wanted certainties, not fresh thinking. Patti hosted an extended news programme and volunteered some to-camera pieces from the British army bases.

'God help us, it is Vera Lynn,' said Sebastian rolling his eyes. Sure enough, Patti's tailored suits had a new military cut to them, while her hair was two shades lighter.

Alex struggled with any ignoble thoughts. Everyone else seemed pre-assigned. Sally coordinated; her daily lists now four times their usual length. (This was not simply professionalism; she needed to work harder to calm her fears for her family whose unexceptional trips to school and work now filled Sally with terror. Potential nerve gas attacks on the streets. Tall buildings at the mercy of aircraft. Security an innocent memory.) Mark had rushed off to America as soon as the airports were opened again. Alex had volunteered herself for Pakistan, shamelessly exploiting her dark colouring and her indigenous name, skimming over the fact that she knew very little about the country. But Sebastian decided to send a more experienced reporter. 'We need you here, love, to deal with the chemical warfare scares.' Alex was both bitterly disappointed and relieved. She could feel her stomach starting to swell and tighten. The rhetoric of war was biologically upsetting. Adam soothed her as they watched television together and she loved him with a new dependency. She spoke to Emily but only to share concern about the new apocalyptic climate. The project was shelved. Instead Alex spent her time interviewing blood donors and hospital staff on high alert. She phoned her parents once a day and Adam every hour. Every conversation ended with the just-in-case sentiment 'love you'. Sally suggested that she worked on a fifteen-minute feature on the flight back to religion but Sebastian countered that the television company must not look pro-appeasement, so it was cut down to five minutes of candlelit church vigils intercut with flag waving.

One day Alex was sent off to Shropshire, with no particular purpose other than shooting some scenes which were not London.

'Speak to real people,' said Sebastian, munching on a sandwich. Adam, who had taken on a protective manliness, looked up the trains from Paddington and booked Alex on at midday so that she could check in with her doctor in the morning. Alex humbly acquiesced, happy to give up her free will. Both she and Adam had quietly ditched their fierce and voluble commitment to the National Health Service in the face of a more precious existence. They did so in the name of convenience. It was simpler and quicker to attend the private doctor down the road. As with private schools, the clientele were markedly better dressed and less stoical. They took conference calls on their mobiles and strode up and down in the waiting room after a ten minute or so delay. Alex sat next to a particularly restless woman executive, who gave her name on her phone as Judith from Lease, Swiss Mercury. In between calls the woman chatted to her, another phenomenon of the private practice. She was emphatically cooey once she established that Alex was pregnant, rather than suffering from an unpleasant or infectious disease. She asked her what she did, confident that all women must work. Alex answered with a bashfulness that distressed her, 'Oh, I'm just a very low-ranking reporter for NTC.'

The woman surveyed her, amused. 'Of course, Alexandra Khan, I've read about you. You are the new thing aren't you? Once all these oldies have had their say on the war.'

Alex bristled and answered primly, 'I think it is too serious to even talk about it in those terms. I mean, thank God we have experienced people in a situation like this.' Judith laughed.

'Don't mind me, I'm an old friend of Patti's, although she wouldn't remember me. Patti has a selective memory. You have to be very important to enter her radar; I've slipped off it.' Alex looked at her with a dark, alert gaze.

'Oh really? How do you know Patti?'

'Ooh long time back. I was in love with her first husband,' said Judith.

'What was his name?' asked Alex itching to whip out her notebook.

'He was called Simon Borkowski, gorgeous, artistic. Don't know where he is now. He went off to Hay-on-Wye or somewhere to write poetry.'

'Hay-on-Wye? You're sure?' asked Alex eagerly.

'Oh God, I always forget what journalists are like. Don't quote me, OK?' said Judith with mock anxiety. The receptionist called out in bright, artificial tones, 'Judith Walker?'

The woman switched off her phone and took a business card from her bag.

'Here, that's me, if you want to know anything about our patronage of the arts give me a call. And good luck with the baby.' She bustled off, led by her umbrella. Alex gave a friendly grimace to the other watching patients, who dropped their heads in magazines.

It was an uncommon coincidence for Alex to have hit upon a second vital connection to Patti, but life throws up such chance encounters, particularly once you have shed the 90 per cent of the country outside your particular socio-economic group. Alex, as a journalist, was accustomed to lucky breaks. Luck was a professional qualification for the job. The lead was all the more promising because Simon had an unusual surname in a provincial town. People outside the cities still glanced twice at Alex for being pretty and dark skinned. The name Borkowski had not appeared in Patti's cuts. There was her fiancé who had died and then the MP. If Patti had not mentioned her first husband then there must be a good public relations reason. Alex tried to argue herself out of following this journalistic bait. Everything had changed since September 11, people's values, their priorities. What was the point of trying to bring Patti to justice when there were much graver, darker threats. She remembered her parents arguing one evening over the wisdom of bringing children into the world. Her father was a proud man and wished to introduce a dimension of grandeur into some racist taunts from a group of foul-mouthed kids at the end of the street.

'I have to ask myself,' he addressed the family, 'whether this is the sort of world I want our children to inhabit.' His wife had dismissed his rhetoric with her courageous brand of common sense.

'What are you saying? It is no worse a world than ever it was. Please don't turn a bad day into a universal condition.' Alex smiled at the memory of the phrase. Now a universal threat intruded on her family. She was truly afraid that her baby would be born into an age of terror. Yet the permanent unease at the pit of her stomach did not stop her loathing Patti. You could not suspend private lives; her small domestic battle could not be frozen. Quite the opposite. As the hideousness of September 11 was bit by bit absorbed, as the population came to terms with the fact that everyday grievances and achievements continue, even against this new dark and evil backcloth, so Alex's sense of purpose returned. It just had to be dressed up a bit, as her father had clothed his slight in a great social anguish.

Alex decided to track down Patti's first husband, not as wounded rival, but as a disinterested journalist. Journalism can justify any intrusion or axe grinding. Sure enough, there were only three Borkowskis listed in the phone book for the area. One man was an engineer, the other a shopkeeper. The third number was an answering machine, with the voice of a gentle-sounding woman.

'Hello, you have reached the Ark, writers and artists centre. There is no one to take your call right now. Please try later or, if you would like a brochure, send a stamped addressed envelope to the following address. Or fax or email us at . . .' the line clicked into a single, piercing tone. Alex held her cellphone away from her ear. She did not like using her phone while she was pregnant, Adam lectured her on this every morning. Also, what was her message? She had neither the time nor the stomach to take on Patti.

Her cameraman, Mike, was waiting for her at the station, in his heavily pocketed combat jacket and red-spotted cotton scarf. Yet another disappointed reject from the war in Afghanistan. 'Do we need visas for Shropshire?' asked Alex jauntily. He shot her a wounded look. It would take hours to get their vox pops in the street. There would be the usual elderly women looking bewildered, and young men who would seize the chance of being on camera for an impromptu audition for MTV. Alex hated the exuberant personality that she forced herself to adopt to convince the public that she was an authentic television character. She thought of Adam, who gave dignity to others just as she debased them, and winced with sorrow and tiredness. On this occasion, however, the public were peculiarly receptive and thoughtful. 'The blitz spirit,' the cameraman kept repeating until she felt like hitting him. They were through by 2 p.m.

'Time for the pub,' said her companion. Alex hesitated.

'You know, I've a friend I would like to look up while I am here. Is it OK if I meet you at the station at six?' She was aware that she was breaking the rules of location camaraderie. If she had a friend in the area she was honour-bound to ask Mike. This was below the salt, Patti-style behaviour. She was surprised by the sliver of ice within her, but she was too close to her prey to be kind. She walked away quickly, leaving Mike blinking at her, weighed down by his equipment. The Ark turned out to be a converted church off the high street. There was a health bar in the lobby with sunken-looking cakes and lurid juices served by a couple of grey-haired women swathed in stripy woollen cardigans. Alex felt suddenly nauseous and sat down too quickly on one of the pine chairs. Her head was swimming as she studied the swirly handwritten recycled menu.

'Could I have some hot water?' she asked weakly. One of the women nodded, then after some whispered discussion with her colleague picked up a telephone receiver on the wall.

'Simon, it's Alicia, how much do we charge for hot water?' Alex felt a rush of journalistic elation which miraculously cured her sickness.

'Is that Simon Borkowski?' she called out. 'I'm a journalist for NTC. I wanted to talk to him about his work.'

Alicia looked flattered. Even the most pure of spirit liked a little recognition now and again. She picked up the phone again.

'Simon, it is a journalist from NTC. She has come to see YOU.'

Minutes later, a tall imposing-looking man with a grey ponytail and sharp cheekbones appeared in the doorway. When he saw Alex he looked disappointed.

'Oh, I thought, I thought that you were somebody else. Would you like to come this way?' Alex stood up heavily, aware of a new centre of gravity within her. She followed Simon into his office, full of pictures of angry-looking nudes and strange, distorted sculptures.

'Is this your work?' she asked brightly. Simon looked at her with fluid, pale green eyes and gestured for her to sit down in one of the two hard chairs.

'We don't claim ownership of work here,' he said. 'What can I do for you?' He smelled strongly of sweat although there were no signs of exertion. For a bohemian, he also displayed a corporate sense of office politics. Alex's chair was much lower than his, giving her psychological as well as physical discomfort.

'I was in the area, interviewing people about the war,' she said defiantly. 'And you are quite a local figure, so I thought . . .'

'Patti tell you about me?' Simon interrupted, his red lips almost forming a smile.

'Well, no, though of course I had heard that you knew Patti.'

'I was married to Patti. You know I was married to Patti?' Alex nodded awkwardly. Well, she might as well get hanged.

'Would you like to tell me about that?' she asked.

Simon considered for a moment. He reached out for a small stone gargoyle on the table and passed it from one big hand to another like an office toy.

'Sure,' he said evenly. 'What do you want to know?' So no chance for the oblique question, for the wide-eyed eliciting of an unsought fact. Alex was after Patti, and Simon could make use of this fact in whatever way he chose.

'Could you tell me why you split up?' said Alex, her cheeks burning with the sudden indoor heat of the room and with the recklessness of her mission.

'The fact that she is a total bitch didn't help,' said Simon calmly, keeping his sea gaze on Alex. Was this a trap?

'What do you mean?'

'Well, for instance, she killed someone,' said Simon, his smile undisturbed.

Uh oh. What was this. A sick joke? A sick man? Alex's eyes slid towards the door.

'I'm not insane,' said Simon leaning back in his chair. 'I'm just answering your question. I discovered in Patti the off-limits of ambition. At some point, in your profession, you have to make a calculation. How much damage is a story worth? Is it worth a life?'

'Sorry,' said Alex. 'I don't know what you mean.'

'OK, here it is. Patti was, is, gorgeous. She is also ruthless, inhuman. She aborted a kid of ours, I'm culpable, I let her do it. But listen now. Whereas I cracked up over this, she became doubly driven. She used that dead baby to get her an interview for her paper with a really good guy, a fertility doctor. He felt sorry for her because she couldn't have children. He spoke to her, told her what he was doing for women like her. And she put him in the paper and she killed him.'

Alex felt the sour bile in her throat. This was a coincidence too many. This did not feel like a lucky break, it felt like witchcraft.

'What was his name?' she asked. Simon blew out his cheeks.

'I won't ever forget him. His name was Berluscoli.'

Alex knew what he would answer. She felt a dull ache in her stomach. She must not upset the baby. She would not distress the baby. 'Simon, I have to ask if you are sure about this?'

Simon shrugged. 'It was Patti. She's a stealth bomber, that woman, she doesn't leave any traces.'

He looked at Alex expectantly but she was too shaken and tearful to think of any further questions. She began chewing at her nails.

'Is that what you came to find out?' asked Simon. Alex shook her head.

'Bad shit,' said Simon. 'You want to know the rest?' Alex shook her head again.

'I think,' she said in a small childish voice, 'that I have to go and get my train now.'

Alex's legs felt weak as she plodded back to the high street. Her immediate concern was a two-hour train journey with Mike, fielding questions, remembering to banter. In her angry, fearful state she wanted to be alone. She felt Patti's presence in a superstitious way, even talking about her, thinking about her, seemed like a curse. She stopped a minicab and asked if it would take her to London. The fare was more cash than she had, so she had to let the cab go and walk back to the station in the drizzling dusk.

She should have told the cab driver she was pregnant, he would at least have given her a ride to a bank, but she felt so protective of the child she did not want to mention it to strangers. By the time she got back to the station, she was spotted by Mike who was waiting patiently outside the ticket office.

'Alex, I was worried about you,' he said kindly, adding unnecessarily, 'we've missed the train.' His simple warmth broke Alex's cordon and she burst into tears on his shoulder. 'I'm just so tired,' she sobbed.

In the fuggy warmth of the train carriage, Alex slept, her head falling onto Mike's shoulder and then jerking upright again as her eyes opened wide. Her dream sequences were vivid and awful. Patti calmly announcing on screen the jihad on Britain, Patti caressing Adam, Patti listening ironically as Alex tried to confront her about the death of Adam's father. 'Stick to the facts, Alex, whose father? My father? Your father? Adam's father? What are you talking about?' as Alex became increasingly incoherent.

Then Patti moving menacingly towards her and starting to shake her, to shake the baby. Alex awoke with a gasp.

'We're here,' said Mike gently. 'I'm so sorry, I had to wake you.' They walked down the station together in silence. Alex had the over-wide-awake feeling she had as a child when the family would leave in the early hours for a holiday. She longed for Adam's quiet, medicinal manner; for him to run her a bath, pour her a drink, soothe her into quietude. Yet, she had to destroy his peace of mind, so she must restore him like a good parent. What should have been a purely professional spat now enveloped her whole life and everything she held dear. She could not find her front door key so rang the bell and leaned heavily against the door. She ached with misery and tiredness. The door opened and Adam caught her in his arms.

'My poor mouse,' he murmured, as she knew he would. 'Darling little mother, come and sit down.' The light in the bedroom shone until the early hours of the morning, and the couple in the flat above started at the rare, racking sound of a man crying. The newspapers were not brought in from the doorstep in the morning; Alex, for the first time, phoned in sick. When Alex did arrive at work early, the day after, it was only to hand in a short typed note to Sebastian's secretary.

I have decided that I can no longer work for NTC. Sorry for the short notice. Could I leave as soon as possible? Thank you for all the encouragement I have received here; I hope that you, Sally and Mark will forgive me and that the network goes from strength to strength. Yours, Alexandra Khan.

Sebastian read the letter with irritation, then called in Sally.

'What do you make of this?' he asked. Sally sat down, put on her reading glasses and sighed.

'Well, she's obviously upset,' she said.

'Yes, that would seem to be the message,' said Sebastian dryly. 'Doesn't the girl realize that there is a war on?' Sally laughed.

'I was waiting for the first person to say that. Did you ever speak to her about what it meant for *The Hour*?'

'I thought she would be mature enough to gather that the last thing I need is a lot of histrionics from the lower ranks.'

'That isn't how you described her a month ago,' said Sally, pursing her lips. 'She was the future of the company then, you can't blame her for feeling a bit deflated.'

Sebastian snorted. 'That is what is so infuriating about you, Sally, you always understand the other side's position. You should be in the Foreign Office.'

'She's young, that's all,' said Sally. 'Do you want me to have a chat with her?'

'Yes,' said Sebastian, lighting up a cigarette.

'When did you start smoking?' asked Sally.

'Oh Christ, we are all smoking now,' said Sebastian. 'Yes, talk her out of this. We'll be back to normal by January. But it is bad taste to talk about it now. Can you encourage her and slap her down? That is the art of people management, no?'

Sally rang Alex on her mobile and arranged to meet her for coffee next to the NTC. The location reflected Sally's dual policy of sympathy and irritation. However, when Alex wandered in, thin and drawn in an oversized coat, Sally felt unconditionally maternal. She stood up and hugged her. 'How are you?'

Alex gave a wan smile and sat down, drawing her coat closer around her. Sally ordered coffee and looked sternly at the thin, dark girl.

'It was a silly letter to have written, Alex, and I think we should just tear it up. You have to learn a little patience, we are a news organization and you can't plan everything. But Sebastian has assured me that *The Hour* will go ahead in January, which isn't actually very far off. I would make use of a bit more reporting experience until then.'

Alex stared at Sally with huge, bewildered eyes. 'It isn't anything to do with the show, Sally. It is personal.'

Sally immediately softened. 'What is it?' she asked.

Alex shook her head. 'I don't want to talk about it, please, just trust me, I can't.'

The coffee came, Sally leaned forward. 'I'm sorry, Alex, but I do have a right to know. I like to think that I have helped you with your career, I have an interest in it. I also like to think that I am a friend. If you don't want me to tell Sebastian I won't, but I need to know. Perhaps I can help.'

Alex struggled to compose herself. She had not meant to confide in the older woman, Patti's friend, but she needed an outlet, maybe a way out. In her unhappiness, she sought some kind of self-mutilation and the sacrifice of her career was a pleasing kind of martyrdom. But, of course, she wanted the villain exposed as well.

'I can't work with Patti,' she said a touch melodramatically. 'It is one thing that she seduced my . . . boyfriend . . . the father of my child,' she paused for effect. 'But now I have found out that she murdered Adam's father. I don't think this makes for a good working relationship.'

Sally swallowed her coffee hard. 'OK, stop,' she said.

'Does this mean you are pregnant?' Alex nodded. 'Oh my dear, congratulations.' Alex's eyes filled with tears. 'I won't ask any more questions about Patti and Adam, that is too horrible for you,' said Sally. 'But what do you mean about his father?'

'Well, Adam's father met Patti and she made him say things about his field of work, fertility, and it got him suspended and then he killed himself, or rather Patti killed him.'

'Stop,' said Sally again. 'Sorry, Alex, I have to take this a step at a time. When was this?'

Alex grimaced. 'Sorry, poor journalism. It was about thirty years ago. She stitched up Adam's dad, and he was so broken-hearted at losing his job and everything that he committed suicide. I just found this out, because I met Patti's first husband and he told me.'

Sally's heart was knocking against her ribs, but she summoned some journalistic logic. 'For a start, Alex, this isn't murder, it is journalistic recklessness, horrible, but unintentional. Some of the worst crimes in life are those with unintended consequences. Second, I remember the case now, I remember the piece, but Patti didn't write it.'

'Yes she did!' shouted Alex. She added in a lower voice: 'She organized it, she only didn't write it because they put a senior journalist on to it. She brought in the story. She betrayed him. God, I can't argue about this, Patti destroyed Adam's father and she came back to try to finish us off too. She is evil.'

'Yes, yes,' said Sally, nervous but persistently fair. 'I know what you are saying. She has behaved wickedly, perhaps she is wicked. I just want you to be clear about what she has done. Patti uses people, sometimes with diabolical consequences. But she does not directly murder people. I mean, this is not a police matter.'

'Morally, she is a murderer, maybe not legally, but morally,' said Alex.

Sally breathed deeply. 'Well, you must fight her morally. Leaving your job is a victory for Patti. You have a moral duty to triumph over her. You stay put, Alex, do you hear me?' Alex nodded wearily, although she was inwardly relieved. It was a pleasing solution to keep her job and the moral high ground.

'Will you say something to Patti?' she asked. She hoped that Sally would recommend full public exposure. She was thrilled and appalled by the prospect of a denunciation by Sally. But instead Sally grimaced:

'Tricky. It is tricky, Alex. I mean I have known Patti a long time but not intimately. She has always had a cordon sanitaire. Frankly, I think she would tell me to fuck off and mind my own business. And in a way she would be right. These are not professional matters.'

Alex's eyes filled with tears, 'Well it is not really further-ing team spirit for her to sleep with my boyfriend and murder . . .'

Sally once more put up her hand. 'Alex, she didn't murder him, you must stop saying that. And she didn't know you at the time, in fact you didn't know Adam. It is a horrible coincidence.' She took in Alex's pained expression and relented. 'I mean, I am trying to fathom how bad a person Patti is. She can be generous and some-times genuinely kind. But I don't think she has much of a sense of other people. We are all a bit of a blur, an audience. But it is different with you, I agree, she seems to have you in her focus. It is as if you are some kind of nemesis. And that makes her bloody in tooth and claw.'

'Yeah well, thank you, David Attenborough,' said Alex bitterly.

Sally gasped, 'Gosh, that sounded like Patti.'

Alex's face crumpled, 'That is a dreadful thing to say. Patti is out to get me and I am afraid. Not for me and Adam, we'll be OK. But, oh, I am pregnant and I don't want her curse on the baby.' If only Alex had played the maternal card before! Sally almost fell on the younger woman with motherly concern.

'No wonder this all looks so cosmic to you. You mustn't upset yourself. Stay still, I will fetch you a glass of milk.' Alex started laughing through tears.

'Milk! I haven't drunk milk since I was about ten years old. Honestly, Sally!' Sally continued to hug her.

'Just forget about Patti. Your family unit is going to be so strong, you can weather a jealous older woman, you can. There is nothing more she can do to you now.' Alex felt reassured by Sally but not entirely satisfied. She still wanted Patti to know that she knew. In fact that everyone knew. This was only justice. As luck, or journalism, would have it, there was a message from Emily on her mobile when she switched it on. Her chum from the *Mail* had been asked to find some entertaining distractions from the war, which was frankly more complicated, less news-friendly than had first been thought. The *Mail* picture desk had been offered some intriguing, although potentially libellous, long-range pictures of Patti in bathing costume and Puffa jacket, kissing a blond youth in surfing gear behind a car. Did Emily know anyone who could shed light on this? A generous tip fee was offered.

'Oh no,' gasped Alex to Emily. 'That has to be Tristan.'

Every catastrophe has a silver lining, and Patti had to admit that September 11 had been good for her. Her position at NTC was re-established. It was not just the airtime, it was the way colleagues subtly acknowledged her shift back to power. The crew were generally more respectful. The grumbling of fellow journalists about her high-handed behaviour, her sense of entitlement from the military top brass, confirmed her superior status. Envy was so much more reassuring than sympathy. Jenny had taken on the role of lady-in-waiting, making sure that Patti got priority in transport, accommodation and food. Patti was also offered exclusive use of the CEO's private bathroom suite to the further irritation of her colleagues.

'What's the movie?' muttered the sports editor as Patti swept by him towards the studio, Jenny pattering loyally behind her. It was 6 p.m. and so Jenny's moment to order the clearing of the two desk telephones, in case Mark was trying to get through.

'That would be Mark Antony, I suppose,' smirked the studio manager.

There were small vexations. Patti was vaguely irked by the drawn figure of Alexandra Khan on the sidelines. 'Looking like a bloody Afghan refugee with those eyes,' mocked Patti to Jenny in the new privacy of the make-up room.

Then there was the inevitable apocalyptic tone that Arthur had begun to adopt in his letters. Copied out passages from Nostradamus. Instructions on the use of a parachute, plus drawings of a bunker hidden in the Welsh hills. Thirty-page letters about the hidden role of Iraq. It was a real problem in times of disaster. It brought out heroes but it also fertilized all the nutters. The other night Patti thought that she had spotted Arthur on the street corner wearing a gas mask. She didn't know whether to laugh or run. On the positive side, her restored professional power, spiced with genuine danger, was doing wonders for her looks, her well being and her relationship with Mark. She had never been happier.

Alex was just leaving for the hospital with Adam for her pregnancy scan when Emily rang. She was phoning from the office so her voice was low.

'I'm going to fax you something. It is the proofs for tomorrow's *Mail*. I thought you might want to see it.'

'How have you got it?' gasped Alex, carefully shutting the kitchen door behind her and lifting herself onto the aluminium stool.

'Well, because I am the main bloody source,' laughed Emily.

'Do you think this is too dangerous?' asked Alex, twisting the telephone wire. 'I mean what have they used? It just has to have come from me.'

'Too late for appeasement now,' said Emily brightly. 'Go and stand by the fax.'

Adam called from the bedroom, 'Are you on the phone, Mouse? We should be leaving.'

'Yes, hang on a minute,' shouted Alex. 'I have to wait for a fax from work. Why don't you go and pick up a taxi?'

She switched the phone and waited. A few seconds later it rang, and the paper started to chug through. There was an indistinct photograph, striped with ink, of a tall woman embracing a youth. Even the blurry photocopy would pass an identity parade. The boy was Tristan. It was captioned: 'The woman in this photograph is Britain's most famous television broadcaster, Patti Ward. The youth is the teenage brother of her boyfriend, the political journalist Mark Wyndham. Are they too close for comfort? See pages six and seven for the secret life of Patti Ward'.

Alex pulled out the following pages with guilty horror. However shocking real life, it was never as bad as the lurid heightened reality of print. Even seeing the names of people she knew in mass-circulation type made her feel sick. Seeing her account of events so faithfully reported felt like an assault. Everything had been thoroughly checked. Patti's father had been interviewed by one reporter, Simon by another. A woman writer had been to see Adam's mother. Mark had been contacted and his stream of anguished expletives asterisked out. The only detail missing was Adam's own relationship with Patti. Alex herself was 'unavailable for comment'. It was an appallingly thorough piece of work. Adam was coming back into the flat.

'Come on, Alex, the taxi is waiting,' he said. He looked so decent in his uncharacteristic suit and tie. So lovely. Alex chewed at her lip. This was a terrible mistake, she had demeaned everyone, without even having the courage to put her name to it. She could hardly bear to think of the damage she must have done to Tristan. She was base and cruel. This was not an appropriate military response. It was murder. The phone rang again.

'What do you think?' asked Emily.

'It is horrible,' whispered Alex.

'Come on, Alex, we have to go,' called Adam impatiently.

'Ems, please, we have to stop it,' pleaded Alex.

'Mouse, put down the phone,' said Adam. Alex rung off miserably and put her hand into Adam's. The consequences would have to be borne.

Most women fall in love a little with their gynaecologists. Alex luxuriated in living with a fertility doctor in training. She begged him to be more clinical in their lovemaking.

'Stop it,' Adam would giggle. 'You are putting me off.' Alex had never loved Adam so much, a passion founded on sorrow and betrayal but now elevated by pregnancy into a sacred bond. As she climbed into the taxi, she hoped this love would save them from her actions, from her act of terrorism. You cannot declare war on someone in isolation. Innocent people get hurt. She ached with fear at what she had unleashed. She prayed in silence:

'God bless Tristan, God bless Mark, God bless Jessica, God bless Kenneth, God bless Adam, God bless our baby and please, please don't punish it.'

In the hospital waiting room, with its high-watt lighting, rows of plastic chairs and boxes of unloved toys, she reflected again on the blessings that she had jeopardized. This was Adam's working environment, he understood the forms and the vending machines. The staff warmed to him instantly and exchanged approving glances with each other. One nurse came over to apologize for the short wait.

'I should have known you were a doctor,' she clucked. The other mothers, worn out and suspicious of preferential treatment, shot angry looks at Alex. Some were on their own, others accompanied by sullen partners. A couple of men did seem good natured but only Adam looked at ease. Alex buried her head into his jacket, and he stroked her hair.

'Feeling OK?'

Alex gave a muffled nod. She could not bare to dwell on his response to the newspaper although she could clearly picture it. He received bad news like a good patient, stoically. He had been the first of the couple to suffer close bereavement. When his uncle had died, it was Alex who had burst into tears and needed to be comforted by him. He was quieter than usual but even more considerate and gentle. When she had told him about Patti's role in his father's death he shook visibly and wept but there was no angry loss of control and strangely no self-pity. He had only repeated, 'Poor mother, my God, poor mother.' Well he would be angry now. Alex was too afraid of this white-knuckled rage to confide in him. Newspapers were usually more censorious about the cover up than the original sin, when the first was a necessary consequence of the latter. She was intellectually confident with her justification, although she would not test out loud her argument. It was the acts themselves that were wicked, rather than the reporting of them. Patti should account for herself and, since her behaviour was immoral rather than illegal, it was proper that she should be judged by the press rather than the courts. Why then the feeling of doom?

'Alexandra Khan?' called the nurse. She jumped up, gathering her coat and bag.

'I'll take those,' said Adam, guiding her towards the narrow, darkened room. Any awkwardness Alex felt at lifting herself onto the trolley bed, unbuttoning her skirt and feeling the cold gel over her stomach was forgotten once she looked at the screen. The strange, subterranean creature, the diagram which took on the gestures of a human being, was exhilarating. She gasped and laughed at the gymnastics, feeling her own heart tilt and soar in response. She looked at Adam and saw his pale face was luminous with love. Everyone in the room was laughing now as the creature scratched its head and shook its toes. The sound of the hurried heartbeat had a mystical beauty.

'Good strong beat,' said Adam to the nurse.

'I think he or she is going to be quite a character,' said the nurse. 'Want a photograph?' The afternoon had a suspended reality. By the time they left the hospital it was getting dark with impending rain.

'It feels like winter rather than October,' said Alex.

'Do you realize, it'll be our last Christmas with just the two of us,' said Adam cheerfully. 'What are we going to call him, by the way?'

'Why do you say him?' said Alex stopping on the pavement.

'No reason. Patriarchal conditioning I expect. Sorry.'

'No, but Adam, do you know? I mean are you speaking as a father or a doctor here?'

'As a father. I deliberately looked away. God, that word makes me proud. Father. Who'd have thought it?' Alex laughed and gave him a push.

'Now you sound like a playground show off.'

'Well, you do look like a school-girl mum come to think of it,' said Adam sweeping her into his arms. He waved one behind her. 'Taxi!'

They headed home to a blissful afternoon and a happy evening stretched out on the sofa in front of the television, the telephone on answering machine. Alex was beginning to exploit her new status, insisting on three romantic comedies in a row.

'I just can't stand violence,' she said cutely.

'That's fine,' said Adam bleakly. 'Really, I love Julia Roberts.' By the third film, Alex was feeling grimly fearful. The rain which pelted against the windows made her nervous rather than cosy. The sky looked unusually vast and black for London. The wind brought down a couple of roof tiles with a fierce crack.

'Shall we go to bed now?' asked Adam, his arm numb from Alex's resting head. Alex was bristling with tension. Her inner drama had speeded up her brain and her body felt saturated by a discordant chemical. She had to go and get tomorrow's paper from the station or the West End, she had to do it now. She searched for a plausible excuse. This was a drawback of living at close quarters with someone who knows you well. There was no conceivable reason for her leaving the flat after 11 p.m. She would have to do a runner.

'You have the bath first,' said Adam.

'No, I want you to,' said Alex. 'I'd like to stay here for a few minutes. On my own. To think about things.' Adam gave her a look that was pure doctor/patient, nodded and walked off quietly in his socks. Once she heard the bath run, Alex crept to the kitchen, got her door key and let herself out.

She probably had fifteen minutes until Adam noticed, another fifteen minutes before he became concerned. She could plead some pregnancy craving; for newspapers. She jumped in a taxi.

'Shaftesbury Avenue, please,' she said, feeling like an escaped criminal. She tried Emily on her mobile but it was switched off. A thought struck her. Would the *Mail* hold the story for its second edition to make sure it was exclusive? She winced with frustration. But no, surely the other papers would have to make their own checks, it was far too legally treacherous to pick it up. And the story needed the photograph, the *Mail* picture desk would be told not to release it to anyone else. She tapped her foot and wiped a peephole in the misted window. Late-night London was always busier than she imagined. A couple of years, her job and her condition separated her completely from the excitable, dressed-up world of the young, single office workers pouring out of pubs or glimpsed through restaurant windows. The taxi braked continuously on St Martin's Lane as groups of laughing, tipsy women crossed the road without looking. Alex asked the driver to pull in, and ran with a new heaviness to the corner of Shaftesbury Avenue. The piles of papers were still bound up, the top copies sodden with rain. She squinted at the *Mail* under the string. There was Patti. She was also on the front of every other paper, broadsheet and tabloid. 'Oh shit,' Alex half sobbed, pulling at all of them. The vendor patiently cut the string and took Alex's damp coins. She looked at the *Mail* front page under the light of a street lamp. It was a file picture of Patti. Why no Tristan? Had Mark intervened, or just the lawyers? What then was the story? The headline went right across the page. **PATTI WARD IN INTENSIVE CARE AFTER SAVAGE STREET ATTACK.** Alex's hands were shaking and she could hear herself breathing, as if it were somebody else.

Patti Ward, the broadcaster, was last night in hospital after being violently attacked outside her home in west London. She had been beaten over the head with a sharp instrument and was unconscious when the police were called by a neighbour, Veronica Little. Miss Ward, aged fifty-three, was taken by helicopter to Chelsea and Westminster Hospital where her condition was described as 'serious but stable'. There are immediate fears of brain damage. The Prime Minister has asked to be informed of developments. The Prince of Wales has also expressed deep concern.

The words started to blur as Alex turned the page. Information gave way to biography and an assortment of photographs. The most recent, taken two days ago, was of Patti interviewing the head of the British armed forces. She looked blazingly alive. The picture had to be more true than the snatched shot of a bloody head above a blanket on a stretcher.

Alex returned weakly to the revving taxi. The bare facts of the story were repeated at a harsh, fast pace on the car radio. The driver pulled back his dividing window.

'I reckon it's the terrorists,' he said. 'Someone like her had to be a target. Bloody murdering bastards, excuse my language. It's like Princess Di all over again, isn't it? You can hardly believe it can you?'

The perhaps fatal attack on Patti certainly had all the marks of a significant public event. It came out of nowhere and yet was in keeping with the time. Patti had been at her most high-profile during recent weeks, which made her seem a target. The public were feeling emotionally porous. Television assumed the greater drama of real life. The list of suspects was especially intriguing.

'Almost anyone you can think of,' said Sebastian swigging a bottle of water as he sat on his desk. The NTC team had assembled unprompted in his office by 8 a.m. the following morning. The mechanistic jokes were contradicted by their expressions of numbness. Sally was not present, having driven straight to the hospital at midnight, and had phoned to say that she would stay there until the afternoon. Mark was also absent, declining to fly back from Washington. Alex arrived a little late and flustered. She had risen early after a sleepless night and dressed in loose, layered velvet for physical and emotional comfort. She spotted a taxi parked with its light on at the end of the road and knocked on the window. She was used to beams from taxi drivers, who were especially susceptible to her pretty-daughter appeal. On this occasion the driver had looked at her suspiciously and turned his head away. She gave a second perplexed knock. The driver had then pushed down his window and asked her brusquely, 'Christian or Muslim?'

Alex stammered, 'Christian, I am Christian and British.' The driver nodded and swung open the door for her. Alex got in silently, wishing she had refused to answer and walked away. Odd how recently she had felt so safe, so subliminally happy and now she was full of arctic dread. Was it her culpability which had brought about this change? Sure enough, the little gathering in Sebastian's office looked at her searchingly as she entered and swung her little rucksack to the floor.

'Any more news?' she asked in small voice.

'The police are meant to be following some leads,' said Sebastian. 'They are coming to us at twelve, which saves us making the calls, I suppose. I wonder if you should be reporting from the hospital, Alex?' He glanced questioningly at her ethnic scarves.

'Sorry,' said Alex. 'I just didn't think. I'll borrow a suit from Wardrobe.'

'Should Alex be wearing black?' asked the young assistant producer.

'Patti isn't the Queen and she isn't dead,' said Sebastian rolling his eyes. 'I don't think we should go over the top about this.'

The head of current affairs put his head round the door. 'Thought you ought to know, the CEO has phoned from the hospital. He said the Patti coverage must be "dignified".'

'Oh, thank you so much,' said Sebastian. 'I was thinking of setting it all to a Kylie Minogue soundtrack, but it's back to the drawing-board.' The room tittered with nervous relief. There was a steady flow of interventions during the morning. Researchers looking for Patti archival material. Urgent requests from the newspapers for unseen photographs. Crews from rival television stations arriving to film the studio. All to fill the vacuum of hard information. Alex filed a lunchtime report from outside the hospital, surrounded by well-wishers – the polite term for the curious and the unemployed. She returned to NTC after a special request from the detective inspector. By the time she arrived, Sally was already making the officers coffee, in a presiding organizational calm. She smiled at Alex. 'You should be sitting down, you look tired.'

Alex swallowed. 'How bad is it, Sally?'

'Oh Patti will pull through. She looks a bit of a mess but as she wisecracked through her stitches, no worse than post-op cosmetic surgery.

'Doctor Sadler told me that he thought at first Patti did not have the will to survive the attack. She refused water and medicine. He said he was in the room during the night watching her blink inside her poor swollen face and cracked skull. She never complained once about the pain. But he saw a tear roll down her temple, onto the bandages. He moved closer to the bed, because he sensed something was in the balance. He said he heard her say, so far as she could move her lips, "OK, one more throw". At least, that is what he thought she said. And she must have said something like it, because she asked for some water soon after. I got in to see her this morning.'

There was a respectful silence. Then Steve, whose role it was to break any silence, natural or unnatural said: 'Are you sure she wasn't asking for me? Maybe she was saying, "Suck my toe"?' Alex gave a frightened snort of laughter. Sally smiled gravely at the little group.

'So you got to talk to her?' asked Sebastian. 'I mean she is obviously acting the broad but she must be in a pretty bad way.'

'Impossible to tell,' said Sally. 'I wanted to cry when I saw her but she glared at me until I composed myself. I think she is very brave and extremely self-reliant. Don't think she is going to come back cuddly.'

'You reckon she'll come back?' asked Sebastian quickly.

Sally shot him a reproachful look. 'Well of course she should, if she wants to. She didn't mention it to me. In fact she seems to have acquired a new hinterland. She said that she wanted to study tropical fish, asked me to get some books for her.'

'Fish?' everyone exclaimed.

'Well, it's a start,' said Sally, flustered. 'Maybe it is because she took some pressure on the brain, fish are probably rather relaxing.'

'So she didn't mention any of us?' asked Jenny anxiously. She was put out that Sally had taken the only visiting time for herself.

'No, she didn't,' replied Sally before hesitating. 'Well she did ask for Mark. I must say, I think he ought to have flown back. It is about time that he took on some responsibility. No one is asking him to marry her for God's sake. Oh, and they've arrested someone, though that is not for broadcast yet, is it gentlemen?' she cocked her head towards the policemen. 'Some local nutter, waiting outside the hospital. His bedsit was full of newspaper cuttings about Patti, and piles of stuff about September 11. He was obsessed by the war and Patti's association with it must have triggered him off. There were disgusting, violent letters he had written to her and all the usual mad conspiracy documents. The police are pretty pleased to have picked him up so swiftly, given all the public interest in the case. NTC will be the first with the story, of course.'

By the time Arthur was named, he had also been released. The blood samples were not his, but from Patti's first husband Simon. The *Daily Mail* were first with the profile and pictures of this vindictive, abusive man, under the headline PATTI'S DARK SECRET. The following day they had uncovered a host of further secrets and contradictions about Patti's life, including her age, which was definitively printed as fifty-seven. The headline was THE RIDDLE OF PATTI WARD. The only statement from Patti was that she intended to put all this behind her and get back to work. Her return, scheduled for January, turned out to be fanciful. To the surprise of the newspapers and her colleagues she disappeared for a month in the Bahamas with her new husband and boss, Sir David Leach. The former Mrs Leach had proved dispensable after all. A second press release announced that she would be returning to NTC in a new role as editor at large. Apart from advising on programming and personnel she would present a flagship weekly news and current affairs programme. At the end of a long, hard session, consultants hit upon the title *Sixty Minutes*. In the light of her changed circumstances, Patti was unable to speak to the press and would not be granting any interviews whatsoever in the foreseeable future.

Three days after the announcement, Pegasus News precipitously called a press conference to introduce their new star Alexandra Khan. Alex had fretted whether mid-pregnancy was the right time for a career move. She had consulted Sally who sighed, put down the plant she'd brought round, and took Alex's small hand in her warm, padded one. Sally said she was old enough to remember the distaste and embarrassment that working women caused in offices. She herself had pretended that she was biologically unchanged and had never dared mention maternity leave. It was only when Sophie was one that Sally had unsteeled herself. A bus conductor had shouted at her for having the wrong change and she found herself unaccountably choked by tears. After that, she had gone part time. 'I think it is an individual choice,' said Sally, her eyes crinkling into little maternal creases. 'But you'll have to prove yourself all over again at Pegasus, it might be better to freewheel here for a while.'

Emily gave different advice. She turned up to visit Alex on her recently acquired pale blue Vespa scooter, balancing the new iMac model on her lap.

'Comfort presents for us getting over that scrape,' she said, her small white teeth reflected in the helmet visor as she lifted it off with her spare arm. 'I thought you could idle away your hours on cranky websites once the baby is born.' Alex hugged her friend and led her into the flat.

'I don't know what to do,' she said, flopping onto one end of the sofa as Emily curled neatly up on the other. 'Pegasus want me to go for some obscene amount of money and not so many hours, so far as I can see. But I'm pregnant and maybe I am safer where I am. It is a fantastic offer but I feel sort of hunted, I don't know, what do you think?'

'I think you sound like Patti bleeding Ward, that's what I think,' replied Emily, fielding the cushion thrown at her. 'Alex, go for it, you don't need to weigh everything up. If it suits you, do it. Didn't you know we have kicked away the career ladder, these days we swing from rope to rope. Have fun.' Mark Wyndham, who had rung the doorbell in the middle of this monologue, agreed with Emily's assessment.

'But you didn't hear what she said,' reasoned Alex, fetching a couple of beers.

'No, but Emily seems a sensible girl,' shrugged Mark. He had come straight from the airport and was unshaven and sheeny. Emily's eyes widened with interest as she raised her can to him. Alex passed her hand over her stomach ruefully. She was out of the game now.

Alex joined Pegasus in the spring. The company was determined to make her into a major signing and so they ingeniously turned her advancing pregnancy into a virtue. She turned down their request to video the birth just as she had politely declined the *Daily Mail*'s persistent demand for a pregnancy diary, accompanied by exercise pictures. She did agree to model some hot new pregnancy jeans for the *Guardian* features pages as a small repayment of Emily's loyalty to her. Alex was also interviewed by Tristan for his school magazine about her favourite music. It would be flung back at her when she objected to some paparazzi shots of her and Adam buying baby clothes together but that was the devil's pact with the press. Nature echoed her ripening condition with citrus freshness. Daffodils opened their mouths like bath ducks and sticky buds unfurled into life. This at least was the laboratory spring of the window boxes. During Alex's third week at Pegasus, the Queen Mother died and Alex fronted a five-hour running news show. The television critics pronounced her competent, although a little underdressed compared to Patti Ward, who appeared in head-to-toe black Chanel and something approaching the crown jewels. This top heaviness was to compensate for Sebastian's exasperated decision to keep her in behind a desk, denying viewers the opportunity to feast upon the quality of her black stockings.

Adam's mother joined forces with Alex's parents to lobby for a summer wedding but their children stood firm.

'Isn't it enough that we love each other?' asked Alex, sleepily nestling onto Adam's lap on a chilly evening in April.

'Hope so,' answered Adam stroking her neck and breasts and belly. 'For the little guy, I hope so.' Alex jerked her head away.

'So you do know, you know it's a boy.' Adam held her in the strait jacket of his embrace, laughing.

'I don't know, I don't know.' She wriggled and he held her even more closely. 'Trust me, Alex.'

*

Alex's stomach was stretched like a balloon by the summer and she acquired the distinctive waddle of late pregnancy. She was expecting. What? She had no concept of a baby as a child in development. She liked Sally's kids but established no connection between them and the somersaulting, pressing baby in her belly. She skipped the postscript chapter at the end of her pregnancy book about childhood diseases and sibling rivalry. She could focus only on the miracle of birth, the expulsion of this secondary being. She enjoyed the dreamy, matronly role accorded to her by her friends. One July evening she was lying on the sofa, propped up by cushions, explaining to Tristan, who had proudly agreed to be godfather, the variety of birth positions. Adam would be home shortly and Mark and Emily would join the group for a local curry.

'So where exactly is the birth canal?' asked Tristan, the feminine seriousness of his expression belied by his T-shirt which said 'Babe Magnet'.

'Sort of here,' said Alex heaving herself up on the cushions to trace a line. She felt a great punch in her lower back, followed by a paralysing ripple, as if she had been stung by a swarm of bees beneath her skin. She tensed, closed her eyes and sucked in her breath: 'Ow, ow, ow.'

Tristan's angular face was close to hers, the pupils of his soft green eyes dilated with alarm. 'Christ, Alex, are you OK, shall I phone a doctor?'

Alex opened her eyes as the pain eased. 'I'm OK, I must have been in a funny position. Tristan, you look so frightened!' Tristan scratched the back of his spiky hair and blew out his cheeks.

'That freaked me out, don't do that again, Alex,

Christ.' Alex's laugh turned into a yelp. The same vicious cramp rushed through her pelvis, tensing every anguished muscle.

'Call Adam, get Adam,' she hissed. Tristan dug out his cellphone from the deep pocket of his jeans. It was on voicemail. Half an hour later Alex was starting to rock with pain, standing, sitting, kneeling, crouching in hopeless flight from it. Tristan's ribs were rising and falling underneath his thin T-shirt but he sounded calm, consciously imitating Adam's voice.

'Alex, I am going to call an ambulance now. Just stay where you are.' He dialled 999, wondering whether you needed a code in front of the number. Nothing seemed to be happening. Finally he got through to an operator but lost her again. Alex was kneeling in front of the sofa.

'What's happening, Tristan?' she moaned.

'Well, I'm trying to get through, I seem to be having a bit of trouble.'

Alex turned her damp, racked face towards him. 'You'll have to drive me,' she said in muffled misery.

'I haven't got my licence,' cried Tristan, his hands clasped over his head. The voice of the emergency services operator attracted his attention and he clasped his phone to his ear.

'Yes, could I have an ambulance. I'll spell the name of the road. Ten minutes? Right. Um, Alex it will be about ten minutes.' Alex gazed at him distractedly. Suddenly inspired, Tristan raced off in search of towels, and returned with a flannel from the bathroom. Alex's whimpering had changed to a harsh, intermittent growl.

'You OK, Alex?' asked Tristan, offering her the cold purple flannel.

'I think I'm starting to pant, I think this is the second stage. Tristan just fucking drive me to the hospital.'

'Right,' he said, folding and unfolding his muscular yet incapable arms. 'Righto, key's in the kitchen, yeah?' He hesitated outside the door, appalled by the primal growl from the room. At that moment, the key turned in the lock and Adam, adult, purposeful, medical, strode in. Tristan moved his lips in a prayer of relief. Adam lifted Alex upwards and looked into her eyes.

'Just keep breathing, Mouse, remember slowly, deeply. How fast are the contractions?' Alex was trembling and restless in his arms, wanting him near her but pushing him away.

'About every twenty seconds, it hurts, it hurts, something's happening, Adam.'

Adam turned to Tristan in the doorway, who was still clutching his flannel and looking on in disbelief. 'Have you called an ambulance?'

Tristan nodded. 'They said ten minutes, I guess about eight minutes now.' Adam glanced back at Alex and made a professional choice, easier when it affected those you loved, oddly, than when it concerned strangers.

'I'm not going to move her,' he said slowly and clearly. 'Alex, listen to me. I'm going to sit you up on the sofa. Then we are going to pant and push, darling. Slowly as you can.' Alex could hear his voice distantly. Her body had become its own mistress, composing itself into thrusting convulsions. The weight and pressure of the pushing descended further and further until she felt the great ball outside her body against her thighs. And then she saw Adam's long hands, coloured by blood and fluids, kneading and tugging until the trunk and limbs slithered out of her and her daughter was pressed against Adam's white shirt. The doorbell coincided with a crash in the hallway. Tristan had fainted.

The following day, Alex was recounting the scene to Emily from her bed, while she cradled her strangely permanent and vibrant daughter in a primrose yellow crochet blanket. This was as far as she had read in her instruction book. This was the after; an exhilarating peace. Outside she heard Adam's low deep voice as he fielded phone calls. From time to time he would poke his head round the door brandishing a fresh bouquet.

'From Sally's garden,' he said, brushing the pollen from his sweater. 'She said not to disturb you but she would pop back after work.' Alex gave a distracted new-mother smile. Emily jumped up and offered to find a vase. A bit later a corporate bouquet arrived from Pegasus News and soon after that a much larger one of such exotic foliage that Adam's face was entirely hidden by it.

'Where the hell is that from?' giggled Emily. 'Brazil?'

Adam felt his way through the stems for the card. 'Ah,' he said in the old weary voice that Alex recognized from a dark phase of their lives. 'It is from Patti. It says: "Thinking of you".'

Alex clutched her crochet bundle.

They were not out of the jungle yet.

SHANE WATSON

The One to Watch

PAN BOOKS

Cold Feet meets the Big Chill in this acutely observed and laugh-out-loud funny novel of friendship, fame and fashion.

When rock-wife and society beauty, Amber Best, dies unexpectedly on the eve of her fortieth birthday, her nearest and dearest are eager to contribute to an in-depth documentary about her life. But who was the real Amber Best?

Everyone who knew her – or thought they did – seems to have a different answer to the question: devoted wife and muse; bohemian mother who allowed her children to run fashionably wild; loyal friend and confidante; elegantly dishevelled celebrity and one-time It-girl … But was there a more complicated and devious character lurking behind the various roles that Amber so convincingly played?

Her friends thought they knew her – and each other – as well as anyone could, but with Amber gone, the delicately spun web of friendship begins to unravel, and damaging secrets threaten to shatter their assumptions.

OTHER PAN BOOKS
AVAILABLE FROM PAN MACMILLAN

SHANE WATSON
THE ONE TO WATCH   0 330 49038 9   £6.99

ANITA DIAMANT
GOOD HARBOR   0 330 49166 0   £6.99

CHRIS BINCHY
THE VERY MAN   0 330 49261 6   £6.99

JENNIFER CRUSIE
FAKING IT   0 330 42030 5   £6.99

All Pan Macmillan titles can be ordered from our website,
www.panmacmillan.com, or from your local bookshop
and are also available by post from:

Bookpost, PO Box 29, Douglas, Isle of Man IM99 1BQ
Credit cards accepted. For details:
Telephone: 01624 677237
Fax: 01624 670923
E-mail: bookshop@enterprise.net
www.bookpost.co.uk

Free postage and packing in the United Kingdom

Prices shown above were correct at the time of going to press.
Pan Macmillan reserve the right to show new retail prices on covers
which may differ from those previously advertised in the text
or elsewhere.